PRAISE FOR THE *NEW YORK TIMES*
BESTSELLING VICTORIA SQUARE MYSTERIES

"Fun plot, fanciful characters, really fabulous crafts. A palette of colorful characters and enticing crafts. Bartlett put her art and soul into this mystery!"

—Laura Childs, *New York Times* bestselling author of the Cackleberry Club Mysteries, the Scrapbook Mysteries, and the Tea Shop Mysteries

"Ms. Bartlett has established a plucky, intelligent heroine in Kate Bonner and has surrounded her with a cast of fascinating multi-dimensional characters."

—Ellery Adams, *New York Times* bestselling author of the Books by the Bay Mysteries and the Book Retreat Mysteries

"A co-op of artisans, one disgruntled artist, and a desperate artifice—the perfect canvas for murder. Lorraine Bartlett's characters come alive in this tightly crafted, suspenseful plot that grips the reader's attention right up to the satisfying conclusion."

—Kate Collins, *New York Times* bestselling author of the Flower Shop Mysteries

"A quaint town square, crafters, quirky characters, and dead bodies. *A Crafty Killing* is sure to be a winner."

—Maggie Sefton, *New York Times* bestselling author of the Knitting Mysteries

"Wonderful . . . Bartlett starts the new Victoria Square series with a can't-miss hit!"

— ng author Mysteries

Berkley Prime Crime titles by Lorraine Bartlett

A CRAFTY KILLING
THE WALLED FLOWER
ONE HOT MURDER
DEAD, BATH, AND BEYOND

Dead, Bath, and Beyond

LORRAINE BARTLETT
with LAURIE CASS

BERKLEY PRIME CRIME
New York

BERKLEY PRIME CRIME
Published by Berkley
An imprint of Penguin Random House LLC
375 Hudson Street, New York, New York 10014

Copyright © 2016 by Lorraine Bartlett

ISBN: 9780425265994

First Edition: December 2016

Printed in the United States of America
1   3   5   7   9   10   8   6   4   2

Cover art by Chris Beatrice
Book design by Laura K. Corless

Acknowledgments

FROM LORRAINE: I'd like to thank my wonderful editor, Tom Colgan, for his incredible patience and faith in me over the years. Thanks, big guy. You're the best!

Working with Laurie Cass on this book was the smoothest collaborative effort I've ever experienced. Thanks, partner!

I'm grateful to my neighbor Tim Cappon, who also happens to be my insurance agent, for suggesting a crucial element of the plot of this book.

FROM LAURIE: Thank you, Lorraine, for the chance to get to know Katie, Andy, Edie, Vance, and all the folks in Artisans Alley.

One

<u>~~~~~</u>

Katie Bonner stepped off the prettiest sloop at Thompson's Landing and onto the dock, juggling a picnic basket, her purse, and a bulging tote bag filled with swim towels and paperback books. She had just experienced the perfect day sailing on beautiful Lake Ontario. She'd also packed and shared a perfect lunch of baguette stuffed with homemade chicken salad, a lovely bottle of sauvignon blanc, and homemade chocolate-dipped madeleines with her lawyer and friend Seth Landers, and was feeling like nothing in the world could possibly spoil her day.

The sun was shining, seagulls were wheeling about, and every one of the people milling around the dock and boats was smiling. It was the nicest Labor Day weather anyone had seen in years. Content with life in general and the day in particular, Katie almost felt like bursting into song.

And then, from out of nowhere, her former boss at Kimper Insurance Agency, Josh Kimper, stepped in front of her. "Well, well, if it isn't the high-and-mighty Katie Bonner." The man didn't seem capable of speaking without a sneer in his voice.

"Hello, Josh," Katie said, hoping her voice conveyed the contempt she felt for the man who had abused her goodwill, treated her like little more than a slave, and was—quite frankly—a horse's ass!

He looked past her to eye Seth's pride and joy, *Temporary Relief.* "I see you've come up in the world since you left my employ."

She didn't bother to dignify the comment with a reply, and instead she forced a smile. "So, what brings you to McKinlay Mill?" she asked, hoping he wouldn't bore her with too long an answer. She didn't really care why he was there—and hoped he would quickly go away.

"Business *and* pleasure," Josh said with a leer. "I've rented a slip here in Thompson's Landing for my boat." He indicated a large yacht tied to the dock. "It's perfect for wining and dining potential clients." His laugh was like fingernails on a chalkboard.

Katie turned and studied the boat so she didn't have to spend any more time looking at her former employer. She'd learned a lot about boats in the last few months. The thirty-seven-foot Carver was slick and spacious and powerful and much too nice for someone like Josh. "I've been out sailing once or twice a week for most of the summer," she said. "Funny we haven't run into each other before this." Not that she was complaining.

"This is only my second weekend here," Josh said. "I tried a few other marinas before I settled in here."

A shout made Katie glance over to the launch ramp. Someone was backing a trailer into the water and taking his boat out of the water for the season. By the end of the week, a lot of boats would be mothballed for the winter. Still, if she wanted to end the conversation—and she most certainly did—she wasn't about to ask any more questions.

"Well, I really must run," Katie lied. "It was—" She hesitated. It hadn't been nice to see Josh. She could've gone years—preferably the rest of her life—without laying eyes on him, and it would have been just fine.

"Good to see you, too, Katie." There was that smirk again. "It's too bad you left the firm, but I'm doing fantastically well without you. Profits are up over forty percent. My new office manager is a whiz. Great little gal."

And did whoever had taken Katie's place despise being referred to as a "gal" as much as Katie had? The edges of Katie's ears started to burn hot. She took a breath, trying to stay calm, and reminded herself that Josh wasn't her boss any longer. He didn't have any power over her, and she didn't want to waste any energy on him.

"That's nice," she said as politely as she could through gritted teeth. "Good-bye, Josh. Have a—" She'd started to say nice life but instead said, "nice Labor Day."

"I will," he said in a nasty tone. "You're the one I worry about."

She'd started to edge away but stopped and swung to face him straight on. "You? Worry about me? You can't be serious."

"Why, Katie, of course I am." He laughed. "Naturally, I care about your so-called success. Sure, you might have made that mess of a flea market your husband left you work for a few months, but that honeymoon's over. The only reason you're still afloat is people felt sorry for you. That's going to trickle off anytime now, and you'll come crawling back to me, begging for your old job." He put on a thoughtful expression. "And maybe, just maybe, I'll think about rehiring you. After all, you weren't the worst employee in the world. A twenty percent pay cut from your old wage would be just about right for a gal like you," he said, winking.

That did it. Katie's temper, which had been rising steadily through his little speech, soared past the breaking point.

"I wouldn't work for you again if you paid me double! You're arrogant and rude and a male chauvinist pig."

Josh's face started to turn an unhealthy shade of red. "Arrogant? You're one to talk. Just because you have that fancy degree doesn't mean you know more than I do about running a business."

For years, Katie had bottled up the things she'd wanted to say to Josh. Keeping it all inside was how she'd kept her job, but there was nothing to hold her back, not now. "You know what?" she asked fiercely. "I might have learned more from you about business than I ever did in college."

The ruddiness on Josh's cheeks faded. "About time you figured that out." He gave a condescending chuckle.

Katie went on as if he hadn't spoken. "Yes, it was from you that I learned how *not* to deal with customers. You taught me that work should never be just about making money, and you taught me that an employer should always have at least an ounce of sympathy for employees. As a negative object lesson, you were an outstanding boss."

Josh's face was now scarlet. "You ungrateful—"

"Tut-tut," Katie said, smiling savagely. "You don't want to swear in front of children, do you?"

He didn't even glance at the family picnicking on the deck of a nearby boat. "I'll do what I want, where I want, and there's nothing you can do to stop me."

She laughed. "Josh, I couldn't possibly care less what you do and where you do it. I don't work for you, remember?"

"What's hard for me to remember is why I kept you on for so long."

Katie's temper, which had started to ebb, came back full force. "Because I knew what I was doing, and I was stupidly willing to work for half what I was worth. The smartest thing I ever did was quit working for you."

"Yeah?" He leaned forward, getting in her personal space. "What are you making now, Little Miss Successful? Who's paying your health insurance? When was the last time you had a vacation? How's that pension coming along?"

Katie felt her head swell near the bursting point. Josh had never so much as contributed a nickel to her 401(k), let alone set up a pension plan. And every time she'd tried to take any of the vacation time he'd grudgingly allowed, he'd manufactured a critical conference, or a supposed family emergency would suddenly surface. The injustice still rankled.

Fury filled her. She knew she was about to say something she'd regret, but at that moment, she didn't care about the consequences. "You are a—"

"Hey." A large male arm draped around her shoulders. "There you are. I wondered what happened. Are you going to introduce me to your friend?"

Katie pulled away from Seth. "He's not a friend," she said, spitting out the consonants. "Never was, never will be. And I hope I never see him again. Ever." She strode down the dock, ignoring the stares and raised eyebrows of the people she passed.

She'd tried to be civil to Josh Kimper. She'd tried to walk away from him. He was the one who'd goaded her into losing her temper. She knew she should feel a little ashamed of herself for the very public confrontation, but on the contrary, she was feeling pretty good.

A small smile quirked her lips. She'd faced down Josh

Kimper and, for once, had told him exactly what she thought of him. Maybe he'd take it to heart and change his ways. It wasn't likely, but at least she hadn't let him intimidate her.

Heavy male footsteps came toward her from behind. She stiffened. If that was Josh, hurrying after her . . .

She swung around, her chin already up, but it wasn't Josh. Her shoulders relaxed, her chin came down, and she waited.

"Who was that?" Seth asked, when he caught up with her.

"My ex-boss."

Seth grinned as he took the tote bag from her. "Josh the jerk?"

"You've got that right." She wrapped her arm around his, and they started walking again. "Thanks for coming up like that, by the way. If I'd kept on going, I might have said or done something I'd truly regret."

"Oh?" Seth asked. "Like what? No, let me guess. You might have called him arrogant and rude. And a male chauvinist pig."

She looked up at him with a rueful expression. "It's easy to forget how sound carries over water."

"Ah, but how good it must have felt to let all those feelings out. Is there anything else you need to add? Something about the small size of his feet, perhaps?"

Katie laughed. "Let's not talk about him. It's far too nice a day."

"Works for me," Seth said cheerfully. "Say, is there anything left in that picnic basket? Sailing all day, you can work up an appetite, you know."

But the picnic basket was empty. They started talking about dinner options, and soon Katie left all thoughts of Josh Kimper behind.

~~~~~

The shrill sound of sirens awakened Katie way too early the next morning. She squinted at the glowing numerals on her clock: six forty-seven. The sun was hardly up, but the volume of the noise told her the sirens were close.

Katie threw back the light blanket and staggered out of bed to look, disturbing her cats, Mason and Della, who'd been nestled against her. Still sleepy, she stumbled into her apartment's living room and pulled up the blinds on the window that overlooked Victoria Square. A clot of police cars and an ambulance had just pulled into the lot in front of Sassy Sally's Inn—what had formerly been known as the old Webster mansion—at the far end of the Square.

"Oh no!" Katie cried. Could something have happened to one of the inn's owners? She watched as the EMTs spilled out of the ambulance, clutching their gear, and raced through the open gate into the yard and up the inn's staircase, disappearing inside the building.

Katie turned, hurried back to her bedroom, where she exchanged her nightshirt for a pair of jeans and a T-shirt, stuffed her feet into a pair of sandals, grabbed her keys, and flew out the door, worried sick that one of the inn's owners, Nick Farrell or Don Parsons, was ill. In only seconds, she hit the bottom of the stairs, exited the building, and ran across the parking lot. She was breathless with a stitch in her side by the time she mounted the stairs and entered the inn's front parlor. Thankfully, she saw Nick.

"I saw the police cars and ambulance," she gasped. "Are you okay? What about Don?"

"We're fine," he said, clasping her hands to reassure her. "But it looks like our first guest has died overnight."

"A guest?" Katie was puzzled. "But I thought the inn wouldn't officially open for another two months."

"He wasn't a paying guest," Nick said. He sighed and

shook his head. "It's too long a story to get into right now." He glanced at the cherry antique grandfather clock that stood against the far wall. "I wonder if it's too early to call Seth."

"Do you really need a lawyer?"

"I don't know. Better to cover our hind ends just in case."

"Where's Don?"

"Upstairs in the only finished guest bathroom with the police."

"Which one of you found him?"

"Don. The guy asked for a six thirty wake-up call. When he didn't answer, Don opened the door. He found him dead in that gorgeous soaker tub."

"How horrible!" Katie easily pictured the scene. She'd spent many hours at Sassy Sally's with the partners Don and Nick, partners in life as well as in business, helping them plan the renovations. For years it had been her own dream to own the mansion and run it as a bed-and-breakfast, but now that her business was a growing success, she was finding it easier to let the old dream fade.

One of the cops thundered down the stairs. "Are you Katie Bonner?" he asked.

"Yes."

"Mr. Parsons said you knew the deceased. If you wouldn't mind, we'd like you to come upstairs and make a positive identification."

Katie looked to Nick. "I know him?" she asked, confused.

Nick nodded grimly. "Do you think you can do this?"

She'd seen several corpses during the past year—and it wasn't something she particularly enjoyed. Still . . .

She nodded and followed the cop up the stairs, noting the bannister still needed refinishing. Nick and Don had made a lot of progress on their renovations list, but there was a long way to go before the inn would open in November.

The EMTs hadn't even unpacked their equipment. "He's been dead for hours," one of them explained to another of the uniformed deputies.

"Stand aside, guys," the deputy said, and Katie threaded her way through the officials crowding the bathroom. Katie hadn't seen the finished bathroom, but she had seen it many times during the renovation. The marble floor and white subway tile looked elegant against the gleaming brass. She kept her gaze fixed on anything but the body in the tub. She could see a man's arm hanging over the edge. She inched forward, allowing her gaze to travel slowly up his pasty flesh, onto his wet shoulder, taking in his stubbled chin, and then—

"Oh my God, it's Josh Kimper." She searched the faces around her until she came upon Don's unsmiling face. "Josh was your guest?"

The dark-haired man nodded.

An officer introduced himself as Deputy Baxter then asked, "What was your relationship with the deceased?"

Katie swallowed. "Uh, I used to work for him. I saw him just yesterday at the marina. He seemed fine." Arrogant and rude, but healthy enough.

"You worked for him?" the deputy prompted.

"Uh, yes. I was his office manager for a number of years. I left the agency last fall. I own a business here on Victoria Square." She looked back at Josh's pale, lifeless body. In death, he'd lost the constant sneer that had usually marred his features. It didn't make him any more attractive. "Did he have a heart attack?" She remembered how red his face had been during their confrontation the day before.

"That'll be up to the medical examiner to determine," the deputy said.

"Poor Marcie," Katie said quietly.

"Is that his wife?" Deputy Baxter asked.

She nodded and then shook her head. "They've got two young daughters. Who will tell her?"

"Someone from the department will make a home visit," the deputy assured her.

Katie nodded in acknowledgment of the awful task. Josh had been a horrible boss and probably hadn't been much of a father, but the girls were much too young to lose their daddy.

"Is there anything I can do?" Katie asked.

Baxter shook his head. "We'll take care of everything from here on out, ma'am."

Katie shuddered. *Ma'am.* But then she shouldered her way out of the lovely bathroom to find Don and Nick waiting for her in the hall.

"Are you okay?" Nick asked.

Katie nodded, but Nick stepped forward to give her a hug anyway. When he pulled back, Katie braved a smile. "Thanks."

"Let's go downstairs and let the officers do their jobs," Don suggested.

Again Katie nodded, and let him lead the way. But as she descended the stairs, she couldn't help but wonder if Josh's death was a bad omen for Sassy Sally's. Too many people had lost their lives within the walls of that house. She hoped that Josh Kimper's death would be the last.

Somehow, she doubted that.

Two

Katie stepped out of the inn's front entryway and onto the porch that wrapped around the front of Sassy Sally's. With his left hand wrapped around a cane, Ray Davenport leaned on the gate at the end of the walk, waiting for her.

"What are you doing here?" she asked.

The older man shrugged. "Waiting for you, of course." He nodded in the direction of Tanner's, the Square's combination bakery and coffee shop. "I'll treat you to a cup of joe. What do you say?"

"I never turn down anything from Tanner's," she said and fell into step as they crossed the parking lot.

"And you found out about the accident at the inn from . . . ?" she asked Davenport. Prior to his retirement some six weeks before, he'd been the Sheriff's Office's lead investigator on several murders that had occurred in McKinlay Mill. Katie had intensely disliked the man when they'd first met, but since he was about to become a fixture on Victoria Square, they now shared common ground, surprisingly affably so.

"I heard it on my police scanner. I figured you'd hightail it across the Square like a fly to sh—"

"Don't say it!" she cried, holding up a hand to stop him.

Davenport shrugged, grabbed the handle on the heavy glass door, and let her precede him into the coffee shop. While they may have been Tanner's first customers of the day, the heavenly aromas of bread, cakes, donuts, cookies, and scones as well as the scent of fresh-brewed coffee already filled the shop.

"What brings you two in so early in the morning?" Jordan Tanner asked. He was dressed in baker's whites, with a coffee-stained apron to match. Embroidered in Kelly green thread was the name of the shop.

"We've just come from the inn," Katie said and wandered up to the big glass display counter, taking in the heavenly delights.

"I saw the cops and the ambulance. I hope Nick and Don are okay."

"They are, but not their first guest."

"Oh? I thought—"

Katie raised a hand to stave off the same question she'd asked of Nick. "Nonpaying guest, although I didn't get a straight answer as to why he was there."

"Was it anyone we know?" Ray asked.

"It was someone I know," Katie said with chagrin. "My former boss."

Jordan looked stricken. "I'd better pour you two a couple of large coffees. Will you be wanting anything to go with?" he asked hopefully.

"I'll have a jelly stick," Davenport said and nodded in Katie's direction.

"I'll have one of those big fat oatmeal cookies, please."

Tanner nodded and opened the pastry case. "It's good for you. Full of healthy ingredients like eggs and oatmeal—which is good for lowering cholesterol—and raisins. That's fruit. All very good for you."

"Uh-huh," Katie said, not buying his spiel but not about to change her selection, either.

"Go sit down. I'll bring you your order."

Katie nodded, while Davenport hung back to pay. She chose a seat by the window so that she could keep an eye on the goings-on at Sassy Sally's.

Ray returned to the table. "You got the seat with the view," he commented and pulled a couple of paper napkins from the chrome holder on the table. He handed one to Katie and then spread one across the table as a place mat for himself. "So, the plot thickens."

Katie looked up at him.

"You knew the deceased," he said. "Why am I not surprised?"

"I suspect nothing on this Earth surprises you, Ray."

He shrugged. "And you'd probably be right."

"You met Josh," she reminded the ex-detective. That was when Davenport had been investigating Ezra Hilton's death just eleven months before.

He nodded, looking toward the counter to see what was taking Jordan so long with their order. "He was an idiot. I'm surprised it took you so long to quit that job."

"In retrospect, me, too."

Jordan finally arrived with a tray laden with their coffee and pastries, which he dutifully doled out.

"Thanks," Katie said.

"Eat hearty," Jordan said and left them alone, although Katie knew he'd be standing behind the counter pretending to work while he listened to their every word. She didn't mind. She had nothing to hide.

"So you haven't seen the poor bastard since you quit your job, right?" Davenport said, removing the cap from his cup and blowing on the contents.

"I saw him yesterday, as a matter of fact. I'd been out on the lake sailing with Seth Landers. Josh was on the dock, as annoying as ever."

"And the cause of death was?"

"Probably a heart attack. Josh always was the epitome of a type A personality. He was uptight all the time. Stress up the wazoo—self-made stress, I might add."

"Will you go to the wake?"

Katie removed the cap to her cup. She dumped in creamer and picked up the plastic stir stick to mix it in. "I don't think so. I'd feel like a hypocrite."

"I assume he had a wife?"

Katie took a tentative sip of her coffee, found it too hot, and set the cup down again. "Marcie. And two young daughters. I always felt sorry for her. She seemed far too nice to be stuck with Josh as a life partner. Then again . . ." Katie frowned. "I wonder what Josh was doing at the inn and not with Marcie on a holiday weekend."

"Maybe she went out of town with the kids," Davenport speculated.

"Maybe," Katie repeated, unconvinced.

"You aren't thinking of calling her or anything, are you?" Davenport asked.

"Why would I?"

He shrugged. "You've got a good heart."

"I will send her a card. It's the very least I could do."

"Uh-huh," Davenport said. He checked the temperature of

his coffee by taking a small sip, apparently decided it was fine, and took a gulp.

"I suppose a few people will be sad Josh is gone, but he wasn't a part of my life anymore, and I'll hardly mourn him." She frowned. "Still, it did seem odd to find him at Thompson's Landing. He lived in Fairport. Why would he rent a slip all the way out here—especially at this time of year? By this evening, half the boats in the marina will be pulled out of the water and mothballed until Memorial Day."

"Odd indeed," Davenport muttered.

"Josh lived near the canal. And even if he wanted open water for his cabin cruiser, Irondequoit Bay is a lot closer." She nibbled at her cookie.

"That it is," Davenport said. He inspected his jelly stick and took a bite. Strawberry filling, or maybe raspberry, clung to the corner of his mouth.

Katie frowned. "Why are you being so quiet, agreeing with everything I say?" she asked suspiciously.

"I'm just being me." He grabbed another napkin from the holder and wiped his mouth.

"Have you got a date for reopening Wood U?" she asked. Davenport had bought the Square's wood gift shop, which had burned six weeks before—just days before he'd been pushed down a flight of stairs and broken his leg.

"I'm still waiting for the insurance company to come through with a check. It could take months, as you well know."

Yes, she did.

"It had better come through before the Christmas rush, or there'll be hell to pay," Davenport added. That at least made Katie smile. Here was the Ray Davenport she knew and . . . well, didn't love, but had taken a shine to of late.

"It'll give me time to make more stock," he said, "but I'll soon run out of room in my rental house. I may have to get a storage unit."

"Haven't you found a house yet?" Davenport was a recent widower, and his two younger daughters were starting high school that week. Sophie, the oldest, had already left for her first semester at the Culinary Institute of America. The three remaining Davenports had decided a new house was in order and listed their house. It sold surprisingly fast, and they'd moved to a short-term rental so they'd have plenty of time to choose the right house to buy.

"I know, I know," Davenport said, almost growling. "But we've all been too busy. The girls just got this place looking like home. I don't want to uproot them too soon, although Sasha and Sadie grab the Saturday real estate section of the paper before I can. They're motivated, and they have a long list of must-haves for the new house. I can see the next couple of months are going to be pure hell."

"If you don't want to wait until Thanksgiving," Katie said, "I've got a couple of booths available at Artisans Alley. I'd be glad to let you have your pick for a steal. This isn't the time of year when sales are at their peak."

"Let me think about it."

Katie nodded and sipped her coffee, her gaze traveling back to what she could see of Sassy Sally's, wondering how long it would be before the authorities removed Josh's body.

"You're not going to poke around that inn, are you?"

"Why would you even ask?"

Ray eyed her speculatively. "Your reputation precedes you."

Katie frowned. "I'll be there for Nick and Don. Emotional support," she asserted.

"Uh-huh," Ray said with skepticism.

Katie's frown deepened. "Josh Kimper hasn't been a part of my life for almost a year. I'm not going to obsess over his death—especially since he no doubt died of natural causes."

"No doubt," Ray agreed, but there was something in his expression that made her wonder.

Katie thought again of Josh slumped in the tub. Had she seen something about the body that indicated a more sinister scenario?

At that moment, she wasn't willing to speculate.

~~~~~~~

A few hours later, Katie slid into one side of a booth at Del's Diner just as the attractive Andy Rust, owner of Angelo's Pizzeria, who also happened to be her landlord and her boyfriend, walked into the restaurant. The Rochester Red Wings baseball cap on his head covered his dark, wavy hair, his T-shirt clung nicely to his muscular upper body, and his jeans had that faded hue that could have come from an expensive purchase in a department store but had instead come from hard use and many washings.

He scanned the restaurant, and when he spotted Katie, he smiled. "Hey," he said, dropping into the seat across from her. "What's shakin', bacon?"

"I didn't know bacon did any shaking." She leaned across the table, and they exchanged a quick kiss. Andy was a sweetheart, but their conflicting schedules made things difficult. Her business, Artisans Alley, was open during regular retail hours, and Andy's pizzeria days were often twelve hours long.

Now that she was renting the apartment upstairs from his shop, they saw each other a little more often, but even when they were snuggling on the couch, watching television, it wasn't easy to forget the work going on downstairs. And certainly the kids down there didn't forget their boss was nearby. More than one romantic interlude had been interrupted by a frantic emergency call.

Katie loved the fact that Andy hired at-risk boys from the local high school. They needed work, he often said, to keep out of trouble, and if he could give them some life lessons at the same time, well, that was all to the good, right?

Having been an at-risk kid himself, he knew what he was talking about, and they were beyond pleased that of all the boys he'd hired, only one of them had found his way back to trouble.

"It's Jim's new catchphrase." Andy pushed aside his menu and went on to talk about the virtues of his assistant manager. When Andy had branched out from pizza into baking cinnamon buns, he'd come to recognize that even he couldn't work sixteen-hour days indefinitely and had hired Jim so he wouldn't work himself into exhaustion.

Katie tried to listen, but she kept getting distracted by the way his hair curled around the edges of his cap. Her husband, Chad, had died in a car accident just about eighteen months before. Though in most situations it would be too soon to think about another relationship, she and Chad had been separated at the time of his death.

The reason for their separation was now high irony, since what Chad had done without Katie's knowledge was take all of their hard-earned savings to invest in Artisans Alley, a rambling old applesauce warehouse converted into an arcade for artists and crafters. Katie had chucked her job at the insurance company to run the place by herself after Chad, then the majority owner, had died. Only now, after months of blood, sweat, and tears, was it making any money at all.

Yes, the business venture that had threatened to break up her marriage was giving her new purpose in life. Katie swallowed away an unexpected lump of grief. Even though she was only thirty-one, she'd had to deal with more sorrow than many people twice her age. Her parents both died when she was young, the great-aunt who'd raised her after the death of her parents had passed away years ago, and then Chad. In many ways, she was lucky to have Artisans Alley and all the friends she'd made there.

Plus there were all the people she'd met from Victoria Square itself. Artisans Alley was anchor to the Victoria Square business district, a quaint shopping area with gaslights and gingerbread facades. Stores ranged from a quilt shop to a tea shop to a place that made scrumptious jams and jellies. For years the district had struggled to bring in shoppers, but Katie's intense efforts to entice customers to Artisans Alley were also bringing people to the rest of the Square, and she couldn't be happier about that fact.

"Have you heard a word I said?"

Katie woke up from her musings. "Sorry," she said. "I was just thinking."

"I kind of figured that," Andy said. "The question is, what were you thinking about?"

"Oh, this and that." She smiled across the table at him, glad they'd started a new habit of eating together at Del's every other day. It was an early lunch for her after a morning in her office, and it was breakfast for Andy, soon after he'd rolled out of bed, but as long as they were together, the names of the meals didn't matter at all.

"You two ready?" Sandy, the morning waitress, stood poised to take their order.

After she'd left, Andy reached out and took Katie's hand. "So are you going to tell me what was going on at Sassy Sally's?"

Katie's eyebrows went up. "What makes you think I know anything?"

His own eyebrows rose to match hers. "Because I've known you for almost a year. Because nothing important goes on in Victoria Square without you hearing about it. Because whatever it was happened at the bed-and-breakfast you've lusted over for years. Because the owners are friends. Because it happened practically outside your bedroom. Because—"

"Because I'm a busybody who can't resist poking her nose into things that don't concern her?" Katie asked.

She tried to pull her hand away, but Andy held on.

"No, because you care," he said. "About your friends and about Victoria Square."

This was true, but Katie wasn't sure she liked it that he could predict her so easily.

"What happened?" he asked gently. "You look a little upset."

"It was Josh," she blurted out. "Josh Kimper, my old boss."

"The jerk?"

She nodded. "None other. It's hard to believe, really. I spent so much time disliking him"—hating him, to be honest—"and now he's gone."

"You mean he's dead?"

Again, she nodded. "He was staying in the one room that was ready. Don found him this morning in the bathtub after he didn't come down for breakfast."

"He drowned in the tub?" Andy's voice was cautious.

She shrugged. "I doubt it was suicide, if that's what you're thinking. They asked me to identify the body, and I didn't see anything that made me think he'd done himself in. Knowing Josh, I'd guess he had a heart attack. He didn't take care of himself, and when I was working for him, I don't think a week passed without him losing his temper over something."

Andy poked at his flat stomach. "Remind me to get more exercise," he said. "I can't die young. I have too many things I want to do."

"Same here," Katie said, and their conversation turned to the top ten items on their own personal bucket lists, none of which included anything about Josh Kimper.

~~~~~~~

A couple of evenings later, in spite of what she'd said to Ray Davenport, Katie pulled up and parked in front of a lovingly restored Queen Anne Victorian home on Church Street in Fairport, one of the prettiest villages on the Erie Canal. She got out of the car and started up the front walk, noting that the wraparound porch was full of cardboard cartons. Each box bore a description in bold black marker: clothes, desk items, tools. Was the Kimper family in the middle of moving? Was that why Josh had been at Sassy Sally's? But that didn't make sense. Why hadn't his family been with him?

Katie climbed the porch steps and strode up to the door, but before she could knock, the door jerked open.

"Katie!" Marcie Kimper said in surprise. "I wasn't expecting you."

"Who did you think it might be?"

"Another reporter," Marcie said bitterly. She stepped back. "Won't you come in?"

Katie entered the home's lovely foyer. The interior had been restored to its former glory, but with a contemporary flair. The once-natural trim had been painted a bright white, which seemed a crime to Katie. Instead of period-specific wallpaper with large, gaudy roses, a more subdued pattern with tiny pink flowers on a white background made for a cheerful entry. Bright sunlight poured through the windows in the parlor, and Katie followed Marcie inside.

"Have a seat," Marcie said, ushering Katie into one of
the comfortable armchairs. She took the matching one. She
looked younger than the last time Katie had seen her, more
than a year before. Had she had her eyes done, or was it
Botox? And her hair color was several shades lighter. While
she'd never been overweight, Marcie also looked thinner,
and it suited her. Though dressed casually, her clothes had
obviously come with much higher price tags than the ones
Katie was wearing.

"I came because—"

"Because you wanted to offer your condolences," Marcie
finished for her. "Well, we both know that's not exactly true."

Katie blinked, startled. "But—"

"Josh treated you like dirt." She settled back in her chair
and sighed. "I was surprised you stayed with him as long as
you did. I always thought you had more on the ball."

"Well, I—" Katie began but wasn't sure where to go from
there. Marcie certainly didn't seem like a bereaved widow.
"I am sorry Josh has . . . passed. In fact, I was asked to identify his body."

"That couldn't have been pleasant," Marcie said with a
scowl.

"It wasn't," Katie admitted. "Marcie, if you don't mind
my asking, why are you—"

"Not distraught because Josh's dead? I am, to some extent. Don't forget, my children's father is dead. The kids have
been so upset—and who can blame them? They loved their
daddy. The fact that I no longer did . . . Well, as you could
see by the boxes out on the porch, Josh and I were no longer
together. He was supposed to come and pick all of them up
on Monday. Now they'll just go to Goodwill."

That explained a lot. "Don't you want to save anything for
the girls?" Katie asked.

Marcie thought about it for a moment. "I don't think so. When they're older, I'll give them all the family pictures. In fact, I took my flash drive in earlier today to have a couple of shots made into photos, and I'll frame them. They seem to want that."

"Where are the girls now?"

"I sent them to be with my mother. I thought a change of scenery might do them good. I'm still not sure what to do about a funeral. Josh's brother and his family live in Oregon. They weren't close, so I doubt they'd want to come all the way here. And I don't want to spend a lot of money on a funeral for someone who was about to become my ex-husband, either."

"Don't you think the girls need some kind of closure?" Katie asked, appalled.

Marcie sighed. "I was thinking a memorial service at the funeral home would be enough. I'm sure some of his clients would make an appearance. I'm having the bastard cremated and hope to quickly move on with my life. I may even put the house up for sale. This is all still so new . . . I'll have to carefully consider my options."

"With a divorce pending, did Josh change his will?"

"I doubt it. I only threw him out last Thursday night, although it wouldn't surprise me if he'd already seen an attorney. I'm sure he was determined to screw me any way he could—since he could no longer do it literally. But even if he talked to a lawyer, there wasn't time to sign any paperwork." Her smile was icy. "It looks like I inherit it all."

"What will you do with the business?"

"Put it up for sale. I've already got some feelers out. Someone needs to go in and take over the day-to-day operations. The girl Josh had working for him is useless—not at all like you. I wouldn't trust her to make the coffee, let alone write a policy." She looked at Katie, her eyes widening. "You wouldn't want to buy the agency, would you? After all, you're the one who made it what it is today."

"That's very flattering, but I already have a business."

"So I heard," Marcie said. "Josh wasn't impressed. But then, his ego was so inflated he didn't have the time or the inclination to give anyone else a compliment, even just to make nice. He said he didn't like to lie." She looked thoughtful. "In the long run, I think it's better that he's gone from Emily's and Alison's lives. They're little girls yet. They'll always have an idealized vision of their father. I'm not going to speak against him, but if he'd lived, they'd eventually have learned what a misogynist bastard he really was."

And what had taken her so long to throw said bastard out of the house?

The doorbell rang, and Marcie got up to answer it. Katie took the quiet moment to look around and saw there really was nothing of Josh in the room. It had been decorated with a woman's touch.

Marcie returned to the parlor with the proverbial tall, dark, and handsome man in tow. He was dressed in jeans and a golf shirt, looking relaxed. "Katie, this is my attorney, Rob Roth. I'm sorry, but we really do need to go over some important papers. I hope you don't mind."

Katie stood. "Not at all. I need to get back to work anyway. Thanks for seeing me."

"It was good to talk to you. I never did like the way Josh had left things with you." She walked Katie to the door. "Unless you come to the memorial service, I don't suppose we'll ever see each other again," Marcie said quite casually.

"No, I don't suppose we will."

"Have a nice life," she said brightly, and before Katie could answer, she closed the door.

Katie slowly turned, fighting the urge to tiptoe along the porch to peek in through the window. She had already gone down one step when she decided what the hell. She tiptoed back up and crept across the porch. She edged around the window just enough to look through and, as expected, saw Marcie and Rob kissing—tongues and all.

Well, no wonder Marcie hadn't been all broken up about Josh's death. She'd already had someone else waiting in the wings.

Katie walked back to her car and got inside. A Mercedes was parked in the driveway. She opened her purse, took out a pen and pad, and jotted down the license plate number.

Just in case.

Three

~~~~~~~~

The next morning, Katie entered Artisans Alley through the front door. To the right, a glass door had recently been installed in what had been a storage area. Inside, instead of a haphazard mess of extra tables, chairs, mismatched flower vases, and, somehow, a hand-lettered sign that had been trying to entice people to buy a used car, there was now the Envy Salon and Day Spa.

Several months before, when Katie had gone to a franchise hair salon to get her hair cut by her favorite stylist, Brittany Kohler, she'd noticed a real estate listing on the counter. Just to make conversation, Katie had asked if she was looking to buy a house, and the young woman had stammered an odd reply. Katie couldn't let that go, of course, and she'd eventually drawn the real story out of the woman at a nearby restaurant.

"I want my *own* place," Brittany had told her over a cup

of coffee, her thick, dark hair showing brassy highlights in the low-hanging lights. "I've been saving and saving and I think I have enough. All I need is the right place for the right price."

Immediately, Katie thought about Victoria Square, and more specifically, Artisans Alley. There wasn't a single hair salon on the Square, and a top-notch stylist like Brittany could turn out to be a huge draw.

After one visit to Victoria Square, Brittany was sold on the idea. An intense few months of planning, construction, and marketing later, the Envy Salon and Day Spa was off to a good start. Not a great start, but Katie was sure that if Brittany could make it through the first year, she'd have a solid business, just like Artisans Alley was turning out to be.

Katie unlocked the door of her closetlike office. Inside was little more than a desk and filing cabinets and enough floor space to walk around the furniture. She kept meaning to spruce up the walls with a new coat of paint, but there always seemed to be more important things to do.

Today, for instance. Now that September was under way, she needed to set up the vendor work schedule for October. The agreement for every vendor's booth stated that the vendor would spend two days a month at one of the various jobs that needed doing, from working the cash registers to walking security to maintenance.

Setting up the work schedule was a huge headache, due to so many of the vendors having complicated lives, and getting it done early was the best way Katie had found to ensure that all the tasks got covered.

She dropped her purse into a desk drawer, sat down in her creaky chair, and got to work. The more she could get done before anyone else showed up, the better off she'd be, because for many vendors, one of the things they liked to do best was talk, and Katie was a prime target. Much of that week had been occupied by calming people shocked with the news of Josh's death, and Katie sincerely hoped that most of the talk was over. She knew it probably wasn't, but it didn't hurt to be optimistic every once in a while.

"Good morning, Katie. How are you this fine morning?"

Katie looked up from the computer monitor, an ancient monster that took up half the space on her desk. Talking did indeed take up a lot of her time, but with some people she didn't mind in the least.

She pushed herself back from the desk. "I'm wonderful, Rose. How are you?"

Rose Nash was a widow in her mid-seventies and was one of Katie's favorite vendors. The jewelry Rose made and sold was delightful, as was the plastic rain bonnet she wore over her determinedly honey-blonde curls whenever there was the slightest chance of rain.

"Looking forward to the Christmas shopping season," Rose said, her pale blue eyes twinkling, "as I'm sure you are, too."

Katie nodded. She certainly was. Labor Day was over, and so was the summer tourist season. The next few weeks would be a serious shopping lull, and as far as Artisans Alley was concerned, Christmas couldn't come soon enough. Katie had some minor sale events planned—a harvest sale, a fall colors sale, and there would be a big Halloween party—but nothing brought in customers like Christmas.

"Are you the first one in?" Katie asked.

"First in and first to start the coffee. That's why I stopped in, to tell you there's a fresh pot in the vendors' lounge."

"You're an angel," Katie said.

"How nice of you to notice." Rose laughed and fluffed her curls. "And how do you like my new do?"

To Katie it looked the same as it always did. "It makes you look twenty years younger." Rose blushed a light shade of, well, rose, and Katie's slight guilt over what wasn't exactly a lie faded.

"That Brittany is a marvel," Rose said. "I wasn't sure at first that a hair salon was a good fit for Artisans Alley, but it's turning out wonderfully."

Rose hadn't been the only vendor against the salon, Katie remembered a little sourly. She'd lost count of the concerned comments and outright protests about how she was going to ruin Artisans Alley. First she'd let crafters in, now this? She was going to confuse the customers.

Katie had gently pointed out that hair salons and spas were a staple in malls across the country. That had calmed most of the vendors; only Godfrey Foster, who made reproductions of master artworks from dryer lint, had harped on Katie to the point where she'd had to remind him that she was the owner of Artisans Alley. The decision was hers, and it was already made.

Godfrey had stomped away. Katie had half hoped that he'd decide to leave for good, but it was not to be.

Rose studied Katie's hair. "You could do with a cut yourself. How long has it been? With Brittany right over there"—she fluttered her arthritic fingers in the salon's direction—"you can't say you don't have time."

"Time for what?" Vance Ingram stood in the office doorway, sipping a mug of coffee. Vance was Katie's assistant manager, and even though she'd known him for as long as she'd been part of Artisans Alley, she couldn't talk to him without thinking that he looked like a skinny Santa Claus—white hair, white beard, gold wire-rimmed glasses, and all.

Rose and Katie said good morning, then Rose added, "Don't you think it's time for Katie to get a haircut?"

Vance's eyes widened. He'd been married for more than twenty years to Janey, a gorgeous woman with a figure Katie envied, and knew when to leave a conversation. "Speaking of time," he said, glancing at his wristwatch, "I really have to get going. I have glue setting up on a project in my booth, and glue doesn't wait." He vanished from the doorway.

"Soon," Katie said, pulling her hair back into a ponytail and tying it up with one of the many hair elastics she kept in her office drawer. "You're right—I need a haircut, and I'll get one soon."

"Excellent." Rose started to leave, then stopped and turned back to look at her. "Katie, dear, why do I suddenly get the feeling that your definition of 'soon' and my definition are two very different things?"

Katie grinned. "Speaking of time, I really have to get this schedule done." Still grinning, she turned back to her computer.

~~~~~~

"What do you think?" Katie asked, patting her hair and turning this way and that.

Her cats, Della and Mason, stared at her and didn't say a thing.

"No opinion? You two are as bad as Vance," she said, giving them both pats on the head. "But with tails and purrs."

"Meow?" Mason jumped off the couch and paraded to the kitchen, where he stood next to the cat food bowl and looked at her expectantly. *"Meow?"*

Katie laughed and followed him. Her apartment was comfortable, reasonably priced, and just along the way from Artisans Alley; her commute took less than two minutes. If she was ever going to have a body like Janey Ingram's, Katie knew she needed to get more exercise than walking to work and back every day, but she'd been so busy with trying to make her business profitable that she hadn't made time.

While opening the bag of cat treats and tossing a few to the bowls on the floor, she caught a glimpse of her reflection in the microwave's door and blinked. Her hair really was getting long, just as Rose had said. A haircut was something else she hadn't made time to do.

Sighing, she opened the refrigerator door. And sighed again. It was time for dinner, and since she hadn't gone to the grocery store in ages, she had nothing worth eating, not unless a leftover calzone counted. Katie pulled it out and peered inside. No, calzones in the fridge long enough to start growing mold didn't count at all.

After tossing the carton into the garbage, she opened the freezer, where dinner awaited in the form of a frozen grocery store pizza.

The cats eyed her as she turned on the oven. "If you don't tell Andy," she said, "I certainly won't."

Mason kept staring, and Della yawned, showing sharp white teeth.

"How about if I bribe you?" Katie opened a can of an especially stinky cat food and scooped out enough for two. The cats went at the food as if they were starving.

Katie smiled and started tidying the kitchen as she waited for her pizza to heat. Cleaning was also something she hadn't had time to do. The dishes were washed and put away, but she had a sneaking suspicion that dust lurked behind the flour and sugar canisters, and she was getting a little concerned about the condition of the under-sink cabinet.

By the time the pizza was piping hot, the kitchen counter was spic-and-span, the utensil drawer was emptied and wiped down, and the under-sink cabinet had been inspected; no need for deep cleaning.

She took her plate and a book—*Nightmares Can Be Murder* by Mary Kennedy—to the small table to eat, but half a dozen bites in, she closed the book, unable to concentrate.

The problem was, she wasn't taking care of herself, not properly. The haircut was the most obvious sign, but now that she was thinking about it, there were lots of others. Poor eating habits. Lack of exercise. Not enough sleep. Too much stress. About the only fun she'd had all summer was going out on Seth's boat, and though that was always relaxing, a few afternoons on the water didn't make up for the many consecutive months of hard work and worry.

Katie started counting the significant life events of the last eighteen months. Her husband had emptied their savings accounts; she'd separated from said husband, become a widow, identified a dead body while simultaneously becoming a business owner, quit a full-time job with benefits, jumped into a completely different life at Artisans Alley, and gained a boyfriend. Oh, and a man she'd despised had died in the house she'd once pined for.

It shouldn't have been a surprise that she felt frazzled, but somehow it still was. The big question, though, now that she was thinking about it, was how to get un-frazzled?

She smiled. There was an easy answer to that.

It was time to get baking.

~~~~~~~

The next morning, Katie put together a plate of the almond cookies she'd made and walked it across the Square to the bed-and-breakfast. Don and Nick were so busy with the renovations that she was sure a few homemade goodies would be welcomed.

As she had for months, Katie felt a small pang of sorrow as she read the wood-carved sign indicating that the Webster mansion was now SASSY SALLY'S INN. Not so very long ago, her sadness would have been due to the purchase of the mansion being forever out of her reach. She'd made so many plans and dreamed so many dreams, but now that she was making Artisans Alley a small success, and now that she saw how much darned work it was to run a bed-and-breakfast, she was content with how things had worked out.

But now her sorrow was for the death of the sassiest Sally she'd ever met, Nick's aunt and the namesake of the enterprise. Sally Casey, who often dressed in a perky shade of pink, had had a sparkling wit and a Kentucky accent that had charmed Katie the first time she'd met her. She'd also had stage four lung cancer and, fortunately, died before her trial for murder had even started.

Katie smiled, thinking of some of Sally's antics, and was still smiling as she gave the oak front door a perfunctory knock and opened it, poking her head inside. "Hello? Is anyone here? It's Katie!"

"Come on in," Don called. "We're in the kitchen."

Shutting the door behind her, Katie traipsed through the foyer, which was decorated just as she'd always imagined, with Oriental carpets on the wooden floor, benches and chairs upholstered with a flower print, a long wood check-in desk with a brass cash register, and globe lights hanging from the ceiling.

She made her way down the hallway, which was covered with framed historic photos of the area, and entered the brightly lit kitchen. This, too, was designed with a period look, but with the acknowledgment that it was a kitchen that had to put out breakfasts for fifteen on a regular basis.

A deep and extremely wide soapstone kitchen sink sat beneath windows that let in the morning sun, but instead of the white lace curtains that would have been in place a hundred years ago, Nick and Don had chosen wooden blinds that were far easier to clean. Similarly, instead of butcher-block countertops, they'd installed stainless steel and softened the harsh look with knife blocks and vases of flowers.

All in all, it was the perfect kitchen for a bed-and-breakfast, and Katie knew she couldn't have done better herself.

Don and Nick were both pulled up to the counter, sitting on tall stools. "I know it's like bringing coals to Newcastle," she said, setting down the plate, "but with all the construction, I thought you might not have had time to make treats."

"Snacks!" Don reached out and peeled back the aluminum foil. "Have a seat, you darling girl. How did you know this was just what we needed?"

"After the morning we've had," Nick said, "this is exactly what the doctor ordered." In seconds, the plate was half empty.

"Doctor?" Katie asked with concern as she pulled out a stool. "Are you both okay?"

"We're fine," Don said, spluttering out a few crumbs of cookie as he talked. "It's—"

His partner jabbed him in the side with an elbow. "Quit talking with your mouth full. It's just an expression," Nick said. "Although after that telephone call, a doctor's visit might be a good idea."

Don swallowed, looked at Katie's face, and gave a short laugh. "We're not explaining this very well, are we?"

"As far as I can tell," she said, "you're not explaining it at all."

The two men exchanged a look that communicated volumes. "First thing this morning," Nick said, "a detective from the Sheriff's Office stopped by. Hamilton, I think his name was. Huge guy."

Don nodded. "He said the medical examiner had sent over

his autopsy report for Josh Kimper, and there was a conclusive cause of death."

"It was drowning, just like everyone thought," Nick said. "Only he didn't drown because of a heart attack."

Katie didn't like the sound of this. She desperately wanted to ask questions, but she didn't want to interrupt their story, so as hard as it was, she just waited.

"There wasn't a heart attack at all," Don said. "Although from what the report said, it was only a matter of time. Kimper had a serious case of cardiovascular disease. Lots of blockages. Either he had a horrible family history or he didn't take care of himself at all."

Nick took another cookie. "But there wasn't any heart damage at this point," he said. "The cause of death was straightforward drowning."

"What?" Katie didn't understand. "So what happened? Was there a head wound? Maybe he slipped and hit his head on the side of the tub."

But the two men were shaking their heads. "All drowning and nothing but," Nick said.

"I don't understand." Katie's frown deepened. "How can someone just plain drown in a bathtub?"

"That's the thing." Don's voice was tight with strain. "Kimper didn't die in our bathtub."

Katie's first instinct was to laugh, but the expressions on the men's faces were so serious that she instead asked the next obvious question. "Then where did he die?"

"In Lake Ontario."

"What?" Katie's mouth fell open. "How? Why? I mean . . ." She shook her head. "That makes no sense. They must have it wrong."

Don and Nick exchanged another glance. "You sound like we did half an hour ago," Nick said, smiling sympathetically.

"The medical examiner tested the water in Kimper's lungs," Don explained. "It wasn't the purified stuff that came out of those brass taps that I polished last week. It had . . . oh, I don't know," he said, sighing. "Lake stuff in it. Silica, calcium, magnesium. Things that wouldn't be in our city water."

"Which means," Nick said, "that Kimper was almost certainly murdered."

The word didn't fit in the cheerful kitchen, and Katie was glad when its last faint echo faded from her ears. "This doesn't make any sense," she said. "I really don't understand."

"Join the club," Nick said morosely.

Don took another bite of cookie. "You are definitely not alone," he muttered.

"Don't talk with your mouth full," his partner told him.

Katie ignored the exchange. "First off," she said, "is why? Why would someone drown Josh in Lake Ontario and then go to all the trouble to bring him here? I mean, that's a lot of work. Josh wasn't a huge man, but he certainly wasn't small."

The two men stared at her, and Nick, then Don, started laughing.

"What's so funny?" she asked, a little annoyed.

"You are," Nick said, chuckling. "Here we've been, starting to worry ourselves sick over this, and you turn it into a logistics class."

Katie smiled at him. "Well, logistics count."

"They certainly do." Don patted her hand. "Thank you for reminding us."

Katie wasn't sure why they needed to thank her, but she said, "You're welcome. But you know, there's something more important than how Josh got from Lake Ontario to your bathtub and even why he was moved."

Though both Nick and Don nodded, neither one said anything.

"The most important question of all," Katie said, "is, who did it?"

But like the other questions, none of them had an answer.

~~~~~~~

"I don't get it," Andy said.

Katie swallowed a bite of toasted cheese sandwich and said, "Don't feel bad. No one else does, either."

Around them, the late-morning clatter at Del's Diner was a low background noise. Few people frequented the restaurant at this time of day. Even so, Katie spoke quietly. "Nick and Don are on pins and needles, afraid they're going to be arrested for Josh's murder."

"That's just stupid," Andy said. "Why would they kill Josh Kimper?"

"They wouldn't, but that doesn't mean the deputies won't consider them as suspects."

"You'd have to be nuts to kill someone staying in your own place," Andy insisted, "and neither one of those guys is nuts."

Katie smiled at him, glad he was defending her friends. "I'm sure the police will figure that out soon enough." She made a mental note to talk to Ray Davenport about the murder investigation. Even though he was retired, he must still talk to his former coworkers. Maybe he'd be able to tell her something reassuring that she could pass along to Nick and Don.

"I just can't figure it out." Andy stuck his fork into a pancake smothered with syrup. "Why on earth would anyone take the time and energy to move a body from the lake to Sassy Sally's? It's nuts."

Katie had been thinking about little else for the last two hours. "It could be someone who has mental issues," she agreed, "but there's one other reason."

"Yeah? What's that?"

"Someone wanted to point the investigation in a different direction. To confuse things."

Andy chewed and swallowed, nodding. "You're right," he said. "But it's weird to think of someone that calculated living here in McKinlay Mill."

The thought had occurred to Katie, too, and she liked the idea even less than Andy did. "Whoever it is could be from anywhere," she said. "Just because it happened here doesn't mean anything."

"I suppose you're right," Andy said, but he didn't sound convinced. "You worked for Kimper for a long time. Was there anyone he pissed off enough to kill him?"

"Other than me?" She laughed, but there was no answering laugh from across the table. "What's the matter?"

"Josh Kimper has been murdered," Andy said, frowning. "You used to work for him. Last year the two of you had a huge argument, and you quit. Last weekend you had another huge argument with him, and now he's dead."

Katie blinked. She hadn't put all the pieces together. "I hadn't thought of how it would look to anyone else." She glanced at her plate, but the congealing cheese didn't appear appetizing in the least. Pushing the plate to the edge of the table for Sandy to pick up, she said, "The police are going to question me, aren't they?"

"Maybe not." Andy shrugged. "That argument you and Kimper had on the dock, was there anyone else around? Maybe no one saw it."

Katie flashed back to the family picnicking on their boat. And the couple walking down the dock. And Seth. Because even though he was one of her best friends, he wouldn't lie to the deputies for her, and she wouldn't want him to.

"They're going to question me," Katie said. She tapped

the table with her fingertips. "It may take a few days, but they'll find people who remember the argument." She considered going in and talking to the police to be up front about it, then decided that was something else she could ask Ray about.

Andy grinned at her. "My girlfriend, the murder suspect."

"I'm glad you can laugh about it," she said a little tartly.

"Aw, don't be like that. The police know you're not a killer, or they will once they figure out that you have a solid alibi." He stopped and looked at her. "You do have an alibi, right? You were with Seth that night."

She nodded. "But I don't know the time of death. Nick and Don didn't say, and I didn't think to ask. I left Seth's house around eleven and probably got home about eleven fifteen."

"Did anyone see you go up to your apartment?" He tipped his head, studying her. "I went home at ten, but didn't you stop in? You usually do."

"I was tired," she said. "All day on the boat, then dinner with Seth, then a couple of his friends stopped by and we played cards. I was beat. It was all I could do to drag myself up the stairs. I don't remember if any of your guys saw me or not."

Andy glanced at his watch. "Got to go." He wiped his mouth with a napkin and started sliding out of the booth. "I'll ask. But don't worry. I'm sure all the cops will do is ask you a few questions and cross you off their list." He opened his wallet and tossed some bills on the table. "My treat today," he said, leaning down for a kiss.

Katie watched him walk out the door. Andy was a great guy, and she appreciated all the things he did for her, but he didn't understand that not worrying was an impossibility. Of course she was going to worry; how could she not?

She scooped up the bills and went to the vacant front counter to pay. But, just exactly the opposite of being on a used-car lot and having sales guys swarm you when all you wanted to do was look, there wasn't a soul in sight. "Hello?" she called. "Is anyone there?"

"Coming!" called a male voice, and Del himself bustled out from the back, a white apron not quite hiding the fact that his white T-shirt was stretched taut around his middle. "Hey, Katie," he said. "How was your lunch?"

"The toasted cheese was toasty, and the tomato soup was tomatoey," she said, laughing. "And Andy paid today, so that was even better." As she handed over the bills, one fell out of her hand and fluttered to the floor.

"I'll get that," Del said.

"No, I'm the clumsy one." She crouched down to pick it up, but the front door opened, letting in a slight breeze that sent the bill even farther under the counter. "Swell," she muttered and got down on her hands and knees, grateful that she wasn't wearing white pants. Without putting her head to the floor—which she wasn't about to do—she still couldn't see the money, but it couldn't be far. Stretching her fingers out long, she reached out, hoping that Del cleaned much better than she did.

Her fingertips touched the corner of what she assumed was Andy's money, but as she started to pull it out, the edge of her hand brushed against something else. Though the surprise made her jerk away, she quickly realized it was just a wadded-up piece of paper.

She gathered up both items and stood. "Got it," she said, slapping the five-dollar bill on the counter. "And this, too." She looked at the ball of paper in her hand. It was shiny, but a little heavier than a page from a magazine should be. Curious, she flattened the paper.

Del grunted. "That was mine," he said in a low tone that made Katie even more curious.

The paper was a brochure for a boat, a good-sized one, if Katie was any judge. Which she wasn't, but she'd spent enough time around boats that summer to know that any boat with the floor plan in front of her had to be more than thirty feet long. Kitchen below deck, master cabin, small second cabin, and a separate head; it all spoke of serious money.

"That's quite a boat," she said, admiring the lines of the photo at the top of the brochure. "I didn't know you were into boating."

"All I've been able to afford for years is a little Boston Whaler," Del said. "Then when I finally get some money saved up, when I finally find a great deal for a great boat, well, doesn't it just figure that the whole deal went to hell and gone and here I am, still in my dinky little tug of a boat."

Katie glanced at his face. He sounded and looked angry. "What happened?" she asked. "Did someone back out on a deal?"

"Worse than that," Del said shortly. "The guy I was going to buy from is—"

"Del, I could use some help back here!"

The voice had come from the kitchen, and it had contained more than a little panic.

Already on his way, Del called, "Coming!" He looked over his shoulder to call a good-bye to Katie, and then he was gone.

~~~~~~

Katie left the diner and walked around Victoria Square on her way back to Artisans Alley. She took a moment to chat with Gilda Ringwald-Stratton, the Brooklyn-accented owner of the Square's basket shop, and her husband, Conrad Strat-

ton, who owned the wine shop that connected to Gilda's
store. The two had been married only a few months—Katie
winced at the memory of the horror of a maid of honor's
dress she'd been talked into wearing—and were still displaying the cooing affection of newlyweds.

The couple stood side by side and hand in hand while they
talked about the upcoming meeting of the Victoria Square
Merchants Association. Katie was the president, albeit reluctantly, and she devoutly hoped to pass the mantle to someone
else when her year was up.

"It doesn't take up that much time," she told them, not
quite lying. Because being president didn't take much time;
not if you didn't have any life outside of Victoria Square.

"We'll think about it," Gilda said, but Katie sensed all the
thoughts would be negative. She said good-bye and headed
into Artisans Alley, wondering how to spin the role of Merchants Association president into something appealing instead of a chore. What she needed was to present it as an
opportunity. A challenge. Something to sink your teeth into.
A chance to make a difference.

"Like subtraction?"

Katie blinked at Ray Davenport, who was standing in
front of her, and realized she must have said aloud at least
part of what she was thinking. "What?" she said blankly.

"You said something about a difference. Subtraction is
the difference between one number and another." The bald-
ing middle-aged man shrugged. "It was a joke. At least that's
how it started out. Now it just sounds stupid."

"Not as stupid as I probably sounded, talking to myself."

Ray grinned. "You're okay as long as you don't start answering yourself, right?"

Katie wasn't so sure about that; she could think of a number of people who weren't okay and didn't talk to themselves. "Do you have a minute?"

"I've got lots of minutes," he said. "I'm retired from the Sheriff's Office, remember? I came here to take you up on that offer of a booth for a couple of months if that cut-rate price you mentioned the other day is still good."

She'd almost forgotten. "Sure," she said. "Wander around and take your pick."

"My pick?" He looked uncertain, an emotion that Katie almost didn't recognize on him. "Which one do you recommend?"

"Well, it depends."

"On what?"

"On if you're a new vendor or if you have established customers that will seek you out. On if you work on the theory that grouping vendors selling the same type of items will increase sales to everyone or if you think the grouping will decrease business." Katie could talk for hours about retail theory. "On if you think that a location near a door helps, or if you think that a location in a corner is better, or if you think that the booth's display can speak for itself. Or if you think that—"

Ray held out a hand to stop her lecture. "Who else sells things made out of wood?" he asked.

Katie thought a moment. "Vance has the only other booth dedicated to wooden items, but lots of others offer a few wood things."

"And Vance sells big stuff, right? Furniture?" When Katie nodded, he said, "Then I'll take a booth near him. My stuff is smaller. Picture frames, animal carvings, toys. We'll complement each other."

"Sounds good." Katie led him down the aisle, past gorgeous hand-thrown pottery, past Rose's beaded jewelry, past stained glass, past greeting cards crafted from handmade paper, past paintings and sculptures, and past weavings, right next to Vance's. "Here it is," she said, gesturing to the ten foot by ten foot square of concrete floor. "Home sweet home."

Ray stood in the middle of the space. "I like it," he said, looking around. "What are you going to charge me?" Katie named the price, and he nodded. "I can do that."

She described how the rental agreement worked, that he needed to sign up for two days a month for one of the appointed tasks, that the utilities were included in the rent, and that there was no cleaning done inside the booths. "Then all I need is a month's rent up front and a signed statement that you agree to everything I just told you."

"Paperwork." He made it sound like a curse. "Thought I was done with paperwork when I retired."

"Benjamin Franklin had it wrong," Katie said as the two of them walked to her office. "There are three things in this life that are certain: death, taxes, and paperwork."

Ray stood back as she unlocked her office door. "You're onto something. There're a few things I miss about being a detective, but filling out all those forms isn't one of them. Whatever happened to that paperless office they promised us?"

"I don't remember that promise." Katie opened the door and they went in. "Just as well, I suppose. If I did, I might try and hold someone accountable." She moved a stack of catalogs from the guest chair and put them on top of the filing cabinet, on top of a pile of trade magazines. She sat at her paper-covered desk, opened a drawer full of paper, and pulled out a letter of understanding.

Seth, who gave her legal advice, had recently badgered her into putting together the simple statement, telling her it was protection for both parties. "Just fill in the name and address at the bottom," she said, "sign it, give me a check, and we're done."

Ray took the pen from her. "As far as paperwork goes, this isn't so bad." He took the time, though, to read everything on the document. Katie's respect for him, which was already fairly high, went up another notch. Few vendors bothered, saying that Katie had explained everything, and were then surprised at the date the rent was due.

"Looks good," he said, filling out the blanks at the bottom of the form. "When can I move in?"

"As soon as you get me a check."

"How about cash?" He reached into his back pocket for his wallet and opened it to reveal more bills than Katie had ever seen outside a cash register. Or a bank.

"Holy cow," she said involuntarily.

Ray handed her the money. "I don't like credit cards," he said. "Even checks. Retailers run them electronically, so you might as well be paying with a credit card."

"What's wrong with that?"

"Nothing," he said, "if you don't mind people looking over your shoulder every time you pump gas, buy groceries, go to the doctor, eat out, or buy a pair of socks."

Katie didn't see the problem. "I don't have anything to hide."

"Neither do I, but I figure that when and why I buy stuff is no one's business but mine."

He had a point. Still, Katie wasn't about to give up the convenience of a credit card. Besides, there was another thing. "Are you sure it's safe to carry around all that cash?"

Ray gave her a slow smile. A dangerous smile. She got an odd feeling somewhere in her middle, and she was very glad that Ray was a friend and not an enemy.

"I'm safe enough," he said. "And I bet it was cash that got Josh Kimper murdered."

Katie's thoughts shifted back to what she'd learned just a few hours ago. "How did you hear that it was murder?"

"I'm retired, not dead. I hear things."

She reached for the candy jar on her desk and took a peppermint from the collection of hard candies she kept at the ready. "Want one?" Ray shook his head, and she unwrapped the treat. "What kind of things do you hear?" she asked.

"That Kimper was murdered," Ray said flatly. "What are you getting at?"

"It's just . . ." She sighed. "Remember I told you that I saw Josh the day before he died?" *Before he was murdered*, she revised mentally. Ray nodded. She took a deep breath and said, "We kind of had a disagreement. Sort of a loud one."

"And you killed him?" Ray smirked. "That means I get to make a citizen's arrest. Please stand up and put your hands behind your back, ma'am."

"Ha-ha," she said flatly. "But it was a very public disagreement, and when that Detective Hamilton starts asking questions, my name is sure to turn up."

"Yeah, so?"

Katie's teeth crunched hard on the candy, and she was rewarded with seeing Ray flinch a little. "So they're going to suspect me of killing him. And depending on the time of death, I might not have an alibi."

"Aw, don't worry about it. Say, can I get a copy of this?" He held up the lease agreement.

She took it and spun around on her chair to open the lid of the printer/copier/fax machine. "Don't worry? That's easy for you to say," she grumbled. "You're not the one who's going to be suspected of murder."

"Sure it's easy for me to say. That's because I know what I'm talking about."

Katie stabbed the "Copy" button but turned her head to indicate that she was listening.

"If what you've told me about Kimper is anywhere close to the truth, and I have no reason to think it isn't, that guy will have had public arguments with a hundred people in the last few months. Yeah, you argued with him the day before he was killed, but I bet you can establish that the two of you had previous arguments that didn't end up with a dead body in a bathtub."

"Lots of them," Katie said. "Sometimes with clients in the lobby."

"There you go." Ray shrugged. "Since you quit working for him almost a year ago, there's no real reason to suspect you. Unless . . ." His eyebrows went up. "Unless there were romantic entanglements?"

Katie's mouth dropped open from pure disgust. "You have got to be kidding. I always found it hard to believe Marcie conceived two children with him."

"Then don't worry about it."

And, though Katie knew she would keep on worrying until the real killer was found, she did start to feel a little bit better.

"Will you be speaking to your former colleagues about this case anytime soon?"

Ray shrugged. "You never know. I suppose you want me to pump them for information."

"Would I ever ask such a thing?"

"Yes."

Smarty-pants. He had no clue about the *real* Katie McDuff Bonner—and it wasn't likely he ever would. Still . . .

"Naturally, I wouldn't ask you to break a confidence—just to share whatever nuggets of information you thought pertinent."

"Why?"

"Because . . ." That wasn't much of a stumper. "Because I'm nosy."

Ray stood, obviously trying not to give in to the smile that tugged at the corners of his mouth. "That you are, Katie Bonner."

Four

It wasn't often that Katie suffered a sleepless night, but the fact that her encounter with Josh had been so public—so strident—kept her awake during the night. Her tossings and turnings had kept her cats awake, too, so it wasn't surprising that all three were grumpy when the sun came up all too soon the next day. And they'd had another repeat the next night, too.

By Tuesday morning, Katie couldn't help herself. She *had* to find out what, if anything, was going on at the bed-and-breakfast. She debated calling but decided that she'd learned so much the last time she'd brought goodies to Don and Nick that she might as well use the technique a second time. If the way to a man's heart was through his stomach, maybe the way to get both men to talk was pretty much the same. Luckily, she had a batch of apple raisin muffins in the freezer and only had to let them thaw half an hour before she had yet another excuse to visit.

That morning, though, she could tell things were going to be different. Three pickup trucks crowded the driveway. All three had beds packed with construction equipment, and there was a tidy pile of lumber on the lawn. With a covered plate in hand, Katie left her apartment to investigate.

The closer Katie got to Sassy Sally's, the louder the noises became. Power saws shrieked, hammers pounded, men called to one another, and underneath it all was pulsing music of a type that set Katie's nerves on edge.

She skirted a pile of lumber and saw a man, already covered with sawdust from the top of his baseball hat to the bottoms of his scuffed work boots. He was sitting on the opened tailgate of one of the trucks and studying a set of what she assumed were plans for the renovations.

"Good morning," she said politely as she started up the front steps.

"Are those for us?" the man asked, smiling, and nodded at the plate she was carrying. He looked to be in his mid-forties, with a stocky but fit frame. "Just kidding. But watch yourself if you go upstairs, okay? The guys are studding out a bathroom."

"Thanks." Katie could just picture the mess a construction crew would be making as they created a new room. Bits of old plaster would be scattered across the floor, sawhorses would be in the way no matter which way you turned, extension cords would be trip hazards, and the men would have to shout to communicate over the noise of a boom box turned up loud enough to loosen the fillings in their teeth.

Inside, someone had laid down thick plastic to protect the floor. There was also a temporary plastic doorway taped around the stairway to keep the construction dust from infiltrating the rest of the house.

Katie thought it was a valiant effort, but she had a suspicion that no matter what, dust would seep into every room. Still, it wouldn't last too much longer, and she hoped Don and Nick owned a super-sucking vacuum cleaner.

The thought of the long-empty mansion coming into its full glory gave her spirits a lift, and she had a smile on her face as she went into the kitchen. "Good morning. I come bearing gifts."

Don and Nick, huddled together at the kitchen island's counter, looked up.

"Aw, Katie." Don patted the stool next to him. "Have a seat and distract us from our labors."

She sat down, putting the plate on her lap and taking the plastic wrap off as she looked at the books and papers that covered every square inch of available counter space.

"Here," she said absently, proffering the muffins. "Have one." Both of the men immediately took her up on her offer. "I take it you're planning menus?" she asked, nodding at the scattered materials: cookbooks, recipe cards, and recipes on full-sized paper printed from various websites.

"Yep," Nick said, grimacing. "And here I thought this would be the fun part."

Katie had always figured the same thing. "It's not?"

Don snorted. "It was great fun until we started taking reservations."

"I'm not sure what you mean." She surveyed the wealth of information. "Seems as if you have a huge selection of recipes." The top layer of paper alone had recipes for chocolate chip pancakes, apple cinnamon French toast, eggplant quiche, herbed hash browns, and . . . really? . . . a recipe for maple-glazed bacon with toasted pecans. Katie's mouth started to water.

"The recipes aren't the problem," Don said. "It's the guests."

"Now, now." Nick gave a sideways smile. "That's no way to talk about the people who are going to run up nice, big credit card bills in our fine establishment."

Don sighed. "I know. But I had no idea we'd get reservations for people who needed a gluten-free meal, people who are vegetarians, people who are lactose intolerant, and people who are allergic to onions."

"Well," Katie said reasonably, "lots of people need special diets. Weren't you expecting this kind of thing?"

"All in the same weekend?" Don asked, his eyebrows raised.

Katie looked from Don to Nick and back again. "You're joking, right?"

"I wish we were." Don pulled a single piece of paper. "The only thing we've come up with that we can serve everyone is soft-boiled eggs."

"And that's not exactly the food you expect at a bed-and-breakfast," Katie said. "And cooking half a dozen different meals would be a logistical nightmare, not to mention far more expensive per plate than you've calculated."

"Bingo," Nick said, sighing.

"I feel for you two." Katie patted both their shoulders sympathetically. "But there is a silver lining."

"Please tell us," Don begged.

She grinned at her friends. "Hearing your problems makes me even happier that I didn't wind up running this place. Chad and I would have been at each other's throats before we even opened. At least you two are working together toward a solution."

"Hear that?" Nick asked. "She thinks we're going to find a solution."

"It's nice to know that someone has confidence in us." Don looked at the piece of paper that was still in his hand. "Soft-boiled eggs. God help all bed-and-breakfast owners."

"You'll figure it out," Katie said. "I'm sure of it."

"I'll drink to that." Nick slid off his stool and headed for the massive refrigerator. "Anyone else want some orange juice?"

"On the rocks, please," said a voice behind them.

They all turned, and Katie recognized the guy she'd seen out front, sitting on a truck's tailgate.

"Hey, Warren." Nick took a pitcher out of the fridge. "How big a glass?"

"Aw, I was kidding," the man said, looking at Katie. "I've seen you around the Square. You run Artisans Alley, don't you?"

"That's right." She stood and, introducing herself, held out her hand. "And you're the contractor Don and Nick hired to do their renovations."

"Warren Noth," he said pleasantly. His handshake was just the right amount of firm, not too tight and not limp, as if he was afraid he'd hurt her hand. "I thought one of the perks of this job would be a good breakfast every now and then, but all I get is this." He nodded at the pile of papers.

"When you're done," Don promised. "We'll make you and your guys something special when the job is finished."

"If we feed you guys now," Nick said, "you might slow down in order to get more meals. It's best to hold it out in front of you like a carrot."

Noth laughed. "With the guys I have, you could be right. Speaking of which, they need a little guidance about where the new pedestal sink is going. I know you said under the window, but we had to put the window in lower than we wanted because of that beam, remember? If the sink goes where you wanted, it's going to look weird."

Don gave his partner a pointed look. Nick sighed. "I know. It's my job to deal with all the renovation issues and it's your job to track the work and pay the bills."

"Equal division of labor," Don said happily. "I'll be here, working on recipes, when you get back." But as soon as the two men left the room, he got off the stool and starting coffee-brewing preparations. "So what's up with you, Katie? Anything new?"

"Not really," she said, "other than I'm guessing the police are going to stop by my office any day to ask me questions about Josh Kimper."

"Oh? Why's that?" Don scooped coffee beans from a canister and dumped them into a small grinder. He pushed a button, and Katie waited for the loud grinding noise to subside before she answered the question.

"The day before Josh was killed, we had a rather loud discussion on the dock at Thompson's Landing."

Don peered at her. "Did you prevail?"

She frowned. "With what?"

"The discussion." He put his arms up into a boxing stance.

"It wasn't like that. We exchanged words, is all."

"Another illusion destroyed." With smooth, economical movements, he set up the ground beans and filter, then added water and started the machine. "But, you know, I bet that during the week before Labor Day half the village argued with Josh Kimper, so I'm not sure why they'd single you out."

Something about the way he said that made Katie look up from the cookbook she'd started to flip through. "Half the village. You mean you argued with Josh, too?"

Don opened a cabinet door and took out two large mugs. "Of course I did. That man would have picked a fight with Mother Teresa."

"What did you and Josh tussle over?"

"The fact that he was the biggest weasel ever," Don said. "He denied it, if you can believe that. Gave all sorts of reasons why he was backing out of the deal."

"What deal?"

Don's glance darted to the empty doorway. "Promise you won't tell Nick?"

She hated promises like that. "If it's not illegal or immoral."

He held up three fingers in a scout salute. "Word of honor?" She nodded her promise, and he came around the end of the island's counter and leaned in close. "I wanted to get a boat," he said softly.

"Okaayyy," she said, drawing the word out. "And Josh had one?"

"He is—was—our insurance agent. Insured this place, our cars, our lives, everything. I stopped in last week to make sure the dates were right, to make sure this place was insured properly when it opens, and there was this boat brochure on the front desk. We got to talking about boats."

"No argument yet," Katie commented, still puzzled.

Don held up his finger, indicating that it would come up in a minute. "He said he could get me a great deal on a thirty-three-footer." Her friend stretched his arms out wide, indicating the hugeness that thirty-three feet would be. "A beautiful boat. Big enough for Lake Ontario, small enough to cruise the canal. Big enough for parties, small enough for the two of us out alone. We could have taken guests out on it, for a small fee, of course, and we might have offered it up to guests as a rental."

"But . . . ?"

"But it never happened." Don scowled in the direction of Josh Kimper's old room. "Kimper called a few days before he was killed. He said he'd left his wife and he needed a place to stay."

Katie remembered that Marcie had told the story differently; she wondered which version was correct. And if it mattered. It probably didn't. It was most likely another he said/she said—two ends of a story with the truth somewhere in between.

"So," Don went on, "I answered the phone and told him that I'd let him stay for free if he could swing me an even better deal on the boat. He didn't have a problem with that, or at least that's what he said."

"I take it the boat never materialized?" Katie asked. She also wondered how Don had the money to be without an income for months, spend a small fortune on renovations, and still have the wherewithal to purchase what was essentially a very expensive toy. Neither Don nor Nick ever seemed to worry about money, a situation she couldn't imagine.

A loud *thump* came from upstairs. Katie and Don simultaneously looked to the ceiling, but there were no shouts, no calls for help, and there was no dust drifting down. Don shrugged and said, "No boat. Kimper stayed here for days, getting a free bed and free breakfasts. He kept talking about the boat, but I never got any details. If he'd even given me a name, I could still work the deal myself."

The coffeepot finished its dripping. Paying little attention to what he was doing, Don reached for the pot, filled both mugs, and restored the pot to the burner, talking all the while.

"I couldn't say anything to Kimper about it when Nick was around, which made getting information about the boat tough for me." He rolled his eyes as he handed Katie a mug. "And that made it easy for Kimper to get away with welshing on the whole deal while he was getting free room and board from us."

There was something Katie didn't understand. She hesitated to ask the question—the answer might be too personal—but Don had mentioned it, so she went ahead. "Why couldn't you talk about it in front of Nick?"

Don checked the doorway again. It was still empty. "Nick has a big birthday coming up, and we've been talking about getting a boat for years. I thought setting up a deal like this would be the perfect present."

Though Katie could follow the reasoning, she wasn't sure committing to a large purchase like that without a partner's consent was the wisest course of action. When her husband, Chad, had withdrawn all their savings to invest in Artisans Alley without consulting her, she'd felt so betrayed and angry that they'd separated. Maybe they would have eventually reconciled, but Chad had died in the car accident before that could happen. "Are you sure that's such a good idea?" she asked. "A boat like you're describing is a pretty big deal."

"It would have been perfect," Don said firmly, "if only it had happened."

Katie had another thought. "Have you told the police about the boat?"

"The boat that's not a boat?" Don asked. "Probably. Or, now that I think about it, yes, I'm sure I did. I don't know if you've noticed, but I tend to talk a lot when I'm upset, and the morning I found Kimper in our bathtub"—he made a sour face—"my mouth ran like you wouldn't believe."

As he sipped his coffee, Katie asked, "Aren't you a little worried that you gave the police a motive for murdering Josh?"

Don's versatile eyebrows went sky-high. "You're joking, right? No boat—or lack thereof—is worth killing someone over. Besides, if one deal falls through, there's bound to be another one around the corner. You just have to be patient about these things."

"Some people don't have any of that particular quality," Katie said.

"Well, that's true enough. But I have an alibi," he said. "And so does Nick."

"Please don't tell me you're vouching for each other?" Katie asked, worried.

Don laughed. "Of course we are. That's what married people do. But that night we were at a friend's house. An end-of-the-summer party. Dozens of people saw us."

A wave of relief that swept through Katie. "That's good to hear," she said, grinning at him. She held up her coffee mug in toasting position. "To alibis."

"To alibis," Don said. "Long may they last."

"Hear, hear," Katie agreed, and they tapped their mugs together. And yet, doubt still niggled at her brain, and she mentally crossed her fingers, because she knew that no matter how logical things seemed to her, the ever-suspicious police might think otherwise.

~~~~~~~

A little later, full of coffee and new recipe ideas for scones, muffins, and biscuits, Katie walked across Victoria Square, greeting the energetic Charlotte Booth of Booth's Jellies and Jams and the not-quite-elderly Nona Fiske, owner of The Quiet Quilter, with a smile and a cheery, "Good morning."

The two women, who were chatting in front of Nona's store, returned the smile and wished her a good morning, too.

Katie and the prim-and-proper Nona didn't see eye to eye on many things, such as the fact that Nona had to abide by all the rules in the Merchants Association charter, not just the ones she felt like abiding by, but for the last few weeks Nona had been, if not friendly, at least polite, and Katie considered that a victory of sorts.

But Katie's smile dropped off her face the second she

stepped inside the door of Artisans Alley. "What is that awful smell?" she asked, wrinkling her nose.

Rose Nash, who was standing at one of the cash registers straightening the various sizes of bags, nodded in the direction of the Envy Salon and Day Spa. "It's coming from *there*."

"What is it?" The smell was astringent and had high, acidic tones that were making the back of Katie's nasal passages start to burn.

"I think it's something to do with nails." Rose shrugged. "I do my own nails, so I'm not sure, but I can't think what else it would be. The products they use to dye hair or give a permanent don't smell anything like this." She sniffed at the air and shuddered.

Frowning, Katie looked at the glass door to the salon. "Brittany didn't say anything about doing nails when we set up her lease. I'll have a talk with her. We can't have this smell permeate the building."

"That's good to hear." Rose glanced toward the main showroom, where they could hear the rattles and chatter of various vendors coming in for a morning check of their booths. "You can bet someone's going to complain about it sooner rather than later."

"Probably more than one person," Katie said. "Because one of them will be *me*."

Katie had planned to spend the morning catching up on financial reports, but that could wait. She stopped at her office to drop off her purse, then made her way purposefully to the salon.

As soon as the glass door shut behind her, Katie realized that she hadn't been inside Envy since before Brittany had officially opened. Katie had been closely involved with the renovations, but once the fixtures were in and the inspections approved, she'd given Brittany free rein to decorate as she pleased.

"Wow," Katie said quietly. The lobby was tiny, but the calming colors and indirect lighting helped her to forget that fact, and a well-placed seascape painting on the far wall drew the eye diagonally to make the space feel much larger than it really was. Even the new age music that played through hidden speakers encouraged thoughts of wide skies and open spaces.

Katie stood there, enjoying the transformation, when a young woman walked into the short hallway and caught sight of Katie. "Oh, gosh, I'm sorry. I didn't know anyone was here. My name is Crystal. Can I help you?"

For a moment, Katie couldn't look away from Crystal's auburn hair. Tied back in a loose braid, her thick locks had richly colored hues and golden undertones. It was hair that looked like a living thing; glorious hair of a kind that Katie had never seen.

"Uh . . ." Katie said, blinking. She shook her head and took in a breath to help pull herself together. "I'm Katie Bonner." Then, since it couldn't hurt to establish her position firmly, she added, "I own and manage Artisans Alley."

"Oh, I'm so glad to meet you!" Crystal crossed the distance between them, beaming and holding out her hand. "Brittany told me all about how you took over this place less than a year ago. She said you took a losing enterprise and turned it into such a big success that all of Victoria Square is feeling the benefits."

"Uh . . . how nice of her." But Katie knew most of that wasn't true. Yes, in the past Artisans Alley had been losing money hand over fist, but she wouldn't call the current situation a big success, not by a long shot. A qualified success, at best. And as for the rest of the Square benefiting? What she mostly heard were complaints about the lack of parking spaces.

Katie shook Crystal's hand and saw that the woman couldn't be much more than twenty-five. She was a few inches shorter than Katie's very average height and had a stocky body that Katie had a feeling made her a natural for playing softball.

"Brittany is the absolute best," Crystal said, still smiling. "I can't believe how lucky I am. I mean, I'm pretty new at all this. How many people would give me a shot like this?" She gestured to the wall behind her, behind which Katie knew stood a fully equipped hair salon station. "This is so great! So far I only have a few customers, but you've made the Square such a cool place that I'm sure I'll have more than I can handle in no time."

"You're cutting hair, too?" Katie asked.

"Hair?" Crystal laughed. "Not me. I get my hair cut twice a year whether I need it or not. I do nails. Acrylic nails." She flourished her own. "And I can do almost any kind of polish design you can dream up. Someone like you?" Tipping her head slightly to one side, Crystal said thoughtfully, "Something understated, but with hints of bold. A traditional deep red base, say, but with small gold glittery stars."

Katie couldn't help it; she glanced at her fingernails, imagining them looking nice for a change instead of ragged and ridden with hangnails. But glitter? Not in her lifetime.

"I'm sorry to tell you this, Crystal," she said, "but there's a problem with the nails." And she was, in fact, sorry. She'd taken an instant liking to the young woman, who was obviously talented and professional in a very sociable way.

"A problem?" Crystal reached around for the end of her braid. As she untied and retied the band that held it in place, she asked, "What kind of problem? Brittany and I have an agreement, honest. You can check with her if you'd like."

Katie certainly would; that would be her first phone call once she returned to her office. "It's the smell," she said. "The air circulation for this building is pretty ancient. Whatever odors you're generating in here are going straight into the building instead of being vented outside." She was sure that's what was happening—none of the noxious odor present in the lobby was inside the salon. "Step out a minute and I'm sure you'll know what I mean."

Katie moved to the doorway. Crystal followed, and they were barely out of the salon when Crystal stopped. "Oh, geez. I am so sorry, Ms. Bonner," she said, sniffing the air. "I had no idea this was happening. I can see why it's a problem."

"I'm sure you can understand why I need you to do something about it?" Katie asked, pleased that Crystal recognized the situation as a problem.

"Oh, absolutely," the younger woman said. "And I know exactly how to take care of this situation."

"That's great." Katie was about to ask what Crystal was planning when she saw Ray Davenport enter the lobby. "Thanks for being so cooperative," she said, "but I need to talk to this gentleman. It was nice meeting you."

Ray had heard her and stopped short. "Gentleman?" He looked down at his old, ratty sneakers, jeans that had seen at least four different painting projects, and a T-shirt advertising a high school football championship from more than a decade earlier. "You sure you're talking to me?"

"Do you see any other man around? And I was using the term loosely."

"It's because of my cane, right? Makes me look dapper."

"That must be it."

"I get to ditch it in a couple of weeks."

"Good for you." She changed the subject, gesturing in the

direction of the booth he'd picked out a few days earlier. "It looks nice back there."

Ray made a wry face. "You call me a gentleman and call that mess nice? Either you want something from me or your standards are slipping."

"You're too hard on yourself," Katie said as they ambled into Artisans Alley and stopped in front of the registers, where Rose was humming and still straightening. "Your space does look nice. No one expects a booth in a venue like Artisans Alley to be Tiffany's, you know. All that's needed is a decent presentation and reasonable prices. If you spent a fortune on fixtures, it would take years to get back the money invested."

Ray studied her, then nodded. "Okay, you're right. But I still don't see the gentleman thing."

She grinned. "Guess I must want something from you."

"Ha!" He pointed his index finger at her, pistol-style. "I knew it."

"How about a cup of coffee?" she asked. "I'm sure there's a pot going in the lounge by now. Rose? Can I bring you a mug?"

"No thanks, dear." Rose patted her chest. "I've already had my cup for the day, and that new doctor of mine has asked me to cut down on caffeine. She's so sweet and earnest; I'm really trying to take her advice."

Katie hoped she'd never wind up with a sweet and earnest doctor. Forgoing her regular morning cups of coffee would be more painful than she wanted to think about. But that wasn't going to happen that day, because in the vendors' lounge, the pot was more than half full. Katie pulled two mugs from the cupboard, checked their insides to make sure they were clean, and poured.

As she added creamer to hers, Ray took a long slug of his.

He thumped the mug down on the table and asked, "Okay. Now I'm ready. What do you want?"

"Your expertise."

"In what?" Ray asked. "My woodworking skills, my lawn mowing talents, or in how I got to be high scorer in my bowling league?"

"None of the above," she said. "It's your detecting abilities."

"Oh, geez." Ray cast his gaze heavenward. "She's at it again."

"Of course I am. Did you really think I'd leave this alone when two of my friends might be suspected of murder?"

"Not to mention yourself," Ray said, taking another sip of coffee.

She shrugged. "No one's stopped by to talk to me. I think I'm off the hook."

"You think?" Ray laughed. "Or maybe they're busy with that double homicide on the other side of the county and will get back to you when they have time. You're not going anywhere, right?"

Katie had heard about the double murder, but she hadn't thought about how it would affect the workload of the Sheriff's Office. "I thought someone had confessed to those murders."

"Yeah," Ray said, "it was one of those love triangle things. Easy enough to figure out who did it, but even still, there's loads of interviews and phone calls and so much paperwork to fill out that your eyes glaze over."

"I suppose so." That part of the job wasn't shown on television. With every hour that had passed without a visit from Detective Hamilton, Katie had drawn easier and easier breaths. It wasn't comforting to know all that easy breathing had been a mistake. She sighed. "Well, anyway, that's not what I wanted to talk to you about."

"So talk." Ray got up and grabbed the coffeepot. "Want another?"

She held out her mug. As he topped it off, she said, "I was just wondering about Josh being found at Sassy Sally's."

"You and me both." Ray dropped back into his chair. "It's just plain weird."

"This is a little scary," Katie said. "I'm not used to the two of us thinking the same thing about anything, let alone a murder."

"Now that I'm a member of the general public and not carrying a badge, I get to say what I think instead of what I had to say to catch the bad guys."

The idea that Detective Davenport might be a much different person than Ray Davenport had never occurred to Katie. She'd always assumed they were one and the same. If they weren't, she was going to have to get to know the man in front of her all over again.

"Weird," Katie said, thinking about doing so. Ray, however, must have assumed she was talking about the murder, because he nodded.

"Yeah, the whole thing is off. You'd think drowning the guy would have been enough. Whoever killed him could have gotten away with it, since there weren't any other wounds, defensive or otherwise. Not even a single clonk on the noggin." Ray rapped his own head with his knuckles.

Katie eyed him. "How do you know there weren't any other wounds?"

"I may be retired, but I'm not dead. A murder happens practically in my front yard, I'm going to ask some questions."

Katie filed a mental note that Ray was still in contact with his former colleagues on a regular basis. She'd suspected as much, but it was nice to have the confirmation. "Don and

Nick have alibis," she said. "But I'm sure they're still concerned that they may be implicated in Josh's death."

"Alibis or not, he did turn up in their bathtub," Ray said.

"Whose side are you on?" Katie bristled. "I thought you were going to help me."

"Help you what? Even though I'm not there, the Sheriff's Office is still competent."

"But like you said, they're busy, and who knows when they'll get around to clearing Don's and Nick's names? It wasn't so long ago that a skeleton was found in there, remember? If word gets around, their business could be finished before it's even started."

"Oh, I remember, all right." Ray glowered at her. "I remember you being an interfering—"

"And here I thought we were getting to be friends," Katie said, smiling, interrupting whatever he might have been going to say. "All I'm saying is, I'd appreciate some help. Just talking things through. With all your years of experience, I'm sure you'll think of things that I don't."

Ray looked at her. "Yeah? That's a switch."

Katie felt her cheeks grow warm. In the past, she'd accused him of not thinking outside the box more than once. "Well, sure."

After a very long moment of silence, Ray shrugged. "Anyway, what I meant was that there has to be some reason Kimper was stuck into that particular bathtub. Otherwise, why go to the trouble of moving him?"

Katie hadn't thought about it exactly that way before.

"Plus, you'd think anyone who's watched any of those *CSI* shows, and that has to be pretty much everyone, would know they'd test the water in his lungs."

She hadn't thought about that, either.

"But what I really can't figure is the drowning," Ray said.

"Anyone who's drowning and isn't catatonic fights it. It's just human nature."

Katie wrapped her hands around her coffee mug and held on tight. She hadn't thought all the way down to the bottom about how Josh had died. He hadn't been much of a human being, but he hadn't deserved to die like that. "Poor Josh," she whispered for the first time ever, and she truly meant it.

~~~~~~

On Wednesday, Katie hurried into Del's Diner a few minutes late for her standing date with Andy. She looked around the dining area but saw no sign of her boyfriend. As she hesitated, Sandy, the waitress passed her carrying a tray of empty dishes.

"Hey, hon," she said. "You looking for that handsome hunk of man they call Andy?"

Katie laughed. "Yes, and he's even later than I am." Just then, her cell phone rang. She pulled it from her purse. "Speak of the devil," she said, as she thumbed it on. "Where are you?"

The clattering noises of the pizzeria's kitchen came through the phone loud and clear over the sound of Andy's voice. "Sorry about this," he said, "but I won't be able to make it over there. Jim's grandmother, I think it was, is having some sort of emergency and his parents are on vacation and his brother is useless, so it's on Jim to make sure she's all right."

Katie blinked at the long explanation. "I understand. I hope everything turns out"—a loud, metallic *bang!* in Andy's background made her wince—"okay for her."

"What's that? Oh, sure." After another loud banging noise, he said, "Sorry, Katie, I have to go. These guys need a little more hand-holding than Jim had led me to believe."

Katie started to say good-bye, but Andy cut off their call in the middle of calling out to his workers, "I don't care if you cleaned it yesterday, this is today and—"

Well. Katie slid her phone back into her purse. Now what was she going to do? Her stomach was already accustomed to eating at this time of day. She didn't mind eating alone if she had a book with her, but since she'd assumed she'd be eating with Andy, she was bookless, and her phone didn't have enough power left in it to let her read off the reading app through a meal.

"Hi, Katie." Across the half-empty dining area, Brittany Kohler, owner of the Envy Salon and Day Spa, was waving at her.

Waving back, Katie walked over. "All by yourself today?"

Brittany made a face. "Wasn't supposed to be, but my friend had to cancel. How about you?"

"Same thing. Andy is shorthanded at Angelo's right now, so he couldn't make it." Katie had known this was likely to happen, now that school was back in session. The college and high school kids who'd picked up all the summer hours they could were back in the classroom, and Andy had a distinct lack of experienced personnel. Though she knew the situation would improve quickly, she was already missing Andy's ready smile.

"Have a seat, then." Brittany gestured to the bench seat across from her. "No reason for both of us to eat alone."

Smiling, Katie slid into the booth. "Thanks. I was just wishing I had a book, but now I don't need one."

Brittany's face lit up. "You're a reader, too? What kind of books are your favorite?"

"Mysteries," Katie said promptly. "I read a little bit of everything, but in a library or a bookstore, it's the mystery section I browse first."

"Historical fiction for me," Brittany said. "And I don't care what time period as long as there aren't any computers, cell phones, or video games."

Katie laughed. "Historicals are probably my second favorite genre. Now, if you combine a nice, long mystery with a big, thick historical, well, that's my idea of a great weekend."

In no time at all, the two women were so deep into a lively conversation about books that they didn't see Sandy standing ready to take their order until she rapped her knuckles on the table. "Sorry to interrupt you ladies," she said, not sounding sorry at all, "but if you want to eat, I have to get your slips into the kitchen."

The two women ordered quickly and went back to their book discussion. By the time they finished eating, though they'd had to agree to have vastly different opinions about the latest bestseller, Katie felt the warm glow of knowing that she and Brittany had gone from acquaintance to friend in the span of one meal. She knew she should have talked to Brittany about Crystal and the pungent odor of acrylic nails, but she easily rationalized it away by telling herself that discussion should more appropriately be held in her office.

"Are you going back to Artisans Alley?" Brittany asked as they left the diner and headed back toward Victoria Square.

"Uh-huh."

"It's such a great location," Brittany said and launched into a soliloquy on just how much she loved the area. Katie half listened. She was already planning the rest of her afternoon.

As they turned into Victoria Square's main entrance, Katie looked across the expanse of parking lot, her attention suddenly on the steps up to the porch of Sassy Sally's. "Um, I just remembered I need to do something. See you later,

Brittany." With a friendly wave, Katie hurried off across the Square.

Halfway there, an unmarked police car passed her. She nodded at the driver, Detective Hamilton, who politely acknowledged her. Once he was out of sight, she started walking even faster. In short order, she was running up the steps and inside the inn.

"Don?" she called, automatically heading for the kitchen. "Nick? Are you here?" She burst into the light-filled room and saw her two friends sitting at the island, both of them staring vacantly into space. "I saw Detective Hamilton leaving. Is everything okay?"

"Katie." Nick gave her a wan smile. "We're fine, honest."

"Just ducky," said his partner sourly. "Couldn't be better. Wouldn't want to change anything in my life, not a single bit."

"He was only was asking questions," Nick said, with the air of someone who'd already said the same thing many times before. "It doesn't mean anything."

"Sure it does." Don pushed back his stool and stood. "Don't you see? It means they think there's something to ask questions about!"

Katie looked from Don to Nick and back to Don. She hesitated, then said, "Well, Josh's body did turn up in your bathtub. Wouldn't it be even weirder if Hamilton didn't have questions? Heck, the times you left and returned from that party could help them narrow things down."

"You're right," Nick said slowly. "I hadn't thought of it that way."

Don shoved his stool forward, making it scrape horribly against the tile floor. "He wants to pin this murder on the gay guys; you know he does. We're targets, like always, just for being different." He stalked out of the room, almost running into Warren Noth.

With a clipboard in one hand and a tape measure in the other, Noth turned to watch him go, then turned back around to face Katie and Nick. "Was it something I said?"

"Hardly." Nick reached out to touch Katie on the arm. "Thanks for stopping by. It's good to know that you're looking out for us."

"You're my friends," she said simply. "If there's anything I can do, anything at all, promise you'll let me know?"

Nick gave her a smile and a nod, but Katie wasn't at all sure that he'd keep his word.

Five

<u>~~~~~~</u>

Katie stopped by Artisans Alley just long enough to tell Vance and Rose that she'd be available by cell phone if anyone needed her, and she hurried out before the questions started. Not that she couldn't take off for a few hours if she wanted to—she owned the place, after all—but she couldn't remember the last time she'd done so. If she'd lingered, someone would inevitably ask, and she didn't want to lie if she didn't have to.

Once she'd settled in her car, though, she decided that "errands" could be her stock answer. It was vague in a polite way and also boring enough that no one would ask further. Would they?

She was still considering the question as she put on the signal to turn into Winton Office Park. It had been months—eleven months, to be exact—since she'd driven into the place, and she was pleased, though not surprised, to find that she hadn't missed it in the least.

If it had been possible to separate her actual job duties from the fact that Josh had been her boss, she might have been able to say that she'd enjoyed her time at Kimper Insurance Agency, but the two were so intertwined that every time she thought about the fifty- and sixty-hour weeks she'd worked to process the claims and write the policies of clients, she still felt a residual anger for how hard she'd worked and how little Josh had recognized that fact.

But while she wasn't going to mourn Josh, she also wasn't going to sit on her hands and watch Don and Nick stress themselves to a frazzle, not if she could do anything about it.

Katie parked in front of her old office—very intentionally not parking in the spot she'd regularly used—and got out of the car. She immediately noticed that no one had planted any annual flowers at the base of the foundation shrubs. And that no one had washed the windows in ages. And that no one had cleaned the spiderwebs off the back-lit company sign. All were jobs that she'd done in the past.

She shook her head, again not at all surprised. She'd been an idiot to do all that, and she was glad that, whoever the new office manager was, she'd been smart enough to set up boundaries. Katie reached for the door handle, remembering that though Josh had said his new hire was outstanding, his wife had said she was useless.

Then Katie remembered the advice of her great-aunt Lizzie, the woman who had raised her after her parents had died. "Form your own opinions," she said more than once. "Don't be lazy and use other people's. Use your own noggin. That's why it's up there taking up space."

Smiling, Katie walked into the office's front lobby. It

looked exactly the same as it had the day she'd stormed out.
Same beige walls, same slightly darker beige carpet. Same
bland furniture, with probably the same magazines on the coffee table. Even the fake ficus in the corner looked the same.

"Hi. Can I help you?"

Katie turned to face the woman who was sitting in what
used to be her own chair. On a normal day, Katie felt confi-
dent that she looked presentable, professional, clean-cut, tidy,
and moderately attractive. On good days, she felt downright
pretty. But even on the best day ever, she would never come
close to the sheer beauty of the woman at the front desk.

A few years younger than Katie's thirty-one, she had
wavy jet-black hair in a short cut that framed her face and
drew attention to her cheekbones. Her nose was small, her
lips were full, and just as Katie was making an instant knee-
jerk judgment, she noticed that the whites of the woman's
eyes were red.

This meant one of two things: She had hay fever allergies,
or she'd been crying. Either way, it was obvious that, in spite
of her physical beauty, she wasn't perfect.

Sneakily cheered, Katie smiled. "Hi, I'm Kate Bonner."

"I'm Erikka," the younger woman said. "With two Ks.
Um, Erikka Wiley." Her voice was high-pitched but friendly.
"Are you a customer here? Because if you are, I think I can
process a claim, but I hope you're not here to get an insurance policy because I can't issue those, I'm not an insurance
agent, Josh was the agent, Josh Kimper like on the name of
the business? Out front? But Josh isn't here, he's gone . . ."
Her steady stream of words came to a sudden stop. "He's
gone," she repeated. "And he won't be coming back. Because
he's . . . he's . . ." She gulped down a sob.

"He's dead," Katie said gently.

Erikka's eyes, big and brown, looked up at her, and the

tears started to flow. "He really is, isn't he? I can't believe it . . . He's gone . . . He's . . ." She shoved her chair back and stood. "I'm sorry, I'll be right . . ." She fled in the direction of what Katie knew was the restroom.

"That's interesting," Katie said to herself. As she waited for Erikka-with-two-Ks to return, she leaned over to look at the papers on the desk. Even upside down, she could tell what they were—forms for processing claims from a car accident. Nothing out of the ordinary, and certainly nothing that would give her any new information about the investigation into Josh's murder.

She sighed and looked at the lateral file cabinets on the back wall. If she was sure Erikka was going to be out of the room for a good ten minutes, she might have tiptoed over and thumbed through the contents.

Not that she knew what she was looking for, of course, but after spending so many years pushing papers of all kinds, she felt sure she would recognize an anomaly if she saw it. And anything out of the ordinary might lead to a clue that might eventually lead to the killer and then Don and Nick would be in the clear.

"Sorry about that." Erikka hurried back to her chair, a tissue in her hand. "How can I help you? Are you a client here? Marcie, that's Josh's wife, she's told me to do what I can to keep the business running. She's going to sell it, probably as fast as she . . ." Erikka dabbed at her eyes with the tissue. "Sorry," she mumbled, "this keeps happening. I'm just . . . It's just so weird, you know?"

"Is anyone interested in buying the business?" Katie asked.

Erikka shrugged. "There was a guy in here this morning, but he didn't ask many questions." She looked up at Katie with hope in her reddened eyes. "Is that why you're here? Do you want to buy the agency?"

Not in a million years, Katie wanted to say, but didn't. Instead she smiled. "No, I just wanted to offer my condolences." And to see if she could learn anything about the murder investigation. "I used to work here. I left about a year ago."

Erikka blinked. "You're *that* Katie? Josh talked about you all the time."

"I bet." Katie laughed.

The younger woman nodded. "He said you were so—"

Katie cut her off, knowing what was coming. "So incompetent?" she asked wryly. "So incapable, so inept, and so unlikely to ever be more than an office manager for a small insurance agency?"

"What? No, of course not!" Erikka's perfectly plucked eyebrows drew together. "Josh kept saying how great you were. He said you were great with clients. And that you'd reorganized the office filing system and made it easy as pie to find anything." She smiled. "He went on and on about the cookies you used to bring in, said he'd never tasted anything so good."

None of that sounded like Josh. Then again, he'd probably been manipulating Erikka, just as he'd manipulated Katie. Once again, she mentally kicked herself for working there for so long. "That's nice to know," she said. "I just wanted to say that I was sorry."

"Th-thanks." Erikka's tears started to flow again. Up came the tissue. "I appreciate it. Very much," she said. "You're as nice as Josh always said."

Katie, who just barely managed not to roll her eyes, told Erikka to take care of herself, but as she got in her car and drove away, her mind was whirring with new possibilities.

At Thompson's Landing that day, Josh had said his new office manager was a whiz. But his wife had said she was useless. What neither one of them had said was how flat-out gorgeous Erikka was. Was is possible that Josh had been having an affair with her? Was that why she'd been crying? Was that why Josh and Marcie had separated? Could Marcie have killed Josh in a jealous rage? Yes, Marcie was already seeing that attorney, Rob Roth, but jealousy didn't always make sense.

"A lot of things don't," she muttered to herself.

But she was going to do her best to figure out what was really going on.

~~~~~~~

The drive to the office park and back had taken longer than Katie had anticipated. She fished out her keys to unlock the side entrance and was so focused on thinking about what she needed to accomplish that she made a beeline for her office, intentionally not looking around. If she caught someone's eye or stopped in the vendors' lounge, she'd get drawn into conversation, and she didn't have time, not right then. After the bills were paid, maybe then. Or maybe not. The schedule still wasn't done, and she still wanted to run projections for the upcoming Christmas season.

After unlocking her office door, she turned and shut it almost all the way. A casual observer would assume she wasn't there, but she'd be able to hear if anything tragic started happening out on the floor.

Katie sat down, put her purse away, and got straight to work. She'd just started making serious progress when there was a knock on the door and Rose Nash poked her head inside. "Hello, there. I hate to bother you, but I have a quick question for you."

"Um, sure." Katie waved Rose in and turned to face her, but her gaze lingered on the computer screen for a moment longer. "What's up?" If only she could have two solid hours without interruptions, she'd be able to zip out the schedule. Maybe she should invest in a laptop so she could work from home. Not now, but if the Christmas season met her projections, she'd be able to afford one and—

"Did you talk to that girl, Crystal, about the smells from her business with the fingernails?"

Though Katie hadn't forgotten Rose was standing there, her thoughts had definitely wandered in those few seconds. "I did. That very day, whenever it was." She frowned, trying to remember, but gave up. "After I brought her out to the lobby, Crystal immediately understood there was a problem and said she knew how to take care of it."

Rose pursed her lips. "Did she give you any details on how, exactly, she was going resolve the situation?"

"No, but—"

The phone on Katie's desk shrilled, startling them both. Katie held up a finger, indicating to Rose that she'd be just a minute. "Artisans Alley, Katie Bonner speaking. How may I help you?" She listened to the voice on the other end for a moment, then said, "Absolutely, but can you hang on just a second? Thanks." She put her hand over the mouthpiece and said, "Sorry, Rose, but this is a potential new vendor I've been playing telephone tag with for almost a week."

"I understand," Rose said, but hesitated. "But please come out to the lobby when you have a moment."

"I will, just as soon as I'm off the phone."

But after that phone call, Katie forgot all about Rose's request and dove right back into setting up the schedule. An hour later, Rose barged into the office and marched over to Katie's desk. "Please come with me."

"Right now?" Katie asked, looking longingly at the computer. "In another half hour, I'll have this almost done. Can't whatever this is wait?"

"Only if you're not worried about what unattended open flames might do to your building."

"What!?" Katie shot out of her chair and all but ran for the lobby. She didn't understand how this could be happening. The lease agreements with all the vendors explicitly stated that they were not to use open flames of any kind at any time for any reason.

Artisans Alley was an old applesauce warehouse, built about a hundred years before from wood. It was drier than plain toast, and Katie's insurance bills were evidence of that. The no-open-flames lease agreements had decreased those rates to some extent, but nightmares of fire had brought her out of a deep sleep more than once, panting and sweating and wishing she had the money to install a sprinkler system.

When Katie emerged into the two-story lobby, she immediately saw and smelled why Rose was so concerned.

Close to a dozen large pillar candles were waving their tall flames and scenting the air with their heavy perfumes. Cinnamon and rose and—Katie sniffed—lilac competed with the astringent smell from Crystal's acrylic nails to create an amalgamated odor that was just short of horrific. But the stink didn't worry Katie. The front door opened, and the flames danced around, guttering high and sending a thin stream of smoke straight to the ceiling where, over time, it would stick tight and accumulate into a black layer that would never, ever come clean.

Katie banished those thoughts from her head as she walked fast to the closest candle and blew out the triple flames that were putting out more vanilla scent than could be found in the bottle of extract in Katie's kitchen.

Next was a ruby-colored candle spewing cinnamon into the air. By the time she reached the purple-colored, lilac-scented candle placed in a frightening location mere inches

away from a stack of fliers that described all the Artisans
Alley vendors, Katie shuddered to think about what might
have happened and gave thanks that she'd put off decorating
the lobby in a harvest theme. Dried corn shocks? Bales of
hay? Scarecrows stuffed with straw? Katie shuddered again.

"Oh no!"

Katie spun around at the sound of Crystal's voice. "The
candles all went out!" she said with dismay. "How did that
happen? I'm so sorry, Ms. Bonner." She reached into her
pants pocket and pulled out a book of matches. "I'll relight
them all right away."

"No, you won't," Katie said firmly.

"Sorry?" Crystal froze, one hand holding a single match,
the other holding the matchbook, strike plate at the ready.

"I can't have you lighting candles in here," Katie said.
"This building was built of wood about a century ago. Everything in here is a fire-starter's dream, and there's no sprinkler
system. If something caught fire, it would spread so fast that
the whole place would burn down before the first fire truck
arrived."

"It . . . would?" Crystal asked in a small voice.

"In a New York minute," Katie replied. "All my leases
include a statement that no open flames will be used anywhere in the building. Brittany signed one, too. I'm surprised
she didn't tell you."

"If she did, I don't remember." Crystal's face was crest-
fallen. "I'm so sorry about the fire danger. I never thought
about that. I just thought lighting these candles would take
care of the stink. It was my best idea. What am I going to do
about the smells from my business now?"

Katie opened her mouth to say it was up to Crystal to
figure it out when a deep male voice asked, "Ms. Bonner? I
need a moment of your time."

Turning, Katie saw Detective Hamilton, who'd replaced
Ray Davenport in the Sheriff's Office. Sudden fear rose up
the back of her throat. Why was he here? She ran through the
possibilities in her mind and didn't like any of them. Unless
he was here to buy something and needed her help to choose
the perfect present for his wife. That would be okay. "Hello,
Detective," she said, sounding more cheerful than she felt.
"How are you this fine day?"

Hamilton, who was tall and wide and thick, looked down
at her. "Is there somewhere quiet we can go? I have a few
questions for you." He wore khaki pants, a polo shirt, and a
navy blue jacket that must have been purchased at a Big and
Tall men's store.

No purchase, then. "Of course," she said. "We can sit in
my office." She turned back to Crystal. "We'll talk later," she
said firmly and looked back to Hamilton. "This way." She
led him to her office.

As soon as Katie had cleared the stack of papers off her
guest chair and they'd both sat down, the detective pulled a
small notebook from his jacket pocket and flipped through a
number of pages. When he got to the one he wanted, he reached
into the same pocket for a pen, clicked it, and looked at her.
"Can you account for your whereabouts on Labor Day?"

The rush of adrenaline suddenly coursing through her
veins took Katie by surprise. Why was she reacting to that
simple question? She'd known they would eventually get
around to talking to her; too many people had seen her at the
marina that day. There was nothing to worry about, just as
Andy and Ray had said. Detective Hamilton was doing his
due diligence, that was all.

"Sure," she said as calmly as she could. "I was out all day
sailing with a friend who keeps his boat at Thompson's Landing. We got back to shore in late afternoon and then went to

dinner at his house. I got home about eleven." Short, simple, concise. She wasn't about to volunteer information he hadn't asked for.

"Uh-huh." The detective was writing in the notebook. "Can anyone corroborate your arrival at your residence and that you didn't leave again?"

"I live above Angelo's Pizzeria. You'd have to talk to the guys who were working that night. I'm not sure if anyone saw me come home or not."

"I will," he said, making a note. "What is your friend's name, the one with the boat?"

She wanted to ask if that was truly necessary, but she knew it was. "Seth Landers."

Hamilton's eyebrows rose. "The . . . attorney?"

"Yes," she said, knowing that the missing word in his sentence was "gay." She looked at him steadily. "Seth is a good friend of mine. He invited me out on his boat once or twice a week most of the summer."

"I see." Hamilton scribbled more notes. "And, upon your return to the marina, did you encounter Josh Kimper?"

"Yes," she said.

The detective waited, but when she didn't say anything else, he asked, "And did you and the deceased have an argument?"

It had *not* been an argument. "We both raised our voices," she replied.

"During that argument, did you or did you not tell him he was rude, arrogant, and a male chauvinist pig?"

"I did."

"And, during that same argument, did you threaten him in any way?"

What? Katie's eyes flew open wide, but she took a slow breath. "I did not."

"No?" Detective Hamilton consulted his notepad. "You didn't tell him that he was a useless human being and that the world would be a better place without him in it?"

Had she? She'd deeply wanted to say something along those lines, but Seth had come up and pulled her away before the words came out of her mouth. "I did not," she repeated, more slowly, trying to remember the incident more clearly. "I did say that I hoped I'd never see him again."

"Interesting." Hamilton looked up from his notebook. "That didn't work out very well for you, did it? You were the one to identify the body."

Katie closed her eyes briefly. "I never wished him dead," she said. "I didn't think much of the guy, but I never wanted him dead. His children . . ." She shook her head and didn't say any more.

"You didn't think much of him," the detective said, "but you worked for him for a number of years. Why did you stay at the insurance agency if you disliked him so much?"

"Because I very much liked getting a paycheck," she said dryly. "Jobs weren't exactly easy to come by in those days."

Detective Hamilton made a few more notes, flipped his notebook shut, and tucked both it and his pen away. "Thank you for your time, Ms. Bonner," he said and grunted with the effort of getting his huge body up out of the chair. "I'll let you know if I have any more questions."

She just bet he would.

Katie watched his departing back. She desperately wanted to ask him what was going on with the investigation, if he really suspected her of murder, if he suspected Don or Nick of murder, and how Josh had drowned without a mark on him and then had been hauled over to Sassy Sally's.

She sighed, knowing that Hamilton wouldn't answer any of those questions. It took her a few moments to reorient herself and realize she had other concerns that needed to be addressed. She got up and headed back to the lobby. Whatever Crystal cooked up next to combat the stench of acrylic nail smells, Katie wanted to know about it ahead of time.

But when she reached the salon, the lights were off and the door was locked with a CLOSED sign hanging from a suction cup on the door's glass.

Katie scowled. So much for that little task.

"How very adult," Ray said and chuckled. "I tell my girls that if they make too many faces like that their muscles will freeze."

Katie turned around, forcing her expression to stay in its exaggerated frown. "Oh no," she said, trying not to move her face. "You're right! I'm stuck this way."

Ray studied her thoughtfully. "I doubt the hospital has ever seen a case quite like this. Maybe I should look it up on the Internet."

"Better do it fast," Katie said. "I'm not sure I can last much longer."

Rose came up between them, carrying half a dozen of Crystal's candles. "You two should go on the road with that routine," she said, smiling and shaking her head. "But before you leave, what should I do with these? If neither one of us happens to be here when Crystal comes back, I don't want her to light them again."

"Absolutely not." Katie took them from Rose. "I'll put them in my office and leave a voice mail for her."

With Ray's help, the candles were soon tucked away on the top of her filing cabinet. "So much for that idea," he said, sniffing the palms of his hands and wincing. "Wonder what she's going to come up with next?"

"As long as it doesn't have open flames, I'm not sure that

I care." Katie dropped into her chair. "Guess what I just found out?"

"That aliens have, in fact, landed and that they've been living among us, undetected, for years? They're just waiting for the signal from their leader before rising up, taking over the planet, and making the rest of us their slaves—or dinner?"

"Um, no." Katie looked at him. "Do your girls think you're funny?"

"Hardly ever." He sat in the guest chair Detective Hamilton had recently vacated. "I get eye rolls like you wouldn't believe, though."

She would, actually. "I stopped by Josh Kimper's insurance agency." Briefly, she told him about Erikka and the differing opinions of her from Josh and from Marcie. "It just makes me wonder," she said in conclusion. "Do you think Josh could have been having an affair with Erikka?"

"There are two great big problems with that," Ray said. "One, why would a young and attractive woman, like you say Erikka is, be attracted to a guy like Kimper?"

"No accounting for tastes," Katie suggested. She'd been about to make a joke that even he'd been able to get someone to marry him, but she was grateful that she stopped herself before the words came out. After all, Ray's wife had passed away only a year before.

"Problem number two is Josh's wife being so jealous over his theoretical affair that she'd kill him." Ray shook his head. "Doesn't make sense, not if what you said is true about her already seeing some other guy."

"Seems to me that anything is possible," Katie said. "Who really knows what could tip someone over the edge?"

"True enough," Ray said. "But I just don't see Josh Kimper

as the type of person who would inspire such emotional passion."

Katie didn't either, not really, but she stood by her statement. "Anything is possible."

"Possible is different from probable, and neither one gets you probable cause. When you get a real theory, let me know and I'll pick that one to shreds, too." He started to stand, then dropped back down into the chair. "Forgot to tell you. Of course, I'm trying not to think about it so my head doesn't explode with frustration, so forgetting is good."

Katie could think of only one thing that could get Ray so irritated. "Don't tell me your insurance check is being delayed even more."

"Worse," he said grimly. "They're promising the check will be cut next month, but now the contractor says he won't be able to finish up my Wood U job until after Thanksgiving because he's too busy with his other project."

"Can't you just switch to another builder?"

He shook his head. "All the approved contractors for the insurance company are booked solid to January, and I don't want to mess with someone who isn't approved."

Katie started to say that just because a contractor wasn't approved didn't mean they weren't reputable, it just meant a little more hassle on his end, but Ray was still talking.

"Besides, this guy Warren has already started some of the work, and I like what he's done, so I'd like to keep him on."

"Warren Noth?" Katie asked, surprised.

"Yeah, that's him. He's doing the renovations at Sassy Sally's. That's why I'm getting such a good deal; he's already here. It's also why I'm not a priority: My job won't make him near that kind of money."

"It's always about money," Katie said, sighing.

Ray stood, nodding. "Pretty much everything. In my

whole career, I hardly ever came across a murder that didn't have cold, hard cash somewhere in the motivation mix. See you later, Katie."

"Yeah."

After Ray left, Katie kept staring into the vacant space where he'd been, thinking hard.

If murder was almost always about money, why had Josh been killed? He'd owned a moderately successful insurance agency, but Katie had done his books and knew he'd been far from making serious money.

Which brought up a question Katie should have thought about long before—how on earth had he afforded a boat like the one he'd docked at Thompson's Landing?

Six

Late the next morning, Katie was upstairs, talking to a vendor about the work schedule, when she heard a heavy tread on the stairs. She turned just in time to see a head covered with a steel-colored crew cut rise above the railing. It was followed by a round head that wore glasses, which was followed by the rest of Fred Cunningham's stout body.

Fred was *the* premier real estate agent for McKinlay Mill and owner of Cunningham Real Estate, and Katie had worked with him on the lease with Brittany and on leases for the other businesses in her building. The owners of the photography and dance studios had both talked to Katie about renewing their leases when they expired, and Katie hoped that trend would continue for years to come.

"Good morning, Fred," Katie said. She made quick introductions between Fred and Godfrey Foster, the vendor she'd been talking to. Godfrey's dryer lint art was, bizarrely, selling well, but his attempts to say his success was so important to Artisans Alley that he shouldn't have to work his two days a month weren't convincing her. "How are you this fine day?"

"I'd be perfect if I could find a renter for that last spot in this building."

Katie laughed. "Fred, that space isn't much bigger than a closet. Who on earth would want to rent that?"

"Well, since you've asked, I do have a couple of ideas."

"Are either one of them any good?" Katie nodded a good-bye to Godfrey. She took Fred's arm and walked him back toward the stairs.

"What do you think about a shop that sells adult novelties?"

"Not much." They thumped down the stairs, one step at a time.

"I figured you'd say that. How about a production studio for rap music?"

Was he serious? "About the same."

Fred heaved a heavy sigh just as they reached the main floor. "I thought you'd say that, too, but I had to ask. If I get anyone else interested, I'll let you know."

Katie held out a hand. "Say, Fred, do you have a couple of minutes?"

"I'm free as a bird until after lunch." He winked at her. "You and Andy looking to buy a house? I have something that would be perfect for two harried business owners. What do you think about a condo?"

"I think you're dreaming," Katie said. "Do all real estate agents have such a rich fantasy life?"

"Part of the licensing requirements." He smiled. "What do you need?"

With Katie in the lead, they headed into the vendors' lounge. Katie took a clean coffee mug off the counter and held it up. When Fred nodded, she poured two mugfuls and handed him one before putting creamer into her own. "Did you know Josh Kimper?" she asked. An expression came and went on Fred's face so fast that Katie wasn't sure she'd seen anything.

"Horrible way to go," he murmured. "Drowning in a bathtub, like that."

Katie didn't correct him. No one had told her to keep the knowledge about where Josh had drowned to herself, but she didn't want to broadcast the information any more than necessary. "You know he was murdered, don't you?"

"Horrible way to go," Fred said again. He blew across the top of his coffee mug and took a couple of long swallows.

It wasn't like Fred to have so little to say, Katie thought. She studied him as she rinsed off a spoon and stirred her coffee. "None of us gets to pick how we die," she said.

"Or when," Fred said. "Makes you think, doesn't it?"

Think about what, exactly, Katie wasn't sure, but she had a feeling it had to do with mortality and lifestyle and a life well lived. Though that was all appropriate, what she wanted from him was a little more specific.

"Speaking of Josh," she said, "what I'm wondering is if you happen to know whether or not Josh's building across town is up for sale." Thanks to the mortgage payments she'd made over the years while working for him, she knew that he'd had a lot of capital invested in the place.

"The office, you mean?" Fred asked. "Or the house? Because they're both listed as being for sale."

Katie eyed him. She didn't want to lie, but she also wanted as much information as she could get. Marcie hadn't said anything about selling the house when she'd stopped by the previous week. "Did you list them?"

"Me? No." He named the biggest Rochester-based agency. "McKinlay Mill is big enough for me."

"Then how do you know they're up for sale?"

Fred shrugged. "Multi-listing. And it's not every day that a business owner is murdered." He took another big slug of coffee, then said, "If you're interested in buying the agency, I bet Marcie would give you a good deal on it, with you having worked for Josh for so long."

Marcie? Katie's eyebrows went up. "I didn't know you knew Josh's wife."

"Oh. Well," The normally silver-tongued man fumbled for words. "I . . . uh . . . well . . . I don't. I guess. Not really."

"Fred Cunningham." Katie gave him a hard stare. "Do not tell me that you've been unfaithful to your wife. She is already far too good for you."

"What!" He stood up straight. "Of course I haven't been unfaithful. I wouldn't dream of doing that to my wife. It's just . . ." He sighed.

"Just what?" Katie prompted.

He sighed again. "I was not unfaithful. I *am* not unfaithful."

Katie sensed there was something more. "But . . . ?"

"But nothing. I like Marcie, that's all." He shifted from one foot to another.

The feeling that there was more to the story lingered in the air. "And have you seen her since Josh's death?"

"Well . . ." Fred stared into his coffee mug. "I did happen to stop by the house a few days after he died to give my condolences."

"And?" Katie prompted.

"And that's when she told me she'd already listed the insurance agency and the house. She apologized, kind of, saying she was sorry she didn't list them with me. I told her not to worry about it, that they were a little far afield of my area. There are lots of fine Realtors closer to her neck of the woods, and I told her the one she chose would probably do an excellent job and get great prices for both the business and the house." He stopped talking and looked at Katie sheepishly. "My wife doesn't need to know about this, does she?"

Either Fred's wife was extremely jealous or he had an overdeveloped sense of shame, which was hard to believe in a real estate agent. "I don't see why," Katie said. "You didn't do anything wrong, right?"

"What? No, of course not." Fred shook his head vigorously. "I'd never cheat on my wife, not even to console a newly bereaved widow."

Katie took the empty mug he proffered, accepted his thanks for the coffee, and watched him go.

But all the while she was thinking one thing: *Hmmm.*

~~~~~~

After a quick lunch from the bakery, a lunch of which her nutritionally minded great-aunt would never have approved, Katie took a brisk walk across the Square to Sassy Sally's. On the way, she thought about how much she loved the month of September. The weather was relatively warm, the snowy chill of winter was months away, and the air was often so clear and still that it reminded her of the set of a play just after the curtain rose.

Shaking away the fanciful idea, Katie walked up the steps and through the half-open door. Once again, pickup trucks filled the driveway and the poundings of hammers and the shrill shriek of circular saws filled her ears.

"Knock, knock," she called. "Is anyone home?" She started down the hallway to the kitchen but stopped short as Don yelled, "We're in the parlor."

She turned around, made her way back to the lobby, and, just before entering the parlor, asked, "Are you decent?"

"Not in the last twenty-three years," Nick said, laughing.

"And who do you think you are," Don scolded, "coming in here without treats. I'm dying for a sweet snack, and when we heard your voice, I thought rescue was imminent."

"Sorry to disappoint you." The two men were seated side by side on a sofa upholstered in a rose-patterned fabric. In front of them was a coffee table stained so dark it was almost black and covered with fabric and paint swatches, and trim samples.

The remainder of the large room was comfortably furnished with a mixture of upholstered and harder seating. A set of glass bookcases lined one wall, vintage prints of McKinlay Mill occupied another wall, and the other two walls were filled with floor-to-ceiling windows. It was a superbly pleasant space with a wood floor and thick area rugs underfoot, and Katie was glad she'd sold all of the items she'd been stockpiling for so long to Don and Nick so she could visit them on a regular basis.

"Still making decorating decisions?" She sat in the comfy chair that Nick waved her into.

"We'll be choosing room and bathroom decor until the day we die," Don said mournfully.

Nick elbowed him. "Oh, come on. This is fun, remember?"

"A year ago, all this was fun." Don gestured at the piled-high coffee table. "Six months ago it was fun. A month ago, even, it was almost the only thing I could think about. But the last week or so . . ." His voice trailed off. He picked up a sheaf of paint samples and shuffled through them, for once silent.

Katie looked from one man to the other. "The last week or so," she said. "Since Josh was killed, you mean."

"It's like a curtain has come down." Don pulled a fabric swatch from the bottom of one of the tumbling piles and held it up. "All of this"—he spread his hands toward the coffee table—"was great fun two weeks ago. Now?" He let his hands drop.

"Our future used to be clear," Nick said. "Now there's just a murky fog ahead. That Detective Hamilton stops by almost every day, asking questions. Sometimes different ones, sometimes the same ones. We have no idea what's going to happen."

Don swallowed. "Every night since Josh died, when I close my eyes, all I see is that arm hanging over the edge of the tub, with those dead fingers dangling down."

Katie shivered. She'd seen the same thing, but she'd known what was coming. To be confronted with that sight unexpectedly? It was no wonder that Don was suffering from posttraumatic stress syndrome. But maybe what she'd stopped by to tell them would help, at least a little.

"Did you know Marcie Kimper, Josh's widow, has already put both his business and their house up for sale?" she asked.

"Already?" Nick's eyebrows shot up. "That's fast work."

"Yes indeedy." Don looked thoughtful. "Makes you wonder a little bit, doesn't it? Everybody says to wait six months to a year after a spouse's death to make big decisions."

Katie squirmed in her seat. She'd quit her job with Josh and moved to working full-time at Artisans Alley within seven months of her husband's death. Then again, maybe that proved the point—she'd wanted to quit her job at Kimper Insurance for ages, and Chad's tragic car accident, followed by the death of Ezra Hilton, the other partner at Artisans Alley, had pushed her in a new direction.

When she mentioned this, Don squinted at her. "So you're saying Marcie killed Josh to, what? Set herself free?" He smirked.

"I'm not saying anything. I'm just tossing out suggestions."

"Suggest away," Nick said. "Don't pay any attention to

him. Don's not getting enough sleep these days and barely knows what he's saying."

Katie saw Don's expression darken and jumped in before a real argument could start. "I stopped by the insurance agency yesterday," she said. "And it turns out that Josh's new office manager, the woman he hired to replace me, is young and extremely pretty. And she bawled her eyes out when I started talking about Josh."

"O-ho!" Don grinned, his sour expression already history. "Methinks there's a possibility there. Love triangle, jealousy, murder!"

Nick frowned. "Josh was having an affair with his employee and Marcie was so jealous she killed him. Seriously? I mean, you'd met Josh, right? He sure didn't seem like anyone who would inspire deep passions."

Had Don been talking to Ray about it?

"What do you think, Katie?" Don asked, grinning. "Did you ever harbor a deep, secret passion for Kimper?"

"Maybe a deep hatred," she said without thinking. Then she saw the looks on the men's faces and hastened to add, "Not that I truly hated him. He was . . ." The words she'd thrown at him on the marina's dock came back to her, and she smiled faintly. "He was arrogant and rude and a male chauvinist pig, but I wasn't filled with hate for him, and certainly not so much that I would have killed him."

Nick nodded. "Maybe in the heat of an argument you might have slapped him silly, but it just doesn't make sense that you'd want to kill him almost a year after quitting that job. And you're nothing if not sensible."

"Um, thanks." Sensible? That made her sound like a pair of shoes.

"It's just as well," Don said. "If Josh had divorced Marcie

and married you, your name would have been Katie Kimper, and that's just too horrible to contemplate."

She made a face. "There's another possibility. What if Josh was killed to get him out of the way? What if Marcie was the one having the affair?" Because even though Fred had protested, maybe he'd protested a little too much? And how long had Marcie been seeing that attorney she'd seen consoling the lovely widow so soon after her husband's murder?

"Well," Nick said, "that's for the police to find out, isn't it?" He looked from Katie to his partner and back. "What?"

Don sighed theatrically. "The poor, misguided soul. Clearly, Nick hasn't been watching the correct television shows."

"Or reading the proper books," Katie added. "The police are shorthanded and can always use some help."

"Leave it to the professionals," Nick said firmly. "It's their job. And we should be out of it, anyway. We have alibis." He looked to his right. "Solid ones, right, Don?"

Don blinked. "Sure. Of course we do. We were at that party. Lots of people saw us."

"Right." Nick gave Don a hard look, one that was filled with something Katie couldn't interpret. "Lots of people."

"But speaking of Josh Kimper," Don said, either not noticing or ignoring Nick's leaden glance, "do you think I should tell the police what I learned this morning?"

"Tell them what?" Katie asked.

"Don," said Nick in a warning tone of voice.

"Oh, don't 'Don' me. Let's try it out on Katie. If she thinks it's police-worthy, I'll tell Detective Hamilton next time he stops by. If she thinks I'm ridiculous, well, so be it."

Nick rolled his eyes. "Suit yourself."

"Okay, then." Don faced Katie. "I was in Rochester yesterday, running some errands, and I decided to stop in at that nifty wine shop near Winton Office Park. You know the one?"

Katie nodded. When she'd worked for Josh, she'd passed it twice a day on the way to and from work. She'd stopped in once when she'd wanted a nice bottle for a dinner party she and Chad were scheduled to attend, but she'd walked out after realizing that the average price per bottle was more than they'd usually paid for a dinner for two.

"Love that place," Don said. "I stopped to order up a case of their best Beaujolais nouveau. I can't get enough of that stuff. It goes perfectly with—"

Nick made a rolling motion with his index fingers. "Moving on, here."

"Anywaaay," Don said, drawing out the word, "when I was in there, checking out the new labels, I overheard a conversation between a customer and the store's owner. It didn't take long before I realized they were talking about Josh. Which wasn't a huge surprise, because it's not every day that a guy in your neighborhood gets whacked. The surprising part was what they were saying about him."

Katie found herself on the edge of her seat. "What were they saying?"

"That Josh had been buying up other insurance agencies. Suburban places, it sounded like, because I heard them talk about Parma and Henrietta." He snapped his fingers. "Greece, too, come to think of it."

"Weird," Katie said, frowning. "Buying even a small insurance agency would cost thousands and thousands of dollars. Josh didn't have that kind of money."

"He didn't eleven months ago," Don said. "Who knows what might have changed since you left?"

Nick blew out a breath. "Probably nothing. And the two guys you were listening to were probably just spreading unsubstantiated rumors. Let's be honest—which is more likely? Rumors or Josh Kimper magically coming up with the wherewithal to purchase two or three businesses."

Don glared at him. "He could have inherited money from . . . from a long-lost uncle. Or his wife could have. Or maybe his wife was the one with the money all along. She finally loosened the purse strings enough to let him buy some other businesses, but when she found out he'd bought businesses that were losing money, she killed him."

"See why I don't take this seriously?" Nick asked Katie. "One scrap of overheard gossip, and he's fabricated a story that has absolutely no basis in fact."

"All anyone would have to do," Katie said reasonably, "is to call the agencies in those towns and see if there was any truth to the rumors or if they're complete fabrications."

The two men stared at her long enough that she got uncomfortable. "Speaking of fabric," Katie said, standing, "I'm sure you two need to get back to—"

"Hang on," Nick said, putting out a hand. "I have an idea."

"Me, too." Don smiled.

"Would you help us out, Katie?" Nick asked. "I know it's an imposition, but—"

"But could you pretty please call those insurance agencies and ask if there's any truth to the rumors?" Don grinned at her.

Nick had the grace to look a little embarrassed. "You're probably thinking that we could do this just as easily ourselves, but I'm betting that having worked in the insurance business, you know those folks. Or," he hurriedly added when she started shaking her head, "at least you speak the same language."

"Please, Katie?" Don asked. "You can say you're a former employee of Josh's and that you're just making sure there aren't any loose ends after his untimely death. No one has to know that you quit working for him a year ago, right?"

"I'm sure everyone I dealt with was well aware that I'd left the agency."

"But you have a knack for this kind of thing," Nick added. "We'd make a mess of it from the get-go."

She looked from one man to the other, trying to come up with a good reason not to do what they were asking. Even as she thought about it, though, she started to warm to the idea. It wouldn't hurt her, or even take that much time, to make a few phone calls. And if she asked the right questions of the right people, she might learn quite a bit about Josh.

"She's hesitating," Don observed. "We're going to have to up the ante."

Nick shot his partner a glance but said, "How about we invite you and Andy over for dinner when the renovations are all done?"

"Deal," she said.

"Hah!" Don snickered. "We were going to do that anyway."

"And I was going to make those phone calls without the dinner offer, so I'd call us even." She laughed at Don's rueful expression. "I'll let you know when I learn anything," she said and left the two to their decorating decisions.

~~~~~~

A few days before, Katie had emailed or phoned all the Artisans Alley vendors to say that she'd scheduled an evening meeting for that evening. She fielded the usual complaints about not being able to make it on such short notice, about having it at such an inconvenient time, and other similar grumblings and said she'd write up notes about the meeting and distribute them within a day.

"You're too nice," Vance told her as they set up folding chairs in the lobby. She'd locked the front door exactly at closing time, and the meeting was set to start in a few minutes. "Ezra never had vendor meetings, and I can't imagine a situation that would have meant he'd spend any time writing up meeting notes."

Katie shrugged and kept unfolding chairs, thinking that if Ezra, the former owner of Artisans Alley, had paid a little more attention to the vendors, she wouldn't have had to spend the last year digging the place out of the massive financial hole it had dropped into.

"Is it time yet?" Gwen Hardy poked her head around the open doorway to the main sale room. Gwen, a middle-aged woman with fantastically pale skin, hazel eyes, and ginger hair, was a talented weaver. She made blankets, wall hangings, place mats, tablecloths, even kilts.

"Have a seat." Katie patted a chair in the front row. She'd debated about even setting up the chairs, since that implied the meeting would run long enough for people to need to sit down, but she knew if she didn't that the first fifteen minutes would be spent discussing whether or not they should get the chairs out. Sometimes it was easier to do something you thought was silly in order to avoid having to do something even sillier.

Joan MacDonald, the creator of clay-based primitive animal figurines, came in next, her silver hair trim and bouncy. Katie put a hand to her own over-long hair and glanced toward Envy's door, but the CLOSED sign was up. Well, maybe she'd get it cut tomorrow.

Other vendors trickled in, coming down from upstairs or from the main room or in from the back door, where they'd parked in the back lot for the meeting. Edie Silver, silk flowers and crocheting. Godfrey of the dryer lint. Liz Meier, stained glass. Duncan McAllister, bird sculptures in clay and wood. Sam Amato, metal work.

As a number of others came in and took their seats, Vance ticked off their names on the vendors' list Katie had printed out earlier. She looked at her watch and, at the exact time she'd told everyone the meeting would be held, stepped up to the front, smiled, and said, "Good evening, everyone."

When the rumble of return greetings faded away, she said, "First off, I'd like to thank each and every one of you for being here. Not only at this meeting, but also here as a vendor at Artisans Alley. Though we've had our ups and downs this last year, I think we're poised for a great fall and an outstanding Christmas season."

A smattering of applause startled her. She blinked at the noise, which had started in Rose's corner, and said, "Um, thanks," feeling the red warmth of a blush on her cheeks. "Anyway, when any one of us is successful, we all stand to gain from that success, so I encourage everyone to work together." She winced internally at the platitude. When she'd been rehearsing the speech the night before, it hadn't sounded nearly so insipid.

She pulled in a breath and went on. "Brittany Kohler, who owns the Envy Salon, told me the other day that she's cautiously optimistic that she'll do well here. As I told you a few months ago, I brought her in here to expand our customer base and get in foot traffic. What I'd like to know from you is if you're seeing any of those effects."

"I am," Liz Meier said, nodding vigorously. "Hands down. I don't even have to ask to know—I've never seen them before and they smell like hair salon shampoo. Where else would they have come from?"

Laughter rippled through the group, and two more vendors shared stories of sales directly related to the salon. Katie smiled, grateful that her plan to allow the salon was actually working. It had been a gamble, and she was relieved it was paying off.

"What about that god-awful stench?" called a male voice.

Though Katie wasn't sure who had spoken, she had a feeling it was Godfrey. "I've talked to Crystal," she said. "That's the young woman who is doing the acrylic nails. She's aware of the issue and understands that it can't continue."

"So what is she doing about it?"

Yes, that was definitely Godfrey's voice. He must have been sitting behind Duncan McAllister, who was large enough for Godfrey to hide behind. Wearing a forced smile, Katie said, "She'll be getting the details to me soon." Or she would be, once Katie could get ahold of her. "But you can be assured that it will be taken care of."

Godfrey started up again, but he was drowned out by another vendor.

"Never mind about all that," Edie Silver said loudly. With her gray eyes and short gray hair, her appearance matched her last name perfectly. Her short stature and solid body didn't exactly go with Katie's own personal vision of silver, but that could be her own limitation. "What I want to know is," Edie continued, "what happened to Josh Kimper?"

A murmur of agreement rippled through the group.

"Are we safe here?" someone asked.

"Have they figured out who killed him?" asked another.

"Is he going to kill again?"

"I heard it was a serial killer."

"A what?"

The comments grew more and more panicked. Katie scanned the group, but there was no sign of Ray. *Swell*, she thought. *I could have used a little police backup here.* Aloud she said, "The Sheriff's Office is investigating the murder.

There hasn't been an unsolved murder in this county in many years, and I have complete faith that they'll solve this one, too." That was a big lie. There were plenty of unsolved murders in Rochester alone—mostly drug related.

Her comments, while not mollifying her audience completely, did quell the questions. She looked at her notes and was about to move on to the next item when her assistant manager raised his hand. When she nodded at him, Vance asked, "Katie, what about our insurance policies? Do you know what happens when the agent dies? Sorry to put you on the spot, but I wondered if you might know since you used to work for Josh Kimper."

Judging from the number of eyes that swiveled her way, Katie realized that many of her vendors hadn't been aware of that particular fact. She had no idea what the protocol was for the sudden death of an insurance agent, but she had to say something—and say it fast—or risk losing all credibility with the artisans.

"The insurance underwriter," she said, thinking fast, "will of course honor all policies already in place. As a business, however, Kimper Insurance won't be able to write any new policies without a certified agent."

"But what if we have a claim?" Vance asked.

Katie looked around. "How many of you have insurance with Kimper's?" She was surprised at the number of hands that went up. Insuring their wares was a good idea, but she'd been under the impression that it was so expensive that most vendors went without. Then, suddenly, she understood.

"Is it insurance for your booths here, or is it car, home, or life insurance?"

The room filled with voices citing different answers to her question, so she asked for a show of hands. In the end it turned out that only two vendors had insured their Artisans

Alley wares with Josh. One or two others insured their booths with other agencies, and of the absent vendors, she was told that two or three of them had booth insurance.

"To tell you the truth," Katie said, "I don't know what would happen if you have a claim." If it were her, she would have already yanked her insurance policies away from Kimper and moved them to another firm. But then she'd worked in the field for a lot of years and had a jaded view of underwriters, which was that they tried to keep from paying anything they didn't absolutely have to.

"But," she went on quickly, seeing the concerned frowns, "you should probably call Josh's office. It's still open, and I'm sure his office manager will be able to give you accurate information." When she wasn't weeping, that was.

"What about the killer?" Rose asked. "Do you think Victoria Square is safe?"

Katie wanted to say of course it was, wanted to say that it had been a personal crime, wanted to say that Josh had been such a jerk that it was more a question of narrowing down all the possibilities than finding the one person who might have had a motive.

But she didn't know any of that for sure. All she could do to reassure them was tell the truth. "I think it is." She left it at that.

"Even with a killer running around?" someone asked.

"Yes." Katie nodded. "Even with." Then, because she felt a need to explain that response, she said, "Josh drowned, but not in the bed-and-breakfast. The water in his lungs came from Lake Ontario."

Some people nodded, others murmured with surprise, two or three looked thoughtful. Katie took it all in, then said, "I worked for Josh for a long time. Please don't spread this around," she said, glancing left and right, "but he was a tremendous jerk."

She was relieved to hear laughter. When it started to fade, she said, "If you have any information that you think has any bearing to the murder, please talk to the deputies." Then, after a moment, she went on to the next item on her list.

But as they went through the plans for the harvest sale, Katie wondered about those two or three vendors who'd worn those thoughtful expressions. What did that mean?

She didn't know, but she vowed to find out.

Seven

Katie encouraged her cat Mason off the dining chair. At the same time, Andy was tipping his chair forward, creating a surface so inclined that Della would be tempted to jump to the floor and find another surface.

Finally, they were both free to sit and eat the dinner that Katie had spent the last hour preparing: chicken teriyaki with vegetables over rice pilaf. She figured it was an excellent combination; healthy enough to keep from feeling guilty, yummy enough to keep from feeling deprived.

"This looks great," Andy said. "All I've had to eat for the last three days is stuff from downstairs. I never thought I'd get tired of eating pizza, but looks like there's a limit, even for me."

Katie smiled. "I know what you mean."

As they ate, they talked about their days. Andy had been shorthanded lately due to unforeseen complications with his employees' schedules, and it seemed as if the situation wasn't going to resolve itself anytime soon.

"I need to hire at least two more part-timers," he said, "but where am I going to find them? The high school and college kids who want jobs already have them, and the adults I've seen who want to deliver pizza as a part-time job aren't exactly the kind of guys I want hanging around my younger guys."

Katie sympathized. "I'll ask Vance," she told him. "His son is a senior in high school. Maybe he has some ideas."

"Thanks." Andy smiled at her, and as per usual, her heart went a little gooey at the edges. "That would be great." He toasted her with a fork full of chicken. "You know, I've been doing all the talking. How was your day?"

She told him about her visit to Sassy Sally's and the volunteer job she'd agreed to.

"Because you need, what, more work?" Andy rolled his eyes.

"It's only a few phone calls," she protested. "And they're right, I speak the insurance language. I'm sure I'll get much better answers than they would." She'd spent the last part of her day on the computer, researching small insurance agencies in the three towns Don and Nick had mentioned, and she planned to start making the phone calls on Monday.

Andy shook his head. "You're a sucker," he said, but he was smiling.

"I'm their friend."

"A friend who's a sucker for more work, then."

"Isn't that a little like the pot calling the kettle black?" she asked.

"A little?" He grinned. "I'd say a lot. That's why I can recognize it so easily."

She returned his grin. "Two of a kind, is that what you're saying we are?"

"Here's to us." He toasted her again. "Say, how did your vendors' meeting go?" he asked, before inserting the laden fork into his mouth.

"Okay, I guess." She frowned, thinking about the concerned questions that had come up. "It turned a little weird, though. They started asking about Josh's murder and if they were safe or not."

Andy shrugged. "Seems like a reasonable concern."

She looked at him. "Really? Are you worried?"

"Me?" He blinked. "Of course not. But I'm not the worrying type."

It was true. Andy worried less than almost any person she'd ever met. She sighed. "I wish more of my vendors were like you. And I wish Ray Davenport had been there."

Andy's fork went still. "Oh? Why's that?"

"Because he used to be a detective," she said. "I'm sure he could have answered a lot of those questions a lot better than I did. Plus, he has a way about him that calms people down and reassures them. I wish I could do that."

Andy didn't say anything for a moment. Then, quietly, he said, "You seem to be spending a lot of time with Davenport these days."

"Well, sure." She looked at him with surprise. "Of course I am. We're working on—"

Just then, Andy's cell phone went off. The pizzeria's ringtone filled Katie's kitchen. "Sorry," he muttered and took the call. "What's up?" He looked into space. "Uh-huh . . . Uh-huh . . . No, don't do that!" He dropped his fork and pushed his chair back. "I'll be right down, okay? Don't do anything until I get there."

He stood. "Sorry, I gotta go." He leaned down to give Katie a quick kiss. "The main oven is down, and my genius assistant manager thinks it would be a great idea to close the place for the night. Seriously?"

Shaking his head, he hurried out, leaving Katie alone at the table.

Mason jumped up onto Andy's chair and sat, blinking wide cat eyes at her.

"How nice it is to see you," she said. "Would you like a glass of wine?"

"Meow."

Katie laughed. Maybe she didn't have a boyfriend who could spend evenings with her, but at least she had cats with a sense of humor.

~~~~~~~~

The next morning, Katie woke up more than an hour before she needed to. She yawned, looked at the clock, thought about what she could do with all that time—read, bake a batch of brownies, go for a nice long walk—then she yawned again and fell back asleep until the alarm went off.

As she got up and ready for work, she started to berate herself for not taking advantage of that extra hour, but then she decided that if she'd fallen back to sleep, she must have needed the rest. Besides, at least she was *thinking* about exercising, and that alone was a big step, considering that exercising hadn't been anywhere on her priority list for the last year.

Soon, she told herself. She'd start an exercise program soon. Did the local high school allow the public to use their outdoor track? Katie made a mental note to ask Vance about it when she talked to him about employee possibilities for Andy. Though the track wouldn't be of much use once the snow started falling in December—if not sooner.

On the way to Artisans Alley, she took an extra turn
around the Square before heading in, waving to Jordan Tanner, the baker, as she went past the second time. Jordan, who
had been cleaning his front window, poked his head out the
door. "Are you lost, young lady?" he asked. "Because I think
you want to go that way." He pointed across the Square.

Katie laughed, a little embarrassed. "Just out for a walk
on this fine morning," she said. Just then, a crash of thunder
made her jump. She glanced up and felt the patter of rain-
drops on her face.

"Fine morning for an umbrella," Jordan called to her as
she began her trek across the Square and finally dashed into
Artisans Alley. Inside, she stood on the front mat, trying to
figure out what would be her next best step.

"Oh dear," Rose said. "Let me get you a towel."

Katie reached up and felt her hair. It was sopped. "Thanks,
that would be great," she said to Rose's retreating back. She
looked down at her clothes. How could she have gotten so
wet in such a short time? Too bad Brittany's salon didn't open
for a couple of hours; what better time to get her hair cut than
when it was a huge, damp mess?

Rose hurried back from her nearby booth and handed
over a fluffy yellow towel. Katie knew better than to ask why
Rose had a towel at the ready; the older woman was always
prepared for any emergency from coffee stains to lost but-
tons to upset stomachs. "Thanks," Katie said gratefully and
blotted her hair with the towel. "Thankfully, I have a change
of clothes in my office."

The T-shirt, jeans, and socks were left over from a project
she'd finished up a few weeks ago, that of cleaning out the
area Chad had been using in Artisans Alley as a living space
in the time they'd been separated. The clothes wouldn't be
exactly clean—she'd meant to take them home and put them

in the laundry, but somehow hadn't gotten around to it—but at least they were dry, which was a huge step forward from what she was wearing.

"See what exercise does?" she asked Rose, still toweling. "I would have been fine if I'd walked straight here, but no, I have to decide that today is the day I'll start taking those extra steps."

"Did you get one of those fitness bracelets, too?" Rose held out a hand, showing off the light blue strap around her wrist. "I try to get in ten thousand steps a day. What's your goal?"

Katie laughed. "To get though the day in one piece."

"Setting the bar a little low, aren't you?" Rose asked dryly.

"Small, achievable goals can build to a substantial future," Katie said.

Edie Silver, who'd just come in through the front door, shut her umbrella and said, "Sounds like something out of a self-help book—or a fortune cookie." She frowned at Katie. "Don't tell me you're reading that kind of crap."

Katie wasn't, but she had in the past and wasn't apologetic about it. "Don't tell me you don't think we're all in need of a little improvement?"

"Honey, I'm too old to improve." Edie rolled her eyes. "If I haven't fixed myself by now, there's no hope for me. Say, you got a second?"

"Sure. What's up?"

Edie looked pointedly at Rose, who took the hint and headed back to her booth. Edie moved closer to Katie, who said, "If this is something you'd like to talk about in private, we can go to my office and shut the door."

"No, no," Edie said, "I can't stay. Got an appointment on the other side of town to pick up some free supplies from a woman whose arthritis is too bad to let her keep crocheting.

But after that meeting last night, there's something I thought you should know." Her voice dropped to a whisper. "Something that might have to do with that murder."

"Edie, you should go to the deputies if you have any information. I don't—"

"It's about Vance," Edie whispered.

"Vance?" Katie asked, starting to look around for the slim Santa.

"Shhh!" With flat palms, Edie made frantic shushing motions. "I don't want him to hear, and I don't want him to see the two of us going into your office together behind closed doors."

Katie didn't see much difference between that and a whispered conversation in the lobby. "What did you want to tell me?" she asked. "Did Vance know Josh?"

"No idea," Edie said. "But I know something about Vance that might change what you think about him."

"Oh?" Katie had a hard time believing that. She'd known Vance for a while, and he'd been her assistant manager for almost a year. She couldn't imagine a more dependable and responsible person. "What's that?"

"He has a boat," Edie whispered.

"A . . . what?" Katie asked. That didn't make sense; never once had she heard Vance mention boating of any kind.

"A boat." Edie stretched her arms out wide. "A great big one. When you said that Josh had drowned in Lake Ontario, I just, you know, wondered. If Josh had been out with Vance and they had an argument, maybe . . . well, you know."

"I didn't know they knew each other."

Edie shrugged. "No idea if they did or not. I just wanted to tell you that Vance owns a boat." Giving Katie a firm nod, she said, "And now my job is done. See you later." She marched to the door, unfurled her umbrella, and went out into the rain.

"Okaaay," Katie said to herself and headed for her office. She wanted to get out of her wet clothes before she started shivering.

Halfway there, Sam Amato stopped her. "Hey, you got a minute?"

Katie closed her eyes. "Don't tell me. It's about a boat."

"Yeah, how did you know?"

"Oh, these things get around," she said, sighing. "Do you know how big it is?"

"Well, I think she said it was thirty-three, but I could be wrong."

Katie's attention, which had been wandering, suddenly focused. "She? We're not talking about Vance?"

"Uh, no. Gwen Hardy. She has this great big sailboat on Lake Ontario. After you said that yesterday, about Josh Kimper drowning there, I thought you might want to know. Gwen gets her insurance from an agency here in town, but still."

Katie thanked Sam and excused herself. She'd just unlocked her office door when Liz Meier, the stained glass artist, sidled up close. "Morning, Katie. Do you have a minute?"

"Is this about a boat?" Katie asked listlessly.

The woman's eyes flew open wide. "How on earth did you guess?"

She smiled wanly. "Just lucky."

With her eyes darting left and right, Liz told Katie that Duncan McAllister, the new vendor who did the amazingly lifelike bird sculptures, had a boat that he kept at a marina not too far from McKinlay Mill.

Katie thanked her for the information and, at long last, shut herself into the office so she could change out of her wet things.

Boats. There certainly seemed to be a lot of boats involved, from meeting Josh for that last time at the marina to all the vendors who happened to have owned one. Not that she really suspected Vance, Gwen, or even Duncan, of course, but it was starting to make her wonder a little.

~~~~~~

On Friday night, Katie stopped by Angelo's Pizzeria to kiss Andy good night and then drove over to Seth's house for dinner. Once there, she leaned against the kitchen counter, sipping a glass of wine, while he cut, chopped, and whisked.

"I could help," she offered.

"No, no," he said quickly. "You're my inspiration, standing there like that. My muse. The reason for cooking at all."

Katie fake-gagged. "More like you don't want me in your way."

"That, too," he agreed. "I am a control freak and don't you forget it. Why do you think I'm still living alone?"

"Because you're ugly," she said.

"Ah." Seth nodded sagely as he continued to chop away. "I had a feeling it was something like that."

Katie laughed. Her friend was slim, fit, still had a full head of hair in his early forties, and was anything but ugly. "I have an even better feeling that you just haven't met the right guy yet."

"I hope I meet him soon," Seth said, "or I'll get so set in my ways that I won't be fit to live with."

Katie held up her glass. "To your future mate, wherever he may be."

"Hang on." Seth looked around for his own glass. He grabbed it, reached out, and their glasses make a tinking sound as they touched. "To my future mate." After they drank, he asked, "Speaking of future mates, how is it going with Andy? Seems as if you spend as much time with me as you do with him."

"We have lunch together every other day," Katie said. *Or almost.* "And once September settles down, he's going to take a couple of nights off a week."

"Tell him he'd better treat you right or your Uncle Seth will get after him."

"Uncle Seth?" Katie giggled and realized that she'd better slow down on the wine if she was going to drive herself home that night. "The only uncle I ever had was named James, and he died fifteen years ago of liver disease."

Seth shrugged. "Andy doesn't need to know that."

Another giggle escaped. Katie put her wineglass down on Seth's granite countertop and made an effort to think of something serious.

Her exercise program?

She did an internal eye roll.

Artisans Alley?

No, she was here to have a good time with her friend, not to think about work. Of course, work had turned a little strange, what with all those people telling her how many vendors owned big boats. Two of those vendors, she'd learned later, had also been clients of Josh's.

"What's going on in that busy brain of yours?" Seth, passing by with a pan of chopped onion in one hand, tapped her forehead with the other. "No prevaricating, young lady. Tell me what's putting furrows into that brow."

Katie smoothed out her face, not wanting it to freeze that way. "Would you like to hear everything I've learned about Josh Kimper?"

"His life or his death?" Seth flicked on one of the cooktop's burners.

"Both."

"Nothing graphic?" he asked.

"Nope."

"Then go right ahead."

So Katie did. She told him about her visit with Marcie, that the new widow hadn't appeared to be grieving and that she was being comforted by a deep kiss from another man. She told him that Josh had drowned in Lake Ontario and been moved. She told him that Marcie was selling both the insurance business and the house. Katie told him that Josh had replaced her with a young and attractive office manager who'd cried whenever Josh's name was mentioned. Told him that after she'd asked her vendors to pass on any information they might have about Josh to the police, she'd subsequently been advised that at least three vendors owned large boats moored on Lake Ontario.

By that time they were sitting at the jet-black dining table with the flames of strategically placed candles reflecting in the table's clear sheen. When she finished, Seth had just picked up his chopsticks and started eating the steaming chicken stir-fry.

Katie's hand hovered over her chopsticks but landed on the fork. "So," she asked, "what do you think?"

He swallowed, then asked, "About what?"

"Any of it."

"Well," he said, picking up another bite of food, "I'm thinking that you don't know that Kimper's agency was one of the biggest in Rochester."

"It . . . what?" Katie's fork stopped moving, and she stared at Seth. "What are you talking about? Josh's agency was midsized, at best."

"Maybe it used to be," Seth said, "but in the last year or so it had tremendous growth."

"How do you know?" Katie asked.

Seth grinned. "I have my sources. And I have complete confidence that they're reliable."

"But . . ." Katie stopped her protest before it got going. *But*, she wanted to say, *I was the only reason he'd succeeded as much as he had.* She had been so sure that he'd lose clients after she left, with her gone and no one to take care of the agency's real business. How on earth could he have grown the business without her?

She poked at her dinner halfheartedly. Her fantasies of the business crashing and burning in her absence had been just that—fantasies. Obviously, her presence hadn't made any difference to the agency. Or, if it had, maybe it had been a negative presence. Maybe, somehow, she'd been the one holding him back.

"And," Seth was saying, seemingly oblivious to her hurt and confusion, "you have a bizarre fixation on boats. Half the people in McKinlay Mill own a boat. Are they all murder suspects?"

"Half?" Katie's eyebrows went up.

"Well, maybe not a half," Seth admitted. "How about a quarter? No? Well, even five percent is still going to be a lot of people."

"Yes, but how many of them had insurance policies with Josh?" Katie asked. "And don't you think it's more than a coincidence that Josh's body was moved to Sassy Sally's after being drowned in the lake, that Artisans Alley has at least three owners of big boats, and that they had policies with Kimper Insurance?"

"Coincidence is one thing," Seth said in his slightly deeper attorney voice. "What the law requires, however, is proof."

"Fine," Katie said. "If that's what they need, then I'll get it." And she knew exactly where she'd start.

Eight

Saturday dawned—traditionally the busiest day of the week at Artisans Alley. Katie bounced out of bed bright and early, and after a quick shower, a thorough cat snuggle, and the subsequent necessary stint with a lint roller, she headed out the door, down the stairs, and landed smack in front of Angelo's Pizzeria. She turned the corner and proceeded down the block, turned at the intersection, and power walked another two blocks to the little strip mall that housed not only the village's sole grocery store, but Del's Diner.

"You're a little ahead of schedule, aren't you?" Sandy asked as she set a glass of water and a mug of coffee onto Katie's table.

Katie smiled. It was nice, going to a place so often that the waitress knew what you wanted without having to ask for it. Next time she went to another restaurant, it was going to take

her a minute to remember that she had to actually order coffee. "I need a couple of minutes with Del," she said. "Is he
busy?"

Sandy, who'd been pulling her order pad from a pocket on
her black apron, stopped and stared at Katie. "Honey, you
know if you have a problem with me or the food, all you have
to do is say so. You don't need to talk to the boss."

"Oh no, it's nothing like that," Katie reassured her. "It's
just that when I was in the other day, Del mentioned something about a boat, and I just wanted to hear a little more."

"Yeah?" Sandy appeared supremely uninterested. "I got
tired of hearing Del talk about boats ten years ago. Listening
to a boat nut talk about boats is worse than hearing my husband talk about his golf game. You getting two scrambled,
raisin toast, bacon, and home fries with orange juice today?"

Katie sighed. "No. Not today. I'd like a bowl of oatmeal.
No brown sugar." If she wasn't going to exercise, she could
at least have a healthy breakfast.

"Really?" Sandy's eyebrows shot up. "That's what you
want?"

Katie laughed. "No, but it's what I'm going to order."

"If you say so." Sandy shook her head and wrote the order
down. "Be back with that in a jiffy, missy." She headed to the
kitchen, her thick-soled shoes soundless on the tile floor.

After adding cream to her coffee, Katie sipped the hot
brew, thinking that she should have brought a book to read.
The restaurant was nearly full, but she didn't see a soul that
she knew. She was on the verge of getting up to borrow an
obviously used newspaper sitting next to the cash register
when Del himself came out of the kitchen and over to her
table.

He was also carrying a tray that held her oatmeal, a tiny

pitcher of milk, and a miniature bowl of brown sugar. "Here," he said, moving the items from his tray to her paper place mat with its scalloped edges.

"I know you said no brown sugar, but that doesn't make any sense to me, so you're getting it anyway." He tucked the tray under his arm and sat on the end of the bench seat. "Sandy said you were asking about boats. What do you want to know? I been spending every second I can on the water since my momma let me go out alone in a fourteen-foot johnboat. Any boat question you got, I bet I have the answer."

"Not boats in general," Katie said.

"No?" Del looked around the room, then, apparently satisfied that he wasn't needed anywhere else at that particular moment, turned back to Katie. "Are you looking to buy something?"

"No, but you were," she said. "Remember I was in here the other day and found that boat brochure under the front counter?"

"Sure do." In the time it took him to say those two words, Del's face went from open and pleasant to closed and unfriendly. "What of it?" he asked roughly.

Katie took in his changed attitude and adjusted herself accordingly. "Well, nothing, really, but it seems like every time I turn around these days I either hear that someone I didn't know was interested in boating at all has one, or that someone I never figured had insurance policies with Josh Kimper actually did."

Del's face was starting to look like a rock, unmoving and unyielding, so Katie hurried to say, "Nick and Don over at Sassy Sally's are good friends of mine, and they're concerned that the murder investigation might hurt their business. I want to do whatever I can to help them, and, like I said, boats keep turning up in a lot of conversations."

"That Don." Del laughed. "He's a nut. A good one, but still a nut. Okay, I guess I see where you're going with this. And you'll never guess the guy who was behind that great boat deal I was supposed to get."

"Josh Kimper," Katie said. Something Del had said that day had lingered in the back of her mind and had finally burst into her consciousness the night before at Seth's dining table.

"Bingo." Del's shoulders heaved up and down as he blew out a heavy sigh. "You know Warren Noth? He's the contractor at Sally's. I was out at Thompson's Landing about a year ago and saw his boat. It would have been perfect. Right size, the right engines, the right cabin setup, everything." He stared off into space, remembering.

Katie waited, but Del didn't say anything for what felt like half an hour. Then, when she was ready to interrupt, he stirred and said, "Anyway, a few weeks ago I ran into Kimper at that big boat supply store in Irondequoit—I needed a new anchor for my dinky little Boston Whaler—and we got talking. I mentioned Noth's boat, and Kimper said he had a line on one a lot like that. He said he'd able to work out a deal for me if I was willing to wait a little bit."

"How long?" Katie asked.

"A few months," Del said. "So I wouldn't get it in time for this season, but in plenty of time for next year." His face twisted. "And now I got nothing. Even now, at the end of the season when prices are the lowest they'll probably get, there's nothing close to what Josh was promising. It's either get a loan, which my wife isn't about to let me do, or accept the fact that any new boat I get is going to be a lot smaller than what Kimper was going to get for me."

Katie, who had by now finished her oatmeal, gave him a sympathetic smile. "Well, I seem to be running into a lot of people with boats these days. If I hear of a good deal, I'll give you a call."

"Thanks, Katie," Del said and pushed himself to his feet. "But I'm not going to hold my breath."

Watching him go, she thought about what she'd just learned. Josh had been brokering yet another boat deal. Why? What did selling boats have to do with the insurance business? And, more to the point, did it have anything to do with Josh's murder?

Once inside her office, Katie got to work on updating her spreadsheets to generate a mid-month report. In a few more weeks she would have a complete year of financial data she'd assembled herself, and she was looking forward to being able to make solid comparisons between this and the previous year.

She was so engrossed in the data that she didn't realize anyone had come in until someone cleared her throat so loudly it make Katie jump.

"Rose!" Katie put her hands to her throat. "I didn't know you were there."

"Sorry," Rose said, not sounding sorry at all. "But you need to know what's going on in the lobby."

"Haven't we had this conversation before?" Katie asked, half smiling.

"Close but not quite." Rose made a come-along motion with her head, her honey-blonde curls dancing as she did so. "Better do this now. The natives are getting restless."

Katie saved her data, then pushed her creaky chair backward and stood. "Isn't it a little early for that?" she asked. "Restlessness, I mean. It isn't even noon."

"You'll see why," Rose said as they walked down the short hallway and turned the corner to the lobby. "Or rather you'll—"

"Holy cow!" Katie stopped dead and wrinkled her nose. "What is that awful smell?"

Rose held her arm out like the ghost of Christmas past and pointed to a cluster of air fresheners. A big cluster. As in a dozen or more, sitting on a small table in the center of the lobby. An orange extension cord snaked its way from a wall outlet to the table, where it exploded in a mass of tangled short extension cords plugged into more extension cords so that each air freshener had its own power source.

The competing smells were even worse than the smell from the candles had been, but to Katie, that wasn't the real problem. It was the incredible fire hazard the extension cords were creating. And the tripping hazard. And the—

Katie stopped listing all the problems in her head and practically ran to the end of the main extension cord. She yanked it out of the wall and started looping it in one hand.

"I've heard," said Rose, who was standing by and watching, "that those plug-in air fresheners are a fire hazard in and of themselves, and studies have concluded their emissions are carcinogenic."

Katie nodded. She'd heard the same thing and had immediately unplugged the one she'd installed next to the cat's litter box. She missed the fresh linen scent, but the possibility of a fire, even if remote, wasn't worth it.

Once she'd finished with the orange cord, she crouched down and started unplugging the tangled mess under the table.

She and Crystal were going to have to have a serious talk. No artificial scent was going to cover up the sharp odor coming from the salon. Although, now that both candles and air fresheners were out, Katie wasn't sure what was left, but Crystal would have to try something else. Katie knew she was going to have to play the bad guy, and she regretted that.

Crystal seemed like a hard worker who, if she was given a chance, would go far, and Katie wanted to encourage that kind of attitude, but she couldn't let it happen at the expense of Artisans Alley.

The last air freshener was just out of her reach. She went down onto her knees and stretched out with her arm, reaching, then saw a pair of very wide and brown shoes come to a stomping halt six inches from her outstretched right hand.

"This can't be allowed to continue," thundered a deep voice.

Katie closed her eyes for a moment. Of all the things she didn't want to deal with right now, talking to Godfrey Foster was in the top ten.

"I want to know what you're going to do about this," he continued loudly.

Or, possibly, the top five.

Recognizing that she was at a huge psychological disadvantage by being on the floor, Katie didn't respond at first. Instead, she finished unplugging the last air freshener and crawled out from under the table while dragging the conglomeration of fresheners and extension cords.

Godfrey went on with his tirade as she got to her feet and dusted off her pants. "This is inexcusable," he said, waving at the pile she'd just created. "How could anyone be so ridiculous as to think cheap little products like this could possibly mask the stench coming out of there?" He pointed at the salon. "It's bad enough that we have to smell the shampoos and conditioners and dyes and whatever horrific chemicals they use for permanent waves, but the reek of those acrylic nails is beyond the pale. It cannot be borne, and I insist that you do something about it right this instant."

Katie, still leaned over in the act of making sure her pants weren't dusty, could have sworn that Godfrey stamped his foot, just like a three-year-old.

"I demand to know your plan," he said. "*We* demand to know."

Katie looked around Godfrey's large, soft body and didn't see anyone except Rose. The few shoppers who'd been in the lobby had vanished either out the front door or into the sales room when Godfrey had started shouting, so she didn't know what "we" he was talking about, exactly. The royal "we" just did not pertain to Godfrey.

Still, much as she'd didn't want to admit it, he had a point. And when he stopped talking, she would tell him so.

"It's got to be a breach of the lease contract to subject the rest of us to this smell," he was saying. "We have a right to safe premises, do we not?"

Katie frowned, her ire rising. "What isn't safe here? Artisans Alley has women's and men's bathrooms, a vendors' lounge with a kitchenette. I've installed fire extinguishers, emergency exit signs, automated external defibrillators, and air-conditioning, at great expense, I may add. And last winter I spent a small fortune on salt for the sidewalks and parking lot. What more can I possibly do?"

Godfrey smiled, and Katie averted her eyes from the sight of his rubbery lips turning upward. "If you can afford all that," he said, "why don't we have an elevator? That should be required in a two-story building. I can't believe you haven't been cited for that."

Katie put her shoulders back and started straight at him. "Are you saying that I'm breaking the law by not having spent over a hundred thousand dollars on an elevator?"

"Well, no," he said, shifting his eyes away from hers. "Not breaking the law, precisely, but skirting it, perhaps."

"There is no requirement," Katie snapped. "Not for a store that hasn't changed from its retail purpose in decades."

"Then you'd best figure out what to do about that place." He pointed at the salon again. "I have allergies, you know. Very bad allergies. And if something happens to me, you can bet that I'll be suing you for every penny you have and then some."

He spun around and marched off.

Katie's shoulders slumped. Now what was she going to do?

~~~~~~~

Katie's early lunch at Del's with Andy didn't provide her with any answers to the Godfrey dilemma, but it did give her a needed respite from the morning's stress. But at the end of the meal—which lasted no longer than the time it took to order, get the food, and eat—Andy got up, said a quick "Got to go, I'll see you later," and left the restaurant.

Katie lingered over her coffee for another five minutes or so before she, too, got up and left the diner. As she walked back to Artisans Alley, zipping up her jacket against air that held a chill, Katie wondered where the relationship between herself and Andy was likely to go. They were good together, but with their work schedules, how were they ever going to spend enough time together to see what they both truly wanted?

Her steps slowed as a new thought occurred to her. Was Andy spending so little time with her because he didn't see that they *had* a future? Was he intentionally pulling away from her gradually? Would their time together be less and less until it just dribbled to nothing?

Katie shook her head and started walking again. Andy

wasn't like that. He didn't play games. He was open and straightforward, and if he wanted something different, he wouldn't beat around any bushes; he'd come out and ask.

With that settled, at least in her own mind, Katie went back to thinking about the latest crisis at Artisans Alley. She thought about it as she walked across the Square, thought about it as she walked in the front door, and was still thinking about it when she stood in front of the door to the Envy Salon and Day Spa, which held a handwritten sign that said, "Out to lunch, back at 1."

"Swell," Katie muttered. Well, she'd have to talk to Crystal later. She made a mental note to get the young woman's phone number from Brittany at the earliest opportunity, and that would be later in the afternoon when she'd scheduled herself to work at the front cash register. She did want to get the financial statements in line first, but Saturday was the busiest day for the vendors, and she wanted to give them as much face time with their customers as she could.

Before heading back to her office, though, she decided to take a walk around the sales floor, something she always enjoyed. But it was more than enjoyment, she realized as she went past a booth of handmade cards, a booth of fused glass jewelry, a booth selling nature photographs, and a booth filled with blown glass. Walking the floor gave her a deep sense of pride and accomplishment for what she'd achieved by turning around a dying business. She'd provided a sales vehicle for her dozens of artists and provided access to original arts and crafts for people not only in McKinlay Mill, but for miles around.

Katie glowed as she watched customers exclaim over the vendors' wares. She was doing good work, running Artisans Alley, and even with the occasional crisis, she was far happier here than she'd ever been working in the insurance business.

"Hey, Ms. Bonner. What do you think?"

It took Katie a moment to realize that she'd been asked a question. She couldn't think of the last time anyone other than the deputies had called her by her last name, and the young voice that had hailed her was no police officer.

She turned from the booth of pressed flowers she'd been looking over and faced two of Ray Davenport's three daughters, Sadie and Sasha. Both were teenaged, blonde, and dressed in jeans, sneakers, and hooded sweatshirts that had the name of the local high school emblazoned across the front. The two were nearly identical in height, and Katie had no idea which one was older, nor did she have any idea which one had spoken.

But it didn't matter, since both had dimpled smiles and were obviously eager to show her something.

"What do I think of what?" Katie asked.

Like a precision team, the two girls stepped apart and flung out their arms, gesturing toward the booth that Ray had recently rented. "This!" Sadie said proudly.

Katie blinked at the transformation. Ray had handed over a month's rent the week before and early that next morning he'd put together a simple booth arrangement of shelves filled with his wooden creations. It had been nice enough, but on the plain side, and anyone not specifically looking for a wooden toy or frame would have passed right by.

That minimalist display was gone, and a spectacularly attractive booth was in its place. The serviceable wooden shelves had been replaced by jet-black displays with indirect lighting that lit Ray's wares crisply. The harsh overhead light was no more; it had a clip-on shade that bathed the booth in a warm glow. The plain white plastic table was now covered with the sheen of a dark gray silk that hung to the floor in luxurious folds, and the plain three-ring binder that had contained photos of other pieces by Ray had vanished. Instead, an electronic picture display set inside one of Ray's wooden frames automatically rotated images of different pieces.

"This is . . ." Katie struggled for words.

"Amazing?" Sasha suggested.

"Stupendous?" Sadie asked, giggling.

"Fantastic," her sister said.

"Awesome."

"Stunning."

"Breathtaking."

Katie laughed, ending the superlative contest. "All of the above. But . . . how?" She gestured at the booth. "And does your dad know about this?"

The girls looked at each other and shrugged. "Sure," Sadie said. "I mean, he doesn't know the details, but we told him he needed to fix up his booth a little."

Katie's eyebrows went up. "This is what you call a little?"

Sadie grinned. "So we inherited the gift of understatement from our dad. Is that our fault?"

No, Katie thought, but she decided brokering communication between the girls and Ray wasn't her job. She moved on to the bigger questions. "But how did you do all this? These fixtures must have cost a fortune."

Sasha was shaking her head. "Hardly cost anything. Out at the mall? One of Dad's friends works security, and he was over at the house the other day, said a store was going out of business and we could pick up stuff for next to nothing."

"That's what gave us this idea in the first place," Sadie said, picking up the story. "One of the guys in my class, his dad has a landscaping business where my friend works in the summer, so it was no big deal to get him to borrow a truck and trailer and haul these things over. We packed it all up last night and got here first thing this morning."

"And that silk?" Sadie pointed, beaming. "I found that at a resale store. Can you believe it? Yards and yards. It was in a back corner and dirty, but still, all I had to do was wash it in the bathtub a few times, dry it out on a clothesline I rigged up, and iron it."

Yes, that was all she had to do. Katie smiled at the girls. Whoever said that the youth of today wasn't willing to work had never met this pair.

"We paid all of two dollars for that lamp shade," Sasha said eagerly. "It was in same resale shop where we found the silk."

"And that electronic picture display," Sadie said, "was a Christmas present Dad had never used. It's just perfect for this, don't you think?"

Katie nodded and anticipated that many of the other vendors would start doing the same thing.

"You know," Sadie said, looking around, "Dad likes it here a lot. This is so nice, I bet he thinks twice about moving to that old barn of a store when that construction is done."

Katie smiled. She had a feeling Sadie was projecting her own feelings onto her dad. "I doubt that. He needs more space than this booth if he's going to make much money. And there's certainly no place here for him to do his woodworking."

"But you'd like it if he stayed, right?" Sasha asked.

"Of course I would," Katie said. If she was any judge of human behavior, a booth like what they'd just created would push other vendors to step up their game, and how could that be bad for Artisans Alley?

"That's what we thought," Sadie said, grinning. "Thanks, Ms. Bonner."

Katie walked off, thinking that Ray was lucky to have children who were willing to work so hard for him.

Halfway back to her office, she saw Vance walking toward her. She snapped her fingers and said, "Vance, there's something I wanted to ask you, but I can't remember what."

He stopped to talk to her. "Hope it's not the price of tea in China, because I haven't a clue."

"No, no." She frowned, trying to think. Who had she been talking to about Vance? And when? Then she smiled. "You know Andy Rust?"

"Sure." Vance nodded. "Your boyfriend. Owns the pizza place the other side of the Square."

"Exactly. He's in desperate need of part-time help, and I was wondering if you or your son might know of any high school kids looking for work."

Vance looked thoughtful. "Not off the top of my head, but I can ask around. This for delivery or for working in the kitchen?"

"Either," Katie said, not sure, but willing to gamble that she was right. "Andy's a great boss, and he pays decent wages, but the kids have to be ready to work hard."

"I'll ask Vance Junior," he said. "And there are a couple of parents I can check with."

"Thanks," Katie said. "I really appreciate this." She smiled. "Maybe I can repay you by swabbing the decks of your boat sometime."

"My boat?" Vance stared at her. "What do you mean?"

"Don't you have a boat?" Katie asked, puzzled. "Someone told me you did. A good-sized one, isn't it?"

"People around here should learn to keep their mouths shut," he said fiercely. "Gossip is a nasty habit. I'm surprised that you include yourself, Katie. I thought you were above that kind of thing, but I guess I was wrong."

"Vance, I—"

But Katie was speaking to his retreating back. She frowned, because despite the whispered comments she'd heard from Edie about Vance's boat owner status, she hadn't truly suspected him of anything.

Until now.

Nine

It was unwise to predict how any given day at Artisans Alley would unfold, and that rainy Sunday brought out scores of football widows eager to max out their credit cards—payback for husbands who were glued to the tube instead of paying attention to their loving wives. Of course, that wasn't a problem for the vendors—or the Alley's bottom line, either. And that was just another sales anomaly for Katie to study in depth . . . one day.

Of course, that also meant Katie had little time to think about murder, mayhem, and bad art made from dryer lint.

At dinnertime, she headed across the Victoria Square parking lot and, sitting on a stool, chatted with Andy as he made and baked a calzone and served it to her with a flourish. After she'd eaten, they'd stolen into a dark corner for a hug and a kiss, which had been interrupted by whistles and catcalls from his staff.

Laughing, they'd pulled apart, and Katie had gone back upstairs for a classic movie night with Mason and Della, who purred all through the scary parts of *The Wizard of Oz*, making the flying monkeys not nearly as frightening as they usually were.

Monday morning, Katie woke up refreshed and energized. She felt ready to tackle the world, and she knew just where to start.

The only other cars in the Winton Office Park lot were parked near the office buildings. Employees, Katie assumed, since it wasn't even eight o'clock. But there was already a car in front of Kimper Insurance. Actually, there was a car and a motorcycle, although the motorcycle was parked on the sidewalk, forcing any pedestrian to walk either onto the landscaping or back down onto the asphalt parking lot.

Katie got out of her car and walked to the front door. It was unlocked, and she pulled it open and started to go inside. Before she got all the way into the small vestibule, however, she heard voices, and they weren't voices that were getting along with each other. She hesitated, but even as she did, Erikka called out.

"Hello? Did someone come in?"

Katie heard a male grumble. She made the quick decision to keep going. In her tenure as office manager, she'd more than once had to face down angry clients, and having someone else in the room had always helped temper the heat of the moment.

"Hi, Erikka," Katie said, walking in with a firm smile on her face. "How are you this morning?"

The dark-haired young woman turned away from the man she'd been arguing with and stared. "Katie! Wow, I . . . I didn't expect to see you again. I mean, I'm glad you're here and everything, but, I'm surprised, I guess is what I mean. That you're here."

Katie smiled at the stumbling rush of words. "I was in the neighborhood"—because she'd driven there—"and I thought I'd stop by. A number of my friends have insurance policies here, and I told them I'd try and get some answers for their questions and save you some time on the phone with each of them individually."

The man leaning against the wall of filing cabinets snorted. "What's to answer? The guy's dead and the business is being sold. Call tomorrow for an update."

Erikka shot him a glance. "Katie, this is Luke Stafford, my boyfriend. Luke, this is Katie Bonner. She used to have my job."

"Hi." Katie gave Luke a polite nod, even though she didn't feel like being polite to someone who was borderline rude to complete strangers. His attire of black jeans and a T-shirt featuring a band she'd never heard of that was so tight it showed off his substantial shoulder and chest muscles also didn't endear him to her. Neither did his hair, which was little more than light brown stubble and a bushy, untidy beard.

She tried to tamp down her instinctive reaction to him, knowing that a lot of it came from her own personal history with men who presented themselves like that, and not necessarily from Luke himself, but since he was undoubtedly the owner of the motorcycle parked on the sidewalk, she didn't feel very guilty about it.

Luke ran his eyes over her and, not saying anything, jerked out a nod.

The slight amount of guilt Kate had been harboring evaporated completely, and she wondered why a nice girl like

Erikka would want to date a guy like that. She mentally shrugged—there was no accounting for tastes—and asked, "Is that true, Erikka? The business is being sold?"

"Yes." Erikka tucked her hair back behind one ear, then another, a completely unnecessary action because her hair was too short to get out in front of her ears at all. "Mrs. Kimper called me Saturday and said she'd just signed a deal with the biggest agency in Rochester. She was all happy about it. She . . ." Erikka's voice broke. She swallowed a couple of times, in obvious emotional distress. Her boyfriend stayed where he was, anchoring the filing cabinets and picking at his fingernails. Finally, Erikka recovered and went on. "Mrs. Kimper said she was making a mint and that she was sure I'd get a job with the new owners, that she'd put in a good word for me."

Luke stared hard at her, then abruptly turned and left the room.

"Sorry about that," Erikka said. "This is hard on him, too. He used to help Josh out sometimes, doing some of the chores that Josh never had time for."

Chores that he never made time for, more like, Katie thought sourly. Because he'd always seemed to have plenty of time for golfing and to attend the Buffalo Bills home games, Amerks hockey, and Red Wings games while she toiled away back at the office.

That line of thinking reminded her of the ostensible reason why she was in her old workplace to begin with. She knew the answer, but sometimes it didn't hurt to play dumb. "So all the people who have policies here will have them transferred to the new owner?"

"That's right," Erikka said, looking past Katie to the hall where Luke had gone. She knew the hall led to a storage room, Josh's office, and a restroom, so Katie couldn't figure out what he was doing back there unless it was taking a nap on the couch in Josh's office—or taking a leak.

"I've heard," Katie said, "that Josh had been buying up some smaller agencies around the area."

"What?" Erikka snapped her gaze back to Katie. "If he was doing that, he didn't tell me about it."

"Really?" Katie tried to remember exactly what Don and Nick had said. "Then do you know if he'd been spending a lot of time in Parma? That was one of the towns that I heard mentioned where Josh was buying an agency."

But Erikka was shaking her head. "Sorry, but I really don't know."

"How about Greece?" Katie asked. "No? Then how about Henrietta?"

Erikka was still shaking her head. "Parma? He was buying an agency there?"

"That's what I heard," Katie said.

"Hmm." Erikka pursed her lips. "The only thing that rings a bell about Parma is that it was one of the boat insurance companies Josh referred clients to."

"Boat insurance?" Katie echoed. "He referred that out? That wasn't the way we did it when I was here."

Erikka shrugged. "He had me give referrals for boat insurance ever since I started, about nine months ago."

"Why?"

"He told me that marine insurance had turned into a sinkhole and he didn't want me to write up any policies that had anything to do with boats. He gave me a list of three companies to send people to." She ticked them off on her fingers. "Fairport Insurance, McKinlay Insurance, and Parma Insurance. So if he was going to Parma, maybe it was because he was working with them on the marine insurance."

Katie didn't understand. She'd never heard of any of those

insurance agencies. New ones popped up every so often, but three in the last year? All in the outlying suburbs? It didn't make sense. "I don't understand," she said. "The entire time I worked here, Josh loved to have me write up boat insurance policies."

"Josh said . . ." Erikka sniffed, pinched her nose, swallowed, and started again. "Josh said there's been a big change in how boat insurance, marine insurance, was underwritten, and new policies were guaranteed to lose money."

It still didn't make sense to Katie. No type of insurance policy was guaranteed to lose money, not across the board. That's why people had insurance, to spread the risk so that no one lost big, not even the insurance companies. Josh should have had Erikka writing up as many policies as possible to reduce the risk even further, not referring any possibility of new ones.

"I still don't understand," Katie said. "More policies means less risk to the agency. Why on earth would Josh want to—?"

Crash!

Katie whirled around at the racket that had come from what she knew was the storeroom.

"Luke!" Erikka cried, rushing past Katie on the way to her boyfriend. "Are you okay?"

Katie instinctively hurried after Erikka, ready to offer assistance if it was needed. A few steps later, they were both in the storeroom, gaping at the mess. The room had been full of freestanding shelving occupied with boxes and boxes of old client files. Now, all the shelves had been tipped over like a row of dominos. Split boxes and the emancipated trove of papers were scattered everywhere. And there, on the floor, was Luke, sprawled facedown on the hard concrete.

"Oh!" Erikka took in a sharp, audible breath and went

down on her hands and knees. "Luke! Talk to me!" she exclaimed as she pawed through the mess to get to him.

"Why?" he asked in a low growling tone. "So you can tell me how stupid I was?"

Katie looked at the horrendous mess, down at Luke, then back at the mess. Someone probably should tell him that he'd been stupid, but she doubted Erikka would, and it wasn't her place.

"Are you okay?" Erikka reached out, but Luke struggled to sit up and pushed her hands away.

"I'm fine. Quit mothering me. All I did was trip on something." He rolled to his knees and stood. "I fell into that first shelf, and it was all over."

Erikka thrashed around, trying to get up, and Katie stepped over to hold out a hand since clearly Luke wasn't going to help. She pulled the poor woman to her feet.

"Are you sure you're okay?" Erikka asked. Luke didn't bother to reply, and she looked over what had formerly been a tidy storage room. She sighed. "Looks like we have a lot more work to do than we did a few minutes ago. I'm glad Mrs. Kimper let me hire you to help me box things up for the new owners, Luke."

Katie was glad to hear that Luke had a reason for being in the agency, but given the frozen look he sent his girlfriend, Katie wasn't sure he was going to be much help during the cleanup.

"I'd better leave you to it," Katie said, but all she received was a distracted return farewell from Erikka and no response at all from Luke. She left the building and headed back to the parking lot and her car. But all the way back to McKinlay Mill, Katie mulled over what she'd been told, because no matter how she looked at it, nothing made sense to her.

~~~~~~

When Katie got back to Artisans Alley, she went straight to her office and fired up the computer, but she couldn't decide what task needed doing the most. She flitted from one thing to another, and when half an hour had passed without her getting anything of any substance done, she pushed herself back from the desk and got up. Maybe a cup of coffee would help her focus.

She was in the act of stirring creamer into her coffee when Duncan McAllister walked into the vendors' lounge, startling her. After all, although the other businesses in the building were open, Artisans Alley was closed on Mondays. Had she left the front door unlocked? "Good morning," she said.

"And a fine morning it is," he replied cheerfully.

Katie eyed him. While she wasn't a night person by any means, she'd never been much of a morning person, either. Afternoons were her best time, but there didn't seem to be a personality classification for that.

"I guess it is nice," she said.

"Autumn is my favorite time of year." Duncan took the coffeepot off the burner and poured the dark stuff into the mug he'd brought along. "Not hot, not cold, the leaves are falling, harvest time is coming. All is right with the world." He beamed at her, and his expression was so contagious that she found herself grinning right back.

"Harvest time?" she echoed. "Are you a farmer?" Katie realized that she didn't know anything about her newest vendor, aside from the exquisite bird sculptures he made. How those big hands could fashion such small and intricate details, she had no idea, and she wasn't sure she wanted to know, since it would take away some of the mystique of his efforts.

"In a way." Duncan put the pot back on the burner with a bit of a thunk.

Katie waited, but he didn't say anything else, so she asked, "In what way?"

He sipped from his plain white mug, then said, "I was a teacher."

"Oh? What did you teach?"

Duncan smiled. "Kids."

"Were you a teacher around here?" she asked.

A shadow crossed his face briefly. "No. Upstate. In the Adirondacks."

She felt a wall close off that subject, so she just said, "Pretty up there."

"If you like trees."

Katie smiled, but he didn't respond in kind. "Trees are nice enough," she said, a little flustered, "but I prefer the water. I wouldn't like to ever live very far from one of the Great Lakes, or maybe an ocean." She took a sip from her own mug, then said casually, "I think someone told me you own a boat. Is that true?"

He gave her a hard look. "Yes," he said shortly. "A wooden one."

"That's nice." She smiled, nodding. "I have a friend who owns a sailboat that he keeps at Thompson's Landing. We went out quite a few times over the summer. He took it out of the water last week, though. Do you keep your boat at a marina, or do you trailer?"

Duncan didn't say anything, so she kept on going.

"It's nice to be able to take a boat anywhere you want to go boating," she said, "but that's so much extra time and hassle. It's a lot easier just to have a boat in a slip, walk right up to it, and go out for a ride on the water."

"Life isn't about the easy way out."

"No, it isn't. But it shouldn't always have to be hard, either." She put on an even wider smile. "So, do you trailer your boat or do you have a slip in a marina?" she repeated.

Duncan emptied his coffee mug into the sink and turned on the water to rinse it out. When he was done, he turned and said, "Ms. Bonner—"

"Please, call me Katie."

He gave a sharp nod. "Katie, I'm sure you're just being the polite and friendly person that folks say you are, but I'm the kind of person who keeps myself to myself. I'm just here to tend to my booth and meet with a few potential customers. I'm not here to make new pals. Nothing personal, but I'd really rather not answer any of your questions."

"I just—"

"Have a good day," he said and walked off.

"You, too. And please lock the front door when you leave!" she called after him, none too happy.

~~~~~~~

"He left me standing there with my mouth hanging open," Katie said to Andy that night. She'd tried not to let the incident annoy her, but every time she thought about it, her temper started rising once again. Though as far as she knew no one else had heard the exchange, going over it in her head made her cheeks hot with embarrassment.

Andy poured dressing on the salad she'd made, studied the effect, then added another generous dollop. "Did any flies get in?" he asked.

"Very funny," she groused. "Don't you think it's weird that someone wouldn't answer some basic questions? It's not as if we're complete strangers. He'd been in a number of times this summer, talking to Rose and Edie and some of the other vendors before he approached me about renting a booth."

"That was all business, though, right?" Andy asked, adding more cheese to his salad.

When he was done with the bowl of Parmesan, Katie reached out for it but pulled back. She hadn't had any exercise that day, other than walking across Artisans Alley, which didn't count for much. Giving up the extra cheese on her salad should make up for at least part of that lack.

"Yes," she said, thinking about Andy's question. "I suppose every conversation I've had with Duncan—Mr. McAllister, I mean—had to do with him being a vendor, but what does that have to do with anything? Business conversations are how you start, then you move into personal conversations. That's how relationships are built."

Andy looked at her. "That's how *some* relationships are built, you mean."

"What are you talking about?" she asked, a little annoyed.

"Not everyone wants to be friends with everyone they meet," he said. "Some people prefer to keep relationships businesslike and never move into personal friendships."

"So," she said, an unreasonable irritation suddenly coursing through her, "are you saying that I'm too friendly? That I make people uncomfortable? That I'm nosy and push people into saying things they don't want to say?"

Andy continued eating.

She sat there, bristling with annoyance. "Well?" she demanded, "what are you waiting for?"

"To finish eating," he said. "This dressing you make is outstanding. If I could sell it downstairs, I'd be begging you for the recipe."

"But I—" She stopped herself, said, "You are—" She stopped herself again, then leaned back into her chair and sighed. "Okay. I'm sorry for flying off the handle like that."

"Apology accepted." Andy smiled. "You've accepted my apologies often enough. I can spot you this one, no problem."

"I'd say it won't happen again, but it probably will at some point."

"You and me both." He tapped the back of her hand. "Eat. I've known you long enough to guess that you didn't have any lunch today, which throws off your blood sugar and is making you cranky as all get-out. It's not you, see? It's the lack of food."

Had she eaten lunch? She honestly couldn't remember, but if skipping a meal was going to do that to her, she'd have to stop skipping meals. Andy didn't deserve that kind of crankiness from her. Katie managed a weak smile. "I like the way you think."

She picked up her fork, and for a couple of minutes, the only sound in the room was that of forks scraping the insides of their salad bowls. After taking in a few bites, she did start to feel better. "And though I believe that all business relationships would benefit from a dose of personal connection, I think I have to agree that there are some uninteresting people out there who prefer to keep business relationships strictly business."

"I have a supplier like that," Andy said. "All business, no fun. It's not the way I want to go through life, but hey." He shrugged. "That's the way he is, and it's his loss. And if our business relationship is improved by me backing away from any personal questions, well, I can do that. I don't have to be friends with everyone."

"You know," Katie said slowly, "maybe that's my problem. I *do* want to be friends with everyone."

Andy leaned across the table and took her hands in his. "And that's one of the things I love best about you. But not everyone is like you. Duncan just happens to be one of them."

Katie nodded. He was right, of course.

Though what she was starting to realize, now that she had relived the scene in her head a dozen times, was that Duncan hadn't gone all standoffish until she'd started asking about his boat.

~~~~~~~

It was half an hour before opening the next morning when Katie, Rose, and Edie assembled in the Artisans Alley front lobby. Their mission? To work on the plan to decorate for the upcoming harvest sale and use as many of those elements as possible for Halloween.

"And Thanksgiving, too," Rose added. "There has to be a way to refresh the theme by rearranging."

Edie spread out her hands. "Halloween, sure, but I don't get the difference between harvest decorations and Thanksgiving decorations."

"They're mostly the same," Katie said, thinking out loud, "but there's still a difference. We're thankful for more than harvest time. We're thankful for all the good things that have happened in the year. We're thankful for everything that we have. We're thankful for family and friends and—"

"That's it!" Edie thrust her hands up into the air. "We can do a family farming theme. We'll use the corn shocks from the harvest stuff, and I bet we can borrow wagon wheels from that booth upstairs. We can also borrow some antique photos of farming families from what's-his-face upstairs and stick them inside some of Ray Davenport's frames, temporarily, of course."

Her face grew animated. "And I bet if we take a walk around the floor we can find a bunch of other stuff to borrow that fits the theme. We can ask everybody to contribute something, that way no one's left out."

Katie and Rose stared at her, then looked at each other.

"I like it." Rose nodded.

"Me, too," Katie said. "I like it a lot."

"I say it's borderline brilliant," said a voice from behind them.

Katie and the two other women turned to see a smiling Fred Cunningham walking toward them. "Morning, Fred," they said, practically in unison.

"And a fine morning it is," he responded jovially, sounding an awful lot like Duncan the morning before. Were they buddies? "I'd intended to ask you ladies how things are going, but I can tell without asking that you have things well in hand. Nicely done."

They chatted for a few moments about the weather. Fred asked them to pass on his name if they knew anyone who was interested in buying, selling, or leasing property, and then he asked, "How's it going with Brittany?" He gestured to the salon. "How's the salon affecting your business at the Alley? Any problems? If it works well, I'd like to set up some other crossover enterprises, but I need to know about any problems, from both sides."

Rose's and Edie's heads whipped around to stare at Katie.

Fred looked from them to Katie and back. "My acute powers of observation point to a potential problem. Would anyone like to tell me about it?"

Katie sighed. "It's not a problem with Brittany or her salon. She's been great, and I've had a number of vendors say that having her here is bringing new customers to Artisans Alley. And she's told me she's cautiously optimistic that her projections were on the low side, which she attributes to being in this location." She tossed her head, and a wisp of hair touched her cheek. She pushed it back. One of these days, she'd make an appointment with Brittany for a haircut. Soon, even.

Fred adjusted his glasses. "That all sounds good. So what's the issue?"

"It's the young woman who's renting space in the salon," Katie said. "She's trying to start up a nail business and—"

"She's really talented." Edie held out her hands, displaying fingernails that were painted navy blue and decorated with tiny American flags. "Don't you just love it? And she does all the painting herself; no stencils, no stickies, nothing but freehand work."

Katie looked at the miniature artwork, and her admiration for Crystal grew. "That's amazing," she said.

Fred nodded at Edie's nails. "Nice. But where's the issue?"

"The acrylic nails." Katie glanced over to Envy's door, but it was still dark. "It's a horrendous smell. The venting in this place is problematic, at best, and the fumes seem to settle in here." She waved to the lobby. "And whenever the front door opens, the smell gets pushed deeper into the sales floor. We're getting a lot of complaints."

"Hmm." Fred rubbed his chin. "Well, if you ladies can figure out such a great autumn theme, I'm sure you'll figure this one out, too."

Katie gave an inaudible sigh. She'd hoped to gain some astute advice from a man who'd been dealing with real estate issues for more than thirty years.

Rose and Edie began discussing who could contribute what for the harvest decorations, and Katie pulled Fred off to one side.

"I have a question," she said. "The other day you told me that Marcie Kimper had put her house on the market."

His neck turned a light shade of mottled pink. "That's right. Are you looking to buy?"

Katie ignored this, as he knew perfectly well that she couldn't even afford to buy a new car, let alone a Queen Anne Victorian in a tony suburb. "Listing a house takes some time and legwork, and I was wondering if you had any idea when Marcie started thinking about selling."

"Well, let me think." Fred pulled his smartphone from his jacket pocket and started scrolling through its calendar. "It was at a Business-After-Hours event last month that the Fairport Chamber of Commerce sponsored. Marcie and I got to talking about Fairport's historic homes. She mentioned something about listing her house in the not-too-distant future."

Katie listened intently, thinking fast. That event must have been held sometime before Labor Day—weeks before Josh had been killed. It didn't prove anything, but it sure made her wonder.

"Then I saw the house on the multiple listing service," Fred was saying. "It couldn't have been two days after Josh died. I was a little surprised that she'd move so fast after a tragedy like that, so I called to see how she was doing."

"I stopped by a couple of days after Josh died," Katie said. "She seemed to be holding up remarkably well."

Either Fred didn't hear her sarcasm or he ignored it.

He nodded. "Yes, wasn't she? When I cautioned her about making such a big move so soon after her husband's death, she said she'd been thinking about it for some time, that she wanted to move the girls to her hometown so they could grow up closer to her extended family. Marcie has a number of siblings and they all have children and it makes sense for her."

Especially, Katie thought, *if her husband was suddenly*

*out of the picture and she was also likely to get a hefty life
insurance check.*

At one time, Katie had admired Marcie, who had presum-
ably found at least one redeeming quality in the man she'd
married. But now Katie questioned all that. Had Marcie had
enough of the pompous little oaf? Good grief—could she
really have wanted the twerp dead?

Maybe.

But there was the fact that whoever had hauled Josh's
dead-weight body out of Lake Ontario had had the strength
to move him to Sassy Sally's. If Marcie didn't have that kind
of strength, her paramour just might.

Ten

By the end of the day, Katie, Rose, and Edie had transformed the lobby of Artisans Alley from its normal, workaday, un-inspired space to the inside of a barn in the midst of harvest time. Corn shocks had been tied in tall bundles and placed in every possible out-of-the-way corner. Edie's wagon wheel idea had been carried out, and colored ears of corn had been wired to the hubs. Baskets overflowed with squash from the local vegetable stand, gourds huddled near the corn shocks and doors, and they'd hauled out the ladders and hung strings of white fairy lights overhead.

"There," Edie said, dusting off her hands as she came down the ladder for the last time. "That'll do until we deco-rate for the holidays, don't you think? One color fits all."

Katie flicked the switch. The lobby had been transformed into a place where magical things just might happen, or so Katie told herself as she stood there, admiring their work.

The lobby's front door opened and closed. "Oooh," Sadie Davenport said, looking all around her. "This looks awesome!"

Her sister chimed in. "It's so totally different than it looked the other day." Sasha turned in a circle, admiring the effect. "I didn't know you'd be decorating for the fall. Look!" She pointed. "There's even a scarecrow! How cool is that?"

Edie grinned. "That's the best reaction we could have asked for, and we didn't even have to bribe you."

"Did you girls just get out of school?" Katie asked.

"Uh-huh. We're free until tomorrow morning," Sadie said. "We thought we'd come by and see how many sales Dad's had today." She glanced at her sister.

Sasha nodded eagerly. "He's here, right?"

"I have no idea." Katie thought she'd seen Ray a couple of hours earlier but wouldn't have wanted to swear to it.

"I'm sure he is," Sadie assured her. "This morning he said he was going to finish up some projects in the basement and bring them over here this afternoon."

Sasha chimed in. "Yeah, that's why we wanted to come by, to help make sure he put the new stuff up right."

"His booth definitely needs a woman's touch," Sadie said with authority. "Poor Dad doesn't have a clue. You wouldn't believe the things he'll try and wear out in public. Things our mother would never let him get away with." The girl's lower lip trembled, and she gave a shuddering breath. It was just about a year since she'd lost her mom.

As though sensing her loss, Edie gave a cheerful laugh. "It's what men do, hon. You'd better get used to it."

The two teenagers nodded, and started off to find their father, but Sasha turned back. "Ms. Bonner, would you come with us? I just know he's going to have put up his new pieces all wrong, and he probably won't listen to what we tell him. He *might* listen to you."

Katie's eyebrows went up. "Do you really think so?"

"Definitely," Sadie said and nodded again, her ponytail bobbing. "He thinks a *lot* of your opinion. He's said so."

Katie found that hard to believe, considering how the former detective had essentially ignored her opinions on more than one occasion, but she let herself be escorted to the Wood U booth. If the girls needed her support in their efforts to humanize Ray Davenport, she was happy to oblige.

"Hey, Daddy-o," Sadie called as they drew near. "Are you in there?"

A grumpy noise emanated from the depths of the booth. Then, "Don't you two have homework?"

"Sure," Sasha said, "but we wanted to see the booth after you brought over the new merchandise."

Katie and the girls drew abreast of the booth and were greeted by the sight of their father standing in the middle, with boxes and packaging strewn across the floor.

Ray held a small wooden box and looked at the new arrivals. "Oh, really?" he asked dryly. "Just wanted to see it? Didn't have anything to do with wanting to make sure your dumb old dad didn't mess up the booth's display?"

"Speaking of mess." Sadie got down on her knees and started picking up the packaging materials.

"Yeah, Dad." Sasha grabbed one of the empty boxes and held it out for her sister to fill. "You yell at us for leaving our room a mess, and then you do this. That doesn't seem fair."

"Well," Ray said, giving the box a polish with a cloth he was holding, "you know what I say to that."

Sadie made a face. "We know, Dad. Don't expect life to be fair."

Ray looked over at Katie. "If they know, why do they keep expecting fairness?"

"Because," she said, trying to keep from laughing, "hope springs eternal."

"Hope was what was left at the bottom of Pandora's box," Ray muttered. "Small consolation, I'd say."

Though Katie actually agreed with him, she was here to support his daughters. "That's beautiful," she said, gesturing to the box he was still dusting. Its lid was inlaid with different shades of wood in the shape of a rose in full bloom.

Ray shrugged. "It's something I thought I'd try. It didn't turn out too bad."

Sadie jumped to her feet. "Sasha and I are going to take this packing material out to your truck."

Her sister blinked at her. "We are?"

"Yes," Sadie said firmly. "Grab those boxes."

In seconds, the two were gone, leaving behind a sort of hazy energy that Katie half believed she could see hanging in the air.

Ray looked down the aisle. "What was that all about?" he asked.

"No idea," Katie said. "They asked me down here to back them up in case you'd done something horrible to their displays." She and Ray looked at each other and simultaneously shrugged. "They're great kids," she said. "You're lucky to have them."

"I know, but don't tell them that." He gave the box one last rub and put it on a shelf. "Think that will pass their inspection?"

She laughed. "I have no idea, but it looks fine to me."

"If only my daughters were so easy to please." He studied the placement of the box, then moved it a fraction of an inch. "So have you learned anything new about Kimper?"

Katie smiled. "Ray Davenport, are you saying that I

shouldn't necessarily leave all the investigating to the Sheriff's Office?"

"Let's just say it's harder to walk away from police work than I thought it would be, especially when there's a murder investigation going on right in front of me."

She thought the "right in front of me" was a stretch but didn't call him on it. "I'm really thinking about Marcie."

"The widow?" Ray crossed his arms and squinted at her. "Why do you say that?"

Katie told him all she'd learned, that Marcie had a love interest three days after the murder of her husband, that she'd sold the business lock, stock, and barrel, and that she'd talked to a real estate agent about selling the house weeks before Josh's body turned up in the Sassy Sally's bathtub.

"I just don't see it," Ray said.

"Oh?" Katie asked, puzzled. "Why not?"

"Do you know how hard it is to move a body? Kimper weighed at least fifty pounds more than his wife, maybe seventy-five. Hauling that kind of dead weight around?" He shook his head. "I just don't see her having the strength."

"Maybe that attorney, Rob, helped her."

"I still don't see it," Ray repeated. "Sure, she'd lose half the assets in a divorce, but murder is too risky for most people. We're all about reducing risk these days. Tamper-proof lids on everything, air bags, warning signs on ladders, for crying out loud."

Katie sensed this was probably a hot-button issue for him and knew she needed to quickly distract him to keep him on topic. "Do you know anything about your fellow vendor Duncan McAllister? I talked to him the other day, and he got all closemouthed the second I asked him a personal question."

"Some people don't like spilling their lives to near strangers," Ray said.

"I just asked about his boat. That's all, honest."

"Hmm. Okay." Ray nodded. "But the only thing I know about him is he moved here from Glens Falls."

"He did?" Katie's eyes went wide. "That's where Josh grew up! Maybe they knew each other there. Maybe they had some sort of past together. Josh was a lot younger, but maybe he'd seen Duncan commit a crime and—"

"Hang on, hang on." Ray made calming motions with his hands. "Those are some big jumps you're making. Let's do a little research first, okay?" He stepped over to the table, sifted through a pile of wrapping materials, and pulled out an electronic tablet. "Let's see what we can find on our Mr. McAllister."

Katie stood close to his elbow and watched as he started up a search engine and typed in the keywords.

"Well, will you look at that." Ray tapped at the screen, enlarging some text.

The search engine had quickly turned up a June newspaper article about McAllister's retirement. "He mentioned he was a teacher," Katie said..

"Middle school, looks like." Ray scrolled through the article. "And he was a high school hockey coach." He tapped again, and the screen was filled with a photo of a smiling Duncan holding a trophy, surrounded by a large group of grinning male adolescents in hockey gear. "Won the state championship a few years back, even."

Katie ran some quick mental math. "The ages aren't right. Josh was too old to have been one of his students."

"Agreed," Ray said. "And it's hard to think that a guy like this could hold a grudge for decades and then come looking for Kimper to get his revenge. Still, you never know."

"No," Katie said slowly, still looking at the photo. "You never do."

~~~~~

As usual, Katie would be the last one out the door at Artisans
Alley that night. She'd long realized that the best way to win
the loyalty of the vendors was to show that she was willing
to do whatever it took to make the place run smoothly, so
she, too, did more than her two days of chores per month.

The job du jour was cleaning, and as she pushed the vacuum cleaner around, she decided that there was no reason not
to consider cleaning as exercise. Her heart rate was certainly
up, and she was using all sorts of muscles, twisting and stoop-
ing. When she had finished putting the vacuum away, she also
decided that she'd worked hard enough to have earned a calzone for dinner. And, if she did a stint of dusting, an order of
breadsticks.

So, after another half hour of cleaning, she left the building just after sunset and locked the door behind her, feeling
tired but pleased with how the sales floors looked. All the
booths were well stocked, the quality of the sales items was
high, and the empty booths she had were few and far between. If they weren't filled for the holiday shopping season,
she could either work to fill them with artificial Christmas
trees and empty boxes wrapped with brightly colored paper,
or offer them at half price short-term to whatever vendors
were interested.

Crossing the parking lot, Katie smiled to herself as she
remembered that during her vacuuming efforts, she'd seen
that either Sadie or Sasha—or maybe both—had repositioned
the box that Ray had so carefully placed on the shelf.

The Davenport daughters certainly seemed to have a good
relationship with their father, and Katie pushed away thoughts
of her own father and mother, who had died so many years
ago. She forced her line of thinking back to Artisans Alley,

which, thankfully, was easy for her to do, since there was so much to think about.

She was glad that Ray was working out so well as a new vendor. Everyone she'd talked to seemed to like him, and Sadie and Sasha were upping the display game with their clever ideas. Katie smiled to herself, thinking she might incite an unspoken competition to make the booths even more attractive to shoppers. This was all to the good, as long as it stayed friendly and as long as no one got carried away with spending too much money. Katie's smile turned into a full-blown grin as she anticipated what might happen in the coming weeks.

"You have to wonder," a voice said out of the dusk, "about a pretty woman, out for a walk all by herself, when she starts smiling for no apparent reason."

Katie started but relaxed when she quickly recognized the sturdy form of Warren Noth, pizza box in hand, approaching his truck in front of Angelo's Pizzeria. "I was having happy thoughts," she said lightly, "and I didn't notice you parked there. Have you been working at Sassy Sally's?"

The contractor nodded. "Was there all day, but I stopped in at Wood U to get in a little work for Ray. Though the boys at Sassy's are decent enough, they keep changing what they want, and that job's taking longer than expected, but it's more money in my pocket. Still, I hate having to delay the reopening of Wood U. Ray's a good guy and doesn't deserve it."

"He just opened a booth at Artisans Alley," Katie said, "and he's already doing fairly well." She knew this because she kept a close eye on sales the first couple of months of a vendor's tenure in the building, trying to figure out trends. Someday, maybe she'd be able to tell if a vendor would ultimately be successful within the first couple of months renting a booth.

"I didn't know that." Glancing over at the old applesauce warehouse, Warren adjusted his Knighthawks ball cap. "Still, it can't be the same as having a real storefront."

While that was true, Katie didn't care for the insinuation that her business wasn't real. The man probably hadn't meant to be insulting, but that wasn't the point. She started to edge away. "What were you working on tonight? I'll probably see Ray tomorrow and can pass it on, if you'd like."

"Sounds good." He took a few steps to the back of his pickup and leaned over to reach into the bed, which had a flat cover hinged at the top and popped up at the back. He pulled out a piece of squashed metal. "This was part of the intake for the HVAC system. I'll take it to my heating and cooling guy, and he'll figure out what we need." Warren smiled. "Ray seemed to think the balance in there was great before the fire, so I'm trying to re-create it."

Katie didn't like the condescending edge to his tone, but she was curious enough to say, "I didn't know heating or cooling was so complicated."

"You'd be surprised." Noth turned to put the chunk of metal back, and Katie, who'd by now moved closer, looked over the side of the truck and saw the expected collection of tools, boots, paint, and wood. She also saw, tucked away in a front corner, a coil of nylon rope sitting underneath a boat anchor.

"Do you have a boat?" she asked innocently, remembering that Del had already told her he did. "It seems like every time I turn around, I learn that someone else I know has a boat."

Noth gave a short laugh that wasn't much of a laugh at all. "I *used* to have a boat. I had it moored in a marina closer to Rochester. It sank in that big storm back in July."

"Oh, that's awful! I'm so sorry," Katie said. Then, because she couldn't help herself, she added, "Did you have insurance?"

He nodded. "Yeah, through McKinlay Insurance, but they're taking forever and a day to pay out. I'll be lucky if I get a check before next summer at the rate they're moving."

Katie made some sympathetic comments about the slowness of insurance agencies, then said good night. Noth got in his truck and pulled out of the lot.

McKinlay Insurance, he'd said. Hadn't that been one of the companies to which Josh had been referring customers?

Katie entered the pizzeria, the heavy brass jingle bells that hung on a leather strap on the door making a cheerful noise.

"Hey there, sunshine!" Andy greeted Katie with a floury kiss. "What's up?"

Katie blushed a little at the display of affection, which was very public, what with his staff listening in. "I was doing cleanup at Artisans Alley today, and it took longer than I thought it would."

Andy grinned. "Can't just give it a lick and a polish and call it good, can you?"

She cupped a hand to her ear. "Do I hear the pot calling the kettle black? Why yes, I think I do."

"Point taken. So did you stop by to help or to eat—or perhaps both?"

As he was talking, the phone rang, and one of his employees hurried to answer it. Katie and Andy both ceased their conversation to listen.

"Angelo's Pizzeria, how may I help you?" Robbie said. "Yes, we're still open, until ten . . . Yes, we . . ." His eyes went wide, and he whirled to face Andy. "Can we deliver five pizzas to the Village Hall? This isn't a joke, is it? . . . Yessir, Mr. Mayor. I do remember you from our government class . . .

Yessir, we can get five pizzas to your work session in . . ."
Andy held up both his hands and flashed them three times. ". . .
in thirty minutes. You can depend on us, sir. Thanks for your
call. Now, what did you want on them?"

"Looks like I'm here to help," Katie said, laughing and
moving to stand behind the sales counter. "I can always eat
later."

Andy, who was already hurrying back to the prep station,
sent her an air-kiss. "I'll love you forever if you cover the
front. Thanks!"

Forever? Katie's chest tightened involuntarily then released as she acknowledged the humor underneath Andy's
statement. He'd been joking, that was all. He wasn't serious
about the forever thing. They'd moved to saying they loved
each other, but there'd been no discussions of permanent
commitment. Katie wasn't ready for that—not yet.

"Hey, what does it take to get some service around here?"

Katie snapped to attention and faced the front of the store.
"Sorry, ma'am, I—" Then she saw who was calling to her
and grinned. "Then again, maybe I'm not so sorry."

"Now is that any way to treat your favorite veterinarian?"
Dr. Joanne asked. "We're here for a pickup. It might still have
a few minutes to go." She was joined by two men and another
woman. "This is my husband, David Perkins, and our friends
Mark and Leslie. Meet Katie Bonner."

"Bonner?" the female friend repeated.

Katie nodded. "Yes, that's right."

The woman smiled. "Don Parsons and Nick Farrell are
friends of ours. They've talked about you, how you've done
such a great job with Artisans Alley in the last year, and almost single-handedly revived Victoria Square."

"They're great guys," Katie said, "but I can't take credit for
the Square's revival. The Merchants Association has worked

together as a team to bring about positive changes. I only hope that having Josh Kimper turn up dead in their bathtub doesn't hurt Sassy Sally's before it even opens."

The couple exchanged a glance. "We're worried about the same thing," the woman said.

"Well, at least they both have alibis," Katie said, sighing. "Having a dead body in your bed-and-breakfast is bad, but it would be a lot worse if one of them was suspected of murder." She smiled, but no one standing before her smiled back. "What's the matter?" she asked.

"We were all at the same party," Joanne said, her expression troubled. "Don left early."

Katie suddenly felt dizzy and rested her hands on the counter. "He . . . what?"

"About an hour into the party, Don left. And he didn't come back for almost two hours," David said.

"Pizza for Perkins," Andy called out, holding a large, flat box. He grabbed a slip of paper and handed it to Katie so she could ring up the sale.

Katie's hands were shaking as she made change. Where on earth had Don been for two hours during the party? And was that enough time to drown a problem guest in the lake and haul the body back to Sassy Sally's? But that would be stupid—criminally stupid.

Still, she wondered . . . and worried.

Eleven

After the revelation about Don's shattered alibi, Katie didn't sleep well. She spent so much time tossing and turning, trying to find a position that would lull her into dreamland, that first Mason and then Della jumped off the bed to find a spot more accommodating to feline slumber.

A weak morning sun, filtering its way through curtains and thin clouds, woke her just as the alarm went off. She slapped it off, blearily, remembering watching the hour change from one to two to three. She hadn't seen four, but that was probably because she'd finally had the sense to flop the clock onto its face so she couldn't see it.

In the shower, she realized that though she'd hoped the warm water would open her eyes past the drowsy stage, it wasn't doing the trick. She gritted her teeth and flipped the knob to cold, gasping at the shock.

She forced herself to endure five full seconds of the arctic blast, then turned it off and hustled into a fluffy towel before she went into hypothermic shock.

"At least I'm awake," she told the cats, as she combed out her hair, "which is more than either of you are."

Della picked her head up, gave her one long blink, and settled back into sleep mode. Mason didn't bother himself even that much, but he did purr when she gave him a pat on the head.

Katie ate a quick breakfast of cold cereal and orange juice, left fresh food and water for her sleepy kitties, then headed out with one purpose in mind: to talk to Don Parsons. A solid drench of rain made her jump into her car to cross Victoria Square. Wet was fine walking home, but she didn't want to sit in damp shoes all day long.

She was only halfway across the Square when she began to question what she was about to do. She wanted to talk to Don alone, and if she barged into Sassy Sally's, how was she going to pull him aside for a one-on-one?

It would be easy enough to ask him to meet her at the bakery or at Del's, but there would be open ears at both places, and she didn't want anyone else to hear the discussion. She drove around aimlessly for a bit, then brightened as she came up with an idea.

Whipping out her cell phone, she tapped at the Sassy Sally's number and waited for the phone on the other end to ring.

"Sassy Sally's Inn, this is—"

The loud whine of a circular saw drowned out the rest of the sentence. The saw was loud enough that Katie heard it from the phone and across the Square in real time.

"Sorry about that. This is Don," he said after the saw stopped. "How may I help you?"

Katie laughed. "This is Katie, and how would you like a break?"

"I will pay you in gold," he said fervently. "How much do you want and where should I bring it?"

"Gold isn't necessary, but I could do with an oatmeal cookie from Tanner's."

"On my way." He paused. "Er, where am I going? I can't bring Nick. He went to Rochester to check on a pedestal sink from a house renovation that might be the perfect fit for that upstairs bathroom."

"You're the one I want," Katie said. "We decorated our lobby for the harvest sale, and I want to get an outside opinion on whether it's cheesy or wonderful."

"Be there in a jiffy."

And a jiffy it was. The first thing Katie had done after arriving was start the coffee, and the pot was only half full when Don knocked on the back door to the vendors' lounge holding the requisite white bakery bag. She let him in.

"Those cookies looked so good," he said, "that I bought half a dozen. You've earned it for saving me from that horror of a construction site. If I had to spend another minute in there I was going to either go insane or kill someone, and neither option was attractive."

Katie stifled a sigh. She knew it was just an overused expression, but this was a bad time for him to joke about murder.

"Okay," Don said, pulling out a chair and ushering her into it. "You sit, I'll dispense goodies, caffeinated and otherwise, and you'll tell me what's going on. I peeked through the front door and the lobby looks outstanding, but you already knew that, didn't you?"

She tucked her chair up to the table. "I did. But it's nice to hear you say so."

In no time at all, Don had two mugs of coffee poured and the cookies arranged prettily on a plate he'd found in the cupboard. "Cheers," he said, toasting her. After the inaugural sip, he pushed the plate of cookies toward her. "Now it's cookie time. Eat two bites and then you can tell Uncle Don all your problems."

Katie shook her head but took a cookie and ate the two required bites. "It's not my problem, but it may be yours."

"Moi?" He put a hand to his chest. "I have no problems. I am deeply in love with my life partner, my new business, though currently noisy, is poised to become a great success, my health is good, I still have most of my hair, and—"

"And you have no alibi for Josh Kimper's murder," Katie cut in.

Don, who'd been reaching for a cookie, stopped cold. "What do you mean?" he asked cautiously.

"The party that you've been saying was your alibi isn't going to stand up if the deputies start looking into it." Katie gripped the cookie so hard that it broke in half and fell to the table. "Joanne Timmer and her husband, David, were there. I spoke to them last night, as well as a couple of their friends, and they said you disappeared for almost two hours."

Don sat back, his expression guarded. "I went for a walk."

Katie glared at him. "You did no such thing."

"I went for a walk," he said again more firmly. "There were so many people there that I needed to get some air and ended up at Thompson's Landing to watch the moonlight on the water and just think." He smiled at her brightly.

Katie gazed at him steadily, and his chirpy look eventually faded to a weary expression.

"Okay," he said. "I know this looks bad, especially since that's probably where Kimper died—or at least where he was transported after he drowned—but there's a good reason why I was gone. A reason that doesn't have anything to do with Kimper's death."

"I never once thought you were involved," Katie said softly.

"Of course not." Don reached across the table to pat her hand. "I thank you for that, very, very much. And though I'd trust you with my life, there are some things I'd rather not share right now, not if I don't have to."

Katie looked at him, still troubled. "It's not me," she said. "It's the police. They're bound to find out that your alibi is far from solid. What are you going to do then?"

Don grinned. "I'm going on the assumption that they'll find the real killer before they get around to poking holes in my alibi. Now, drink your coffee before it gets cold, and eat those cookies before they get stale."

"But—"

"My darling Katie," Don said. "It will be fine. Don't worry."

But Katie knew that she would.

~~~~~~~

The clouds that Katie had woken to had blown off by midmorning, but there was a distinct chill to the air that somehow translated into one of those days that defy retail lore and expectations.

Normally, on weekdays there was no need for more than minimal help at the checkout registers and on the floor. That particular Wednesday, however, Artisans Alley was deluged with shoppers who had questions, who wanted to purchase items, who wanted gift wrapping, and who wanted to gush to anyone present about how wonderful it was to find so many fantastic artists and artisans under one roof.

Katie had hurried out to help after a panicky summons from Liz Meier, who was spending the day at Cash Desk 1, and there wasn't a single break in the action until late afternoon.

"Wow," Liz said, leaning back against the counter and blowing out a breath. "What a day! I can't believe how busy we've been."

"It's been wild," Katie agreed. She was also wondering why it had happened. Had it been a freak occurrence, or was it something else? Her marketing classes had taught her not to jump to conclusions on the basis of one day of sales, but there had to be a reason. There was always a reason. Well, unless there wasn't. Sometimes things just happened.

Brittany Kohler poked her head out of the salon's door. "Have you guys been bizarrely busy, too?"

"Beyond belief, for a Wednesday," Katie said. "You, too?"

"Sure have." Brittany nodded. "And I think I know why. There was an article about Victoria Square in Rochester's Sunday paper."

"There was?" Katie was surprised. Months ago, as part of her duties as president of the Victoria Square Merchants Association, she'd sent all the newspapers in the area a press release about the changes in the Square. One or two had picked it up, but Katie had never been sure it had done any good.

Brittany smiled. "Half a page, pictures and everything."

"That's funny," Liz said. "I don't remember hearing about any reporter coming around."

"Or seeing any photographer taking pictures." Katie frowned, then shrugged. "But I guess I don't care," she said, starting to smile, "since it must have been written by someone who liked the Square."

"A number of them told me they'd come back to shop for Christmas," Liz said.

Katie held up her hands and crossed her fingers. "Here's hoping!"

The women laughed, and the happy sound filled the lobby.

It gave Katie a warm, fuzzy feeling deep inside, and she sent up a wish that all their hopes would come true.

"Well, I have to get back," Brittany said. "See you ladies later."

Just then, a wisp of hair fell out of Katie's ponytail. She hurried toward the salon and caught the door just before it closed. "Brittany, do you have time to cut my hair?"

The other woman shook her head. "Sorry, I have an appointment in ten minutes. Do you want to schedule something for tomorrow?"

"I'd better not," Katie said regretfully. "I can't count on having the time. I'll just have to wait and catch you when there's an opening."

"Happily, they're getting to be few and far between." Brittany, behind the counter now, tapped at a computer. "If this keeps up, I'm going to have to hire someone early next year." She rolled her eyes. "Then I have to learn about doing payroll and keeping back taxes and workers' compensation and who knows what else."

Katie laughed. "The high price of success." Then she sobered, because hoping for a haircut hadn't been the only reason she'd followed Brittany into the salon. "There's something I need to talk to you about."

"Sure," Brittany said. "Highlights? A new cut?" She looked at Katie's hair judiciously. "There's a pixie cut that I bet would look great on you."

Katie flashed on an image of herself in short hair. Not a chance. Then again . . . She shook her head. "It's about Crystal."

"Isn't she great?" Brittany smiled. "She's really good at nails. It's almost artwork, which is why I thought she'd fit in well here."

"She does," Katie said, "but the smells don't belong at all."

Brittany went still. "Smells?"

So Katie explained that the pungent aromas were permeating the lobby of Artisans Alley and the sales floor, surprised Brittany hadn't noticed it herself. "It's a real problem," she said. "One of the vendors has severe allergic reactions to it. And if a vendor does, who knows how many customers might. I'm sorry, but it's just not working out."

"Not working out?" Brittany's voice was tight. "You mean she has to leave?"

"I'm sorry," Katie said, "I really am, but I can't risk anyone's health."

"There has to be a solution. Can't she . . . ?" Brittany's eyes darted around, looking for answers. "How about if she uses something to mask the smell, like air fresheners? That would help, wouldn't it?"

But Katie was shaking her head. "She's already tried that. What really needs to happen is to get a ventilation system installed, and that would cost thousands. If the two of you could come up with that money . . ."

Now it was Brittany who was shaking her head. "I've already borrowed all I can to pay for this." She waved at the walls around them. "There's no way I can get any more."

Katie figured it was a vain hope, but she asked the question anyway. "How about Crystal? Could she borrow from somewhere? Or someone? Her parents, maybe?"

"Not Crystal's." Brittany made a rude noise. "Her dad hasn't been in the picture since she was conceived, and her mom bounced from wonderful new boyfriend to wonderful new boyfriend, dragging her daughter along until Crystal turned eighteen and went out on her own."

"No grandparents? No aunts or uncles?"

"None that were willing to step up. Sounds like they washed their hands of Crystal's mom when she turned up pregnant at sixteen."

"But it wasn't Crystal's fault she was born out of wedlock."

Brittany gave a helpless head-shaking kind of a nod. "I know that and you know that. Try telling that to people who think premarital sex is a sin."

"Poor Crystal," Katie said quietly.

"Yeah. It's a miracle she's turned out as well as she has. She's my little sister's best friend, and I've always liked her. She's one of those people who sees the best in everyone, you know? Always has a cheerful disposition."

"I like her, too."

"Then can't you cut her some slack?" Brittany pleaded. "There has to be some way this can work. All she needs is a little help to build her clientele and she'll be out on her own in no time."

"I'd love to," Katie said, trying to stay firm. "But I can't risk anyone's health. I'm sorry, but I can't."

"Just a few more days? We'll wrack our brains, talk to people, figure out something, I promise. Please? All Crystal needs is a chance."

Katie caved—but only so far. "No more than a week," she said. "If there's no solution inside of a week, she has to go."

~~~~~~~

As the day wore on, Katie's mind kept summoning images of a younger Crystal dragged from pillar to post by her ne'er-do-well mother. Her mind's eye saw the wan look of the child Crystal when her mom said they were moving yet again, that she'd be going to yet another school, and wouldn't it be fun?

But Katie knew for a fact that it almost certainly hadn't been. It's never easy being the new kid, and harder for some more than for others. After her parents had died she'd been the new kid when she'd gone to live with her great-aunt, and then again when her great-aunt had retired and moved to a smaller house with less upkeep.

Katie tried to stop comparing her story with Crystal's—they were two different people, and she barely knew the younger woman—but it was hard when she kept walking across the lobby and seeing the salon.

She truly wanted to give Crystal that break, truly wanted to help someone struggling to make it, wanted to be supportive of a new business owner, yet . . . how could she? If any customer or any vendor fell sick due to the noxious odors from Crystal's nail business, and it was shown that Katie had known about the problem and failed to do anything about it, she would undoubtedly be liable for who knew what.

Which meant that, unless Crystal and Brittany came up with a magical solution, Crystal had to leave.

"Penny for your thoughts?"

Katie was taking a ten-minute break in the vendors' lounge, staring into her last cup of coffee for the day, thinking about Crystal and Don and Nick and Marcie and Rob and Del and Erikka and Duncan and all the things she'd learned in the last couple of weeks, much of which she would rather have never learned at all. She looked up at the kindly words and smiled. "Hey, Gwen. How are you? I don't think I've seen you since the vendors' meeting last week."

The fiftyish woman returned her smile, but it didn't last long. "I'm fine, how about you?"

Katie, whose greeting may have been more perfunctory than deeply meant, caught a tone in Gwen's voice that wasn't usually there. "Busy," she said carefully, studying the pale-skinned woman. "But that's pretty normal, so it had better be fine."

"I know what you mean," Gwen said, but it was a vacant statement that lacked feeling.

"How about I buy you a cup of coffee?" Katie asked. She had long since instituted an honor system for coffee payment; if everyone put in a quarter for every mug they drank, Katie would purchase the supplies and stock the break room with coffee and tea fixings. And she was no exception. She dropped a dollar into the jar every morning and rationed herself accordingly. Thus, the coffee in front of her was the last of the day unless she put in more money. And if Gwen wanted one . . . She felt her pockets for loose change.

"Oh, no, thanks." Gwen took a mug from the cabinet and turned on the faucet. "I wanted water, that's all. Trying to get in that two liters a day my doctor is always scolding me about."

Katie grimaced. Right. Water. Like Gwen and practically everyone else, she knew she should be drinking more water. And she'd think about that right after she started exercising more. "I like water just fine," she said, "as long as I'm out on top of it in a boat."

She'd happened to be looking straight at Gwen when she spoke, and she was surprised to see a sad look cross her face. *Hmm*, she thought, then said, "Speaking of boats, I think someone told me that you have one. What kind is it?"

The look on the hazel-eyed woman's face changed from sadness to something that looked like desperation. "A sailboat," she said, so quietly that Katie almost didn't hear. "A thirty-four-foot kit boat we built ourselves after the kids were out of the house. It's . . ." She looked at the glass she was holding, blinked, then turned and heaved the contents into the sink.

"Sorry," she muttered, putting the glass upside down onto the drying rack. "I have to go."

Katie, who had half stood in preparation for offering

whatever emotional assistance Gwen might have needed, sat back down with a light thump.

Hmm, she thought. Was it just her, or suddenly did everyone in McKinlay Mill who owned a boat look perpetually guilty?

The rest of the day remained busy with shoppers. Katie was exhausted down to the marrow in her bones. She didn't know how Andy worked his long days after long days without having to check himself into a restful spa for a week.

"Holy cannoli, what a day!" Edie smiled, her round face flushed red with exertion. "We have more days like this and we're going to have to hire some staff to give you a hand, Katie."

"One day does not a hiring decision make," she said. "It was probably an anomaly."

"Want to bet?" Edie asked, looking smug.

"If I were the betting kind," Katie said, "but I'm not, I'd . . ." Her voice trailed off.

"You'd what?" Edie prompted.

"Um . . ." She tried to concentrate on what she'd been saying, but it was hard because of what she'd just glimpsed back on the sales floor: two people standing close, their backs to her and their heads together, clearly deep in conversation.

Gwen Hardy.

And Duncan McAllister.

~~~~~~~

Since Katie had spent almost the entire day out front, working a cash register, wrapping and bagging goods, she hadn't had a minute to spend in her office until the front door was locked and all the vendors were gone.

She flicked on the light switch and sighed at the pile of

mail she'd plopped on her desk that noon. Her email box would undoubtedly be full, and in her hand was a small stack of special requests from customers about which she'd promised she'd follow up.

The requests were mostly simple things like "Does the lady with the stained glass do commissions for personal homes?" and "Is there anyone here who would make a Santa outfit for the cement goose my husband gave me for my garden?" But there was a question about selling baked goods that she had a feeling would require a complicated answer that might take her a full day of research and a discussion with the county board of health.

"Tomorrow," she murmured, firing up the computer. Maybe Edie was right; maybe she did need to consider hiring someone. A college student, perhaps, who needed some practical bookkeeping experience. Or someone who'd recently retired and wanted to get out of the house a couple of days per week.

Katie fantasized about this for a few minutes, even to the extent of starting up a fresh spreadsheet and running some numbers. In the end, though, she repeated what she'd told Edie earlier; that one high-volume weekday didn't mean anything on a long-term basis. She'd track the data, watch the revenues and expenditures, and maybe consider hiring someone next year. The vendors often brought in family members to help during the holidays, so that wasn't an issue. Next year, though . . .

Smiling, Katie starting working on the email in her inbox.

Lost in the work, it was hours later when Katie finally surfaced, and that was only because the emptiness in her stomach was starting to give her a headache. She stretched, yawned, and only then noticed the time on the corner of her computer screen.

Half past eight? No wonder she was hungry! And, now that she was noticing things, she was also tired and stiff, too. It was definitely time to go home and rustle up something to eat.

She saved her documents, shut down the computer, gathered up her purse and the light coat she'd worn that morning, locked the door, and headed out of Artisans Alley.

But prior to opening the back door, her ears picked up the clues before her eyes saw what was going on outside. "Oh, swell," she said out loud. Rain was dropping from the heavens as if it would never stop. Big, fat drops that would drench her to the skin the moment she stepped out into it. She pulled on her coat and rolled out the hood she hardly ever used and was grateful for the large brass stand that sat near the main entrance and was filled with brightly colored golf umbrellas used to usher happy patrons to their cars during inclement weather. She grabbed one.

The rain drummed down, and Katie looked through the Alley's plate glass door at a dark, watery world. The sun had set some time ago, and with the rain clouds, there was no lingering afterglow. All she saw were the vague shapes of the Victoria Square buildings and the dim light from the ornate street lamps. Not a soul was moving; not a single living thing was in sight.

Katie shivered involuntarily. She needed to get to Angelo's and see Andy. She was about to leave the building when she paused, squinting to focus on a blur to the east. What was that? Or rather, who was that?

The murky darkness concealed a lot, but across the Square, she detected movement. Movement that could only be made by a human being, coming from the direction of Sassy Sally's. But who would voluntarily go out in this weather? Katie dodged under the eaves and out of the light but leaned forward, watching the figure move along the asphalt. It was an odd movement, too. Whoever it was would trot along, then stop and look back. Trot, stop, look. Trot, stop, look. The only thing Katie could think was that someone was headed off on a nefarious mission and kept checking to make sure he—or she—wasn't being followed.

Katie moved away from the side of the building, despite knowing the security lighting might reveal her presence. The figure was a male, she decided, after the shadowy shape passed close to one of the Square's gas lamps. The shape itself, the walk, the clothes, the stance; everything suggested the male version of the human species.

She moved back and then peered around the edge of the building at the man as he neared another gas lamp. If he would just get a little closer, maybe she would recognize who it was and maybe she would be able to figure out why he was acting oddly. She reached into her purse for her cell phone. If she needed to call 911, she wanted to be ready.

Timing was everything, and she needed to wait as long as possible without alerting the hurrying dark shadow. He moved a little closer, a little closer . . .

"Oh!" The gasp was involuntary. She stood straighter and stared at the furtive figure. *Don Parsons! What are you doing out in the rain?*

She couldn't think of a single reason. Not one that she liked, anyway.

Puzzled and more than a little concerned, she continued to watch Don scurrying along the parking lot and looking over his shoulder. Where on earth was he going? Frowning, she edged farther forward, worried now about losing sight of him. Then . . . she did.

"Swell," she muttered and moved along Artisans Alley until she reached the end of the building and saw headlights flare. She'd let both Don and Nick park in Artisans Alley's back lot for the past couple of months while more than one Dumpster had been planted in front of Sassy Sally's.

A car rolled out of the parking lot and turned right toward Main Street, away from her.

It took her all of half a second to decide what to do. Katie ran for her car, unlocked it, and jumped in. She started the engine and eased it into gear but did not turn on the head-lights.

She waited until Don had gone a couple of blocks, switched on her lights, and started following him.

Through the pouring rain they drove, a very short parade of two cars, one of which didn't even realize it was part of the event. Katie switched the windshield wipers to high and closed the gap between them to one block, figuring that Don wouldn't have a clue the car in his rearview mirror was fol-lowing him.

Because why would he? Normal people living in a small village didn't pay attention to the vehicles behind them—especially when the driving conditions were less than optimal—unless it was to check if it was someone they knew.

So Don drove, and Katie followed. She glanced at her gas gauge, grateful to see that the tank was almost full. Where was he headed? The hardware store? That would make sense, really. She could come up with an easy half a dozen reasons for him needing to stop there . . . but, no. Not only was it closed, but he passed that, too.

As Don drove past every business on Main Street, Katie began to run out of ideas. Where on earth was he going? The rain, thankfully, was dribbling off to a sprinkle, and there was enough traffic that Katie was sure he didn't suspect her presence, but . . . where was he going? Where—

The left turn signal on Don's car blinked, and he went

down Parma Townline Road. Katie slowed to increase the
gap, then made the same turn. They were outside the village
limits now, and the area was a mix of residential homes and
small farms.

There were also fewer cars, so Katie let the gap between
them increase further. She wasn't worried about losing sight
of him; there weren't that many places for him to go.

One mile, two miles . . . then at close to three miles down
the road, Don's blinker went on again. The brake lights flared,
and the car turned into a driveway that led to an odd cluster
of buildings with varying shapes and sizes.

Katie's foot came off the gas pedal, and she let her car
coast. She'd get the address of this place, whatever it was,
and come back later to check it out.

As she drew closer, she watched as Don jumped out of his
car. Yard lights flicked on, and a man Katie didn't recognize
walked out of the largest building. Don hurried toward him.
Katie could see that the men were talking, and then, just as
her car passed by, she watched, wide-eyed, as Don held out
his arms and the two men gave each other a huge hug.

Twelve

Katie spent another night tossing and turning as she replayed the events over in her mind.

One. Don sneaking down the sidewalk.

Two. Don driving through a rainstorm by himself.

Three. Don greeting another man—a man who clearly wasn't his life partner—with a huge hug.

Four. Katie suddenly suspicious of Don's actions. He'd asked her to trust him, but could she after what she'd seen? Though she wanted to trust her friend—yearned to trust him—how did she reconcile that wish to trust with the possibility that . . .

Pushing away the thought, she determinedly thought about sitting on a beach listening to the soft wash of waves on the sand, concentrating on her breathing, and fell into a sleep that was punctuated by unwelcome dreams.

The sun brought her awake from a blurry chase scene that

involved boats, faceless bad guys, candles, and, oddly, cats in a bathtub.

"Was it you two?" she blearily asked Mason and Della, who'd wrapped themselves into two furry circles at the foot of her bed. Two untouching circles, that was, because though the two unrelated cats tolerated each other, they weren't best buddies. "It was mostly dark in the dream, so it was hard to tell."

The felines stared at her, unblinking.

"Right," she said snarkily, but sliding out of bed in a way that didn't disturb her pets. "You're cats. You wouldn't tell me even if you wanted to, because it could lead to the destruction of the mysterious allure that is the hallmark of your species."

"Meow?" Della asked.

Katie stopped, a little ashamed of herself. "Sorry about that," she said, turning back to give her cats quick snuggles. "Looks like I got out on the wrong side of the bed." After they'd closed their eyes and started purring, she kissed them both on top of their heads and headed for the shower. Maybe a few cold shots of water would help to wake her up.

An hour later, she was sitting in her office, sucking down coffee as if it was the last liquid left on the planet. The caffeine helped her body to function, but it wasn't helping her to focus on the pile of tasks that needed doing.

Out on the main sales floor, a number of customers circulated among the booths. More than normal, but not nearly what they'd seen the day before. As Katie had expected, that had been an anomaly, and with a wry smile, she started to delete the spreadsheet she'd worked on the evening before, the one that showed her calculations of when she'd be able to hire someone to fix the gutters by the side entrance that needed to be done before winter. She didn't want the water to freeze and become a slipping hazard.

At the last second, though, she stopped herself from deleting the document. After all, you never knew. Instead, she slid it into a folder titled "Long-Range Planning."

"Someday," she said out loud and was pleased at the sense of optimism that washed through her. "Someday," she said again, promising herself. Then she shook out her hands, took a deep breath, took another one, and got down to work.

Once again, the hollowness in her stomach brought her to the realization that she hadn't eaten lunch. She was tempted to skip the meal, since Andy had texted her that morning that he wouldn't be able to meet her at Del's due to being short-staffed once again, but she knew that skipping meals wasn't the wisest way to lose weight. Yet, it was tempting.

Still thinking about it, she got up from her desk and, stiff from sitting so long without moving anything except her hands, almost fell over. "Whoa!" She grabbed the edge of the desk. Looks like what she needed more than anything was to walk around and stretch her legs. She'd been warned by numerous older friends that she would need to start taking care of herself better now that she was in her thirties, but somehow she'd assumed that need would be at the end of the decade, not at the beginning.

Grimly, she stood and leaned over in an attempt to touch her toes. It was an epic fail. Her hands barely reached past her knees. After a little effort and light bouncing, she managed to touch the tops of her shoes, but that wasn't exactly satisfying.

How on earth had she let this happen? Okay, the separation from Chad had sent her to ice cream more than once, and then his death had pushed her to add chocolate syrup. And then Ezra's death and her immediate plunge into making Artisans Alley a money-making enterprise, and then . . . and then there she was, having been either too emotionally bereft or too busy to do little more than minimal maintenance on herself for well over a year.

Still, it was only a year. And she was still young, since there was no way that thirty-one could be considered old. All she had to do was work a little. That wouldn't be so hard. She vowed to take a walk around the sales floors once every hour. A few minutes was all it would take, and wasn't she always thinking she needed to get to know her vendors better? And right that moment would be a perfect time to start.

But the moment she stepped outside her office door was the moment she saw the empty vendors' lounge, which was the moment she remembered talking to Gwen and, after that, seeing Gwen in deep conversation with Duncan. Her new and uncomfortable knowledge of Don's activities had pushed all that out of her head.

She went back inside her office and grabbed her purse, jacket, and the new sign that she'd ordered the week before. Locking the office door, she hung the new WILL RETURN sign on the door, moved the clock hands around to an hour away, paused, moved them to an hour and a half away, and headed out.

~~~~~~~

Thanks to the willingness of people to talk about wooden boats, it only took her two phone calls to find the name of the marina where Duncan kept his craft. She'd started with the manager of the marina where Seth kept his boat, who had in turn provided the name of a marina that he knew kept a lot of wooden boats.

The manager of North Coast Marina frowned. "Duncan who? McAllister? Nope, not sure I—"

Katie had interrupted him to describe Duncan and what she knew of his boat.

"Oh, I got it," the manager had said. "You're talking about

Mac! Sure, his boat is here, but I doubt he's interested in selling." Wanting to purchase a large wooden boat like Duncan's
had been Katie's cover story to everyone but Seth. "Still, I
don't suppose it would hurt to talk to him. He's around most
mornings."

She'd written down directions to the marina, but as she
neared the location, she tossed the piece of paper onto the
passenger's seat. There was no need for a specific address
when there were so many signs of a pending marina in front
of her. Large warehouses, expanses of flat grass crowded
with boats on trailers, trailers without boats, pieces of boats,
even, and half a dozen trucks, tractors, and cranes moving it
all around.

Katie parked off in a far corner of a parking lot and hoped
her car wouldn't be in anyone's way. After dodging three
trailered boats being hauled across the lots, she was grateful
to enter the door of the marina's office and get out of the way
of the hustle and bustle.

Inside, however, it wasn't much better.

The man at the desk hung up the phone, looked at her, and
growled, "Where the hell is he?"

Katie blinked. "I'm sorry?" She was pretty sure this was
the guy she'd talked to on the phone earlier, but his question
didn't make any sense.

He stabbed his index finger in the air, indicating he'd be
right with her, and picked up the phone. "Chris, where the
hell is Trevor? He was supposed to be at the Langdons' at
noon . . . No, I don't care if it took longer at the Garfields'
than he thought. The Langdons needed him there at noon,
and it's almost one o'clock. Get him there now!" He slammed
the phone down, but just as he looked up at Katie, the phone
rang.

The man glared at the instrument. "I love my job," he

muttered. "I love my job." Picking up the phone, he said, "North Coast Marina . . . Yes, ma'am, we're absolutely getting your dock out of the water this week . . . Yes, I realize it's already Thursday afternoon, but—"

Behind Katie, the office's door opened and a well-dressed couple in their sixties stepped in. The man's face was stormy, and his fists were clenched.

"Now, honey," said the woman, "I'm sure there's a reasonable explanation. There's no need to get all upset about this."

"I'll take them to court," the man said tightly. "I said last year if it happened again I'd sue. I've had enough of their excuses, and you should have, too."

Katie decided to get away while the getting was good. She smiled at the man on the phone, edged away from the couple, who were now in a quiet but fierce argument, and went back outside.

Pulling in a breath of fresh air, she looked around the marina and considered what to do next. She'd intended to ask about Duncan in the office, see if she could get some impression of him, anything that might help her figure out what was going on, but that obviously wasn't going to work out.

"Now what?" she asked out loud. A loud burst of laughter made her look in the direction of the lake. At least she assumed there was a lake out there somewhere since she was mostly seeing paths that must lead to floating docks. She was surprised to see so many sailboats still in the water; she'd been under the impression that most boats came out right after Labor Day.

Then again, maybe this was where boats hung out if the marina was doing some extra work. Or maybe this marina happened to have a lot of people who didn't mind boating in the chillier weather of fall.

She decided to walk around for a little while, then head back and see if she could catch a few uninterrupted minutes with the manager. A wide concrete sidewalk flanked the line of covered boats closest to her. Off to the right, she caught sight of some wooden boats, so she set off that way.

Only a few of the slips were empty, and she smiled to see some of the names people had painted on their boats. *Sodium Free. YachtSee. Deeper in Debt. Idle-Ours. After Math. Whatever Floats Your Boat.* Hang on . . . "*After Math*?"

She walked back a few steps and studied the boat, a large wooden job, remembering that Duncan had been a teacher. Had he been a math teacher?

"You looking for someone?"

Katie turned. "Hi," she said, smiling. The gray-haired woman standing nearby was lugging two big buckets of soapy water and had towels slung over her shoulders. "Do you need help with that?"

"If you'd asked thirty yards ago, I would have said absolutely, but since I'm here, I'll say thanks, but no thanks." She thumped the buckets down on the dock that ran between *After Math* and its neighbor, also a wooden boat, and reached down into the bucket. Pulling out a sponge, she squeezed out the extra water. "You looking for Mac? He was here this morning."

Katie's breath quickened. "Do you think he'll be back today?"

The woman shrugged. "No idea. He comes and goes, like most of us retired folks." She shot Katie a look. "If you're looking to buy Mac's boat, you're wasting your time. He's not interested in selling."

"I've heard that," Katie murmured. Thinking fast, she said, "But let's pretend that he is. Does Dunc—I mean Mac, does he take good care of his boat?"

A snort started off her reply. "I wish my husband took care of me like Mac takes care of *After Math*."

Katie laughed. "I know what you mean." She paused, then asked, "Does he take the boat out often?"

"Often?" The woman stood there, soap suds dripping onto the dock in small plops. She smiled, and the corners of her eyes went all crinkly. "If by often you mean he's out on the water every chance he can get, then I suppose he's out often enough."

"Even on the weekends?" Katie asked. "I mean, I can imagine a lot of people wouldn't want to take out a really nice wooden boat on a weekend. Especially holiday weekends, when there're so many people boating that don't really know what they're doing."

"Ain't that the truth." Her new friend rolled her eyes. "Take Labor Day weekend. Remember how nice it was? This place was packed. All my husband and I wanted was to get out of here and out onto the open water, and I swear it took us an hour when it normally takes five minutes. Holiday boaters kept getting in our way. It's enough to drive you to drink." She grinned. "Which, luckily, we happened to have on board."

"How about Mac?" Katie nodded toward *After Math*. "Was he out that weekend, too?"

"None of your damn business."

Katie flinched at the sound of Duncan McAllister's voice but held her ground. "What makes you say that?" she asked.

"You stay away from my boat," he said, stepping close to her. "And from me."

She shook her head. "I don't know if you've noticed, but there's a murder investigation going on."

"And that's your business how?" His voice was low and growly.

"Because my friends are involved," she said, keeping her chin up and her gaze fastened on Duncan's face. She would not, repeat would *not*, let the size of this man intimidate her. "If my friends are involved, I'll do what I can to help them, including asking questions about you." She pointed her index finger at him but stopped short of poking him in the chest, even though he was close enough—and she was sorely tempted.

"You stay away from my boat," he repeated. "And stay away from me." He pushed past her, strode onto the dock, stepped up into his boat, and disappeared from view.

"Well," Katie said brightly to her new friend. "Looks like—"

But the woman gave her a baleful glare, and then she, too, retreated to her boat.

"Swell," Katie said under her breath. "Just swell."

~~~~~~

Instead of doing what a responsible owner of a close-to-thriving business would do, which should have been return to the location of said business and get back to work, Katie decided that since she was out and about, she may as well take a joyride to Fairport and stop at Marcie Kimper's house for a casual chat.

She'd come up with a couple of decent explanations for stopping. One, seeking reassurance for her vendors that the purchasers of the insurance agency weren't going to sell their policies to a huge, uncaring corporation; two, that she'd met and liked Josh's new office manager, Erikka, and hoped that Marcie would give her a solid letter of recommendation.

What she wanted to know, of course, was if Marcie had suspected Josh of having an affair with Erikka, and, if so, had Marcie killed Josh in a fit of jealous rage. Or, if not that, then had Marcie killed Josh to get the insurance money and clear the way for her to marry Rob Roth, the tall, dark, and handsome attorney who had been comforting her in such a personal way so soon after Josh's death.

Katie thought either option was possible. All she needed was a little evidence, one way or another, that she could hand over to Detective Hamilton. Of course, she also thought it was possible that Duncan McAllister might be involved, and then there was how both Gwen and Vance had reacted when she'd asked about their boats. And, if Josh and Erikka had been involved, was it possible that Erikka had killed him when he'd, say, refused to divorce Marcie? Wouldn't that be high irony.

But all of that was, as the television attorneys said in court, sheer conjecture. She had lots of theories; what she needed was proof.

She parked at the curb in front of the Victorian house and climbed out of the car. But even before she set foot on the porch steps, she realized something was wrong.

The porch was empty of furniture, yes, but that wasn't completely unusual for this time of year. Lots of people stored their summer furniture after Labor Day, getting it out of the way of falling leaves and the inevitable snow.

No, it was more than an empty porch. The living room's lace curtains were pulled shut—Katie was certain they'd been wide open when she'd stopped by after Josh's death—and the cheery WELCOME sign that had hung next to the front door had disappeared.

Katie slowly climbed the porch steps, but she knew there was little point. The house was empty. Marcie and her daughters were already gone.

She put her face close to the tall, narrow windows that flanked the front door. Peering through the sheer curtain, she could see that her suspicions had been correct. Boxes with labels "Master Bedroom," "Kitchen," and "Downstairs Bath" were piled high. Not a single picture remained on any wall, and what furniture she could see was clustered together, awaiting the moving van.

"They're gone."

Katie turned. Standing at the bottom of the porch steps, his hands in the pockets of his suit pants, wearing a loosened tie and a woebegone expression, was none other than Rob Roth. "Marcie and the girls, you mean?" she asked.

He nodded.

Katie gritted her teeth, trying to think kindly of Marcie and failing. Maybe Marcie had taken into consideration that ripping her kids away from their schools would be the second major trauma they suffered in less than a month, but somehow she doubted it. "Where did they go?" she asked. "Did she say?"

Rob sighed and mentioned a town Katie had never heard of. "It's in Maine," he added. "That's where Marcie grew up. All her family is there, and she felt she needed the support, now that . . ." He faltered. "Now that she's alone."

The stumble in Rob's words pricked Katie's curiosity. She thought about what, exactly, to say here, then said, "You were good friends with Marcie and Josh?"

Rob's face went stiff. "I don't like to speak ill of the dead, but Josh Kimper was an arrogant jerk."

Since Katie wasn't about to disagree with that statement, she nodded and waited for him to continue. It didn't take long.

"Marcie only stayed married to him for so long for the sake of the girls," Rob said. "I fell in love with her practically the moment we met. That was two years ago at a party given by a mutual friend, and it's been the longest two years of my life. I asked her and asked her to divorce Kimper and marry me.

Pleaded with her. Begged her. All I want is to share my life with her and the girls. Is that so wrong?" His expression begged Katie to agree with him.

"It sounds," she said, "as if you love her very much."

"I'd do anything for her. Anything." He pointed his chin at the house. "I told her I'd keep an eye on this place, if she wanted, so I drive past a couple of times a day. When I saw you, I stopped." For the first time, he seemed to take in who she was. "You used to work at the agency, didn't you? Marcie spoke highly of you." He smiled faintly. "Said you were smart to quit working for Josh, but that you should have done it years earlier."

"The time wasn't right," she said, since it felt like she had to say something.

He nodded seriously. "Timing is everything, isn't it? If only I'd met Marcie before she'd married Josh, or at least before she'd had the girls. If only . . ." He shook his head, sighed, and wandered back to his car.

After the lovesick attorney pulled away, Katie walked back to her own car and got in, thinking hard.

Marcie was gone, moved out of the area. If Marcie had killed Josh, and who was more likely than the victim's spouse, how on earth was anyone ever going to prove it? And there was Rob to consider. What was it he'd said?

I'd do anything for her.

Thirteen

The next morning when Katie was dutifully doing her walk around the sales floors in Artisans Alley, she spied Ray Davenport in his booth, adding a few more pieces to his display.

She stopped. "You do know your daughters are going to change whatever it is you do."

"Got to give them some reason to come hang out with me." He stepped back, studying the display, then pushed everything slightly out of line. "What do you think? I'm aiming for a look that's not unattractive to shoppers, but bad enough that it'll make my daughters think I need their help."

"Why, Ray Davenport," Katie said, surprised and more than a little shocked. "You are a schemer and a manipulator!"

He shrugged. "I was a cop for thirty years and a detective for fifteen of those. It's hard to turn all that off."

"But to your own flesh and blood?"

"Hah. From that statement alone I can tell you've never had children."

"Too young," she said quickly. "There's lots of time." Then, to stave off any further kid-oriented discussion, she asked, "Do you have a few minutes? There are some things I've found out about Josh's murder that I'd like to talk over."

He eyed her. "If you have any real information—"

"I'd be calling the Sheriff's Office," she cut in. "Of course I would. What I mostly have are theories."

"Ah, theories." Smirking, he rubbed his hands together then grabbed his cane, which stood against the wall. "Nothing I like better than poking holes in other people's theories. Lead me to them."

Katie rolled her eyes and led him to her office after a quick stop in the vendors' lounge for two coffees. She didn't intend to discuss Gwen, Vance, or Duncan with him, but even so, a conversation about murder belonged in a private setting. She closed the door behind them, scooped a stack of mail off the guest chair, and settled in behind her desk.

"So what do you have?" Ray leaned back, lacing his wide fingers around his mug. "Please tell me you suspect an alien abduction gone wrong. That would brighten my day like nothing else."

"Not yet," Katie said. "Although I do have a friend who visited Roswell a while back."

"New Mexico?" Ray's face lit up. "Seriously? What was it like? How much do they let you see?"

"No idea. She was there on a business trip. But she did bring home a baseball hat that had the alien image on it."

Ray slumped back in the chair. "Here you had me all excited." He sipped at his coffee and said, "Back to the more mundane murder of McKinlay Mill. Anything new?"

"I don't think murder should ever be called mundane," Katie said stiffly. "That's callous and—"

"Yeah, yeah." Ray waved her off. "Callous and unfeeling and not showing respect for the deceased or the family and friends of the deceased. I was just working on the alliteration, see, and that was the best I could come up with on short notice."

Katie squinted at him. "If that was a joke, it wasn't very funny."

"Story of my life." He shrugged. "Anyway, what's up?"

So Katie recapped what she'd previously told him about the quick sale of the insurance agency, how Fred Cunningham had said Marcie had been looking to put the house up for sale before Josh's death, and that Marcie had already moved. And she reminded him that Marcie had been involved with another man for two years, a man who'd begged her to divorce Josh and marry him.

All the while she was talking, Ray listened intently, but when she finished, he asked, "Okay. What else have you got?"

"What else?" For a moment she was at a loss for words. "Isn't that enough?"

"Not even close. You're talking suspicions, sure, but where's the proof? And you're mixing up motives. Last week you were thinking Marcie killed Josh over jealousy about Erikka. Now you're saying she killed him to avoid a divorce?"

Katie's hackles rose, then she subsided, sighing. He was right. "You must think I sound like an idiot."

He laughed. "Better me than my successor. Because if you call the deputies with this, they'll laugh you out of the station. Not in front of you, of course, but I can guarantee you they'll do it behind your back."

She narrowed her eyes. "Are you saying that's what you did to me, before you retired?"

Once again, he laughed. "I refuse to answer on the grounds that it may incriminate me. Now, unless you have some other information, I have to get back to ruining my display so my girls can feel superior to their dear old dad."

Using his cane, he pushed himself to his feet and looked down at Katie, his expression suddenly serious. "You do realize the Sheriff's Office will figure out who killed Kimper eventually, right? They really don't need your help."

Katie thought about how she'd seen Don hugging a strange man. She shook her head, trying to push it away. "My friends are under suspicion," she said. "Don and Nick are the easy answer. If there's anything I can do to keep them from being arrested for something they didn't do, I'll do it."

"And what would you do if you learned one—or both—of your friends was guilty of murder?" Before she could answer, Ray continued. "I can't tell you how many times a friend or relative has told me, 'I never would have thought he—or she—was capable of murder.'" He gave her a parting nod and exited her office.

~~~~~~

Later that morning, when Katie was out doing her laps around the sales floor, she saw Rose in her booth, working on her jewelry displays. "Lot of restocking going on today," Katie said, slowing to a stop.

Rose looked up and smiled. "Oh, hello, dear. Yes, the last couple of days have been busy, haven't they? And the weekend is coming up. If this continues I'll have to start putting together some new designs."

"Time will tell," Katie said. "I wouldn't worry about it right away, though."

"Spoken like a born retailer," Rose said, laughing. "No counting those chickens until they're well and truly hatched."

"And laying their own eggs." She started off, but the elderly woman called her back.

"Is everything okay with your young man?"

Katie looked left and right but didn't see anyone, let alone a youngster who might be in need of assistance. "Sorry?"

"Andy," Rose said. "He was here earlier, wanting to talk to you."

"He was?" Katie frowned. "I never saw him. When was this?"

"Let me think." Rose tapped her chin. "Oh, I remember. It was when you were shut up in your office with Ray Davenport. Are you going to tell me what that was all about?"

"Nothing, really." There wasn't much Katie wouldn't tell her friend, but she didn't want to start speculating about murder suspects with Rose, especially when three of those suspects could be standing around the corner of an adjacent booth. Not that she really thought Vance would murder anyone, but why had he gone all weird when she'd asked him about his boat? Same with Gwen. And then there was that episode with Duncan . . .

She shivered and looked at Rose. "Did Andy say what he wanted?"

"Just that he wanted to see you about something." Rose studied her. "He went back to your office but was walking back through the lobby thirty seconds later, saying that your door was shut. I told him you were just talking to Ray and to barge right in." She tipped her head. "Andy said he didn't want to disturb the party and left."

A prickly sensation ran down Katie's back. "That's weird," she said, not liking what she'd just heard. "Thanks, though. I'll stop by Angelo's and see what he wanted."

"I don't wish to be intrusive," Rose said, "but would you mind a piece of advice?"

The prickly feeling was replaced by a chill in the pit of her stomach. What had she done wrong now? "Go right ahead."

"It's about your—"

A panicked voice interrupted them. "Katie! Katie, is that you?"

The two women turned. Approaching them was a wet and bedraggled young woman, her clothing in tatters, her mascara streaking down her face.

"Can you help me?" Erikka asked. "He's gone and I need . . . I need . . ."

But before she could say anything else, she collapsed.

~~~~~~~

"I'm fine," Erikka protested, a few minutes later. She'd woken from her dead faint almost as soon as she'd hit the ground, and she wouldn't hear of anyone calling an ambulance. Rose and Katie had half carried her to the vendors' lounge, where Katie had dug through a back closet and hauled out the folding cot she'd remembered seeing in there, once upon a time.

Since there wasn't time to clean it, she grabbed a painting tarp that vendors often used when redecorating their booths and spread it over the cot. "Lie down," she ordered, "and we'll consider not calling nine-one-one."

"But, really, I'm okay," Erikka said, but then obediently settled back. "I'm probably just dehydrated, you know? I don't think I've had anything to drink today."

"Or eat?" Rose asked. She'd conjured up a brightly colored fleece blanket and was draping it over Erikka. "When was the last time you had food?"

"Um, I had a bagel?"

"This morning?" Rose's eyebrows went up.

"Uh, no, ma'am. I guess that must have been yesterday."

Rose motioned Katie to the other side of the room. "I take it you know this young woman?" she asked quietly.

"An acquaintance at best." Katie sent a concerned glance toward the cot. "She was my replacement at Josh's insurance agency. I stopped in a couple of times to . . . to chat with her."

"Hmm." Rose looked at her speculatively. "Do you have any idea why she's here?"

Katie shook her head emphatically. "Absolutely none. Do you think we should call for an ambulance? Or the police?"

"If she says not to, then we don't." Although Rose said the words lightly, Katie could tell she was concerned. "You can't force people to do what is so obviously best for them." She brightened. "However, between the two of us, I bet we can gently browbeat her into doing the right thing, at least in the short term."

"And that would be what, exactly?"

"Well, my completely inexpert medical diagnosis is she just needs food and water."

Katie thought fast. "How about if you get her something from the bakery? I'll stay here and try and get some fluids into her."

"Good idea. I'll be just a jiffy." Rose took one step, then turned back. "Is Ray still here?"

"No idea." Katie had been wondering the same thing, though. "Maybe you can stop at his booth on your way out, see if he has a minute." The two women looked at each other and, without saying a word, communicated volumes. They were both worried that Erikka might have been attacked and that there was a chance her attacker might be nearby.

"I'll do that," Rose said and hurried away.

Katie went to the sink and filled the largest cup she could find with water. She pulled a chair close to the cot and sat down. "Here," she said gently. "Let me help you sit up. There you go, now drink this . . . That's right, all the way down."

With loud swallows, Erikka drank it down. Sighing, she eased herself back onto the cot. "I'm so sorry," she whispered. "I didn't mean to make a scene. It's so embarrassing."

"Don't you worry about that." Katie got up and filled the glass with more water. Erikka sat up to drank half the glass then shook her head that she'd had enough. "All right," Katie said. "Rose went to get you something to eat, and sorry, you don't have a choice about that. You're going to eat what she brings you—unless you'd rather we called nine-one-one?"

Weakly, Erikka shook her head. "I'm feeling a lot better already," she said. "Honest."

"That's good to hear." Katie glanced toward the sales floor but saw no sign of Rose. "Can you tell me what happened?"

Erikka gave the faintest of smiles. "You mean, why am I here, making trouble for someone I hardly even know?"

"You're not making trouble," Katie said, "but essentially, yes, that's it." She waited, but Erikka didn't say anything, so she went on. "When you came in, you said, 'He's gone.' And you said you needed my help."

A single tear flowed from Erikka's eye and trickled down the side of her lying-down face. She turned her head so Katie couldn't see and wiped it away.

Though Katie felt like a heel, she knew she was going to have to push. She'd be as gentle as she could, but she anticipated more tears. "You were talking about Josh, weren't you? That he's gone and now things won't ever be the same. That you think you won't be able to go on without him, that you loved him so much and—"

"What?" Erikka sat bolt upright. "Josh Kimper? You think I was in love with Josh?" She stared at Katie with an incredulous expression. "Seriously?"

Uh-oh. "You seemed so upset that first time I stopped in," Katie said. "You'd obviously been crying. I just assumed you were crying over Josh."

"Well, sort of." A still pale Erikka lay back down. "But it wasn't because I was in *love* with him." She made a face of such distaste that Katie had to fight down the urge to laugh. "It was because I was out of a job."

"Marcie said she'd put in a good word for you with the new firm."

"Yeah, that and a buck fifty will buy me a cup of cheap coffee." Erikka stared at the ceiling. "I'm not counting on that. I can't. And now . . ." Her voice cracked. "And now Luke and I had this huge fight. It was his apartment first, so I'm the one who has to leave, and I just maxed out my credit card because I had to put a new transmission in my car. I need a new place to live, I don't have the money for a deposit on an apartment, and I don't have a job. I am so screwed." She turned away, but silent sobs wracked her body.

Katie's heart ached for the younger woman, but there was something that had to come first. "Did Luke hurt you? I'm just asking because your clothes are ripped."

The short black hair moved from side to side in a negative way. "Luke's a jerk, but he's not that much of a jerk. It happened when I was moving my stuff out of his place. My arms were full and I tripped. I must have caught my sleeve on something.

Katie breathed a short sigh of relief. "I don't know about

a place for you to live, but I can talk to a friend of mine about
a job. Not a great one, mind you, but something that might
tide you over."

"You . . . what?" Erikka faced her. "Really? I mean, really
and truly?"

"The pizza place across the Square is in dire need of help.
So like I said, not a great job, and I can't promise you anything, but I can introduce you to the owner."

"That would be so cool!" The strain on Erikka's face was
still there, but at least it had toned down a notch. "Thanks,
Katie, thanks so much! I didn't mean to put you to any trouble." She looked around apologetically. "All I really came
here for was to ask if anyone here does consignment. I need
some money fast for an apartment, and I thought maybe I
could raise some cash by selling some of my stuff."

Katie shook her head. "Not here, but I can give you a
couple of names." She paused. "What are you going to do
about a place to live? Your parents?"

But Erikka was already shaking her head. "I was raised
by my mom. Met my dad maybe twice, and I have no idea
where he is. Mom moved to Texas with her new boyfriend,
and all she does is complain about the heat." A flicker of a
smile appeared. "I hate hot. I'd rather stay here and deal with
snow than be hot."

Katie disagreed with that statement, but she let it go.

"I just need to make some calls," Erikka said. "If I can
sleep on a friend's couch until I make the money for a rent
deposit, I'll be good."

"Sounds like you have a plan."

"Oh, I always have a plan." Erikka's smile was bigger this
time. "It's the timing that's the hard part."

"I know exactly what you mean." As the two women

smiled at each other, Katie felt sorrow and sympathy for all the people who were so close to being without a roof over their heads. She'd been close to it herself, once or twice, and knew how frightening it felt.

Rose came in, carrying a white paper bag and looking grim. "Katie, I'm sorry to have to tell you this, but the fumes are back."

"What?" Katie shot to her feet. "I thought . . . Never mind. Rose, can you make sure Erikka eats everything in that bag? And Erikka, I'll call Andy today about that job, but right now I have to go deal with something."

She charged out of the lounge and into the lobby. The fumes were indeed back. Not nearly as pervasive as they'd been, but still there, bright and sharp and making the insides of her nose crinkle.

But just as her hand was on the salon's doorknob, she heard an odd, choking sort of noise coming from behind her. She turned and saw the tall, portly form of Godfrey Foster stagger and crash into the cash register's counter.

"Godfrey!" She ran to his side. "What's wrong? What do you need?"

His breaths struggled in and out. "Air," he rasped, clutching at his throat. "I need air. Can't . . . breathe . . ."

"Call nine-one-one!" Katie shouted. She'd left her cell phone in her office and didn't want to leave Godfrey alone. "Someone call nine-one-one! He's having an allergic reaction!"

Sam Amato, whom she remembered seeing in his booth earlier that morning, hurried toward them. "Got it," he said, tapping at his phone and holding it to his ear. "I need an ambulance," he told the person at the other end of the phone. "Allergic reaction. Breathing difficulties."

With that taken care of, Katie's attention went back to Godfrey. He was wheezing, and his face was turning red.

"Need . . . air!" he gasped. "Can't . . . breathe!"

She took his arm. "We need to get you outside and away from these fumes." With Sam's one-handed help, because he was still talking to the 911 dispatcher, they ushered the large man outside and into the fresh air. But Katie knew essentially nothing about allergies and had no idea if Godfrey was still in danger.

Frightening thoughts tumbled about in her head. What if he was seriously hurt due to Crystal's nail business? What if he sued Artisans Alley? What if he sued her? What if he . . . died?

She tightened her grip on his arm. "Take deep breaths," she advised.

"C-can't," he stuttered. "Hurts . . . so . . . much . . ."

Katie and Sam exchanged worried glances. "How much longer?" Sam asked into the phone. But even as he asked the question, Katie heard the distant, but very welcome, sound of a siren.

Between them, they eased Godfrey down onto the concrete pad at the entrance to Artisans Alley. After what felt like an eternity, the McKinlay Mill Fire Rescue Unit pulled up in front of the building, and two emergency medical technicians hopped out, one male and one female.

"Breathing difficulties?" the female asked, opening the storage units on the side of the squad.

"Any chest pains?" the male asked, grabbing two boxes of equipment.

Katie gratefully relinquished her place at Godfrey's side and watched as the pair went to work. After a few minutes of evaluation, a Rural/Metro ambulance arrived, and its EMTs took over. The firefighters helped them transfer Godfrey to a gurney. "We need to take you to the hospital," the female said. She looked at Katie. "Are you his wife?"

"No! But I have her phone number." She had all the vendors give her emergency contact information, just in case.

"You might want to call her," the male EMT said, jumping up easily into the back of the ambulance to help Godfrey in from above.

"I'll do that," Katie promised, and in short order, the EMTs shut the back doors of the vehicle and started off, with lights flashing.

"No siren," Sam commented. "That's a good sign."

"It is?" Katie watched the vehicle cross the Square and head east toward Greece and the nearest hospital.

"Sure. If it's truly life-threatening, they'll turn on the siren and go a lot faster." He grinned. "And then charge a lot more for the ride."

Katie wondered if Godfrey carried health insurance. Had he had any policies through Josh? She couldn't remember, but that wasn't her problem. She thanked Sam for his help and went back inside.

In the vendors' lounge, Erikka, who was now sitting up and had much better color, and Rose were chatting away as if they'd known each other for years instead of less than an hour.

"Is everything all right?" Rose asked.

"Yes, but no." Katie slowed but didn't stop. "I'll give you an update later." She went into her office and shut the door behind her. She sat at her desk and unlocked the drawer that contained her private files. She flipped through the vendor folder and found Godfrey's home number.

For a moment, she just stared at it. Then, after taking a deep, calming breath, she picked up the phone and dialed.

"Hello, is this Godfrey's wife? Hi, this is Katie Bonner . . ."

Five minutes later, she hung up the phone and fervently hoped she'd never have to make a call like that again in her life. Once had been more than enough. She shook away the fear she'd heard in the woman's voice, dug into her purse for her cell phone, and scrolled through her list of favorite numbers.

"Hey, Seth, it's Katie."

"And this is Seth. What can I do for you on this wonderful Friday morning? If you're calling about dinner tonight, I'm actually booked up, if you can believe it."

"Of course I can believe it, but this time I have a legal question."

"My favorite kind. What's up?"

Katie described to him the situation with Crystal and her nail business and the complications that were arising. "What can I do, legally?" she asked. "I want to help her, but this situation can't continue."

"Of course not," Seth said, and Katie heard the tapping of his computer's keys. "I'm just pulling up your lease . . . Ah, here it is. Hang on a second . . ." There was a long pause. Katie waited as patiently as she could, which wasn't very, but before she went completely insane from waiting, Seth said, "There's nothing in the lease about termination for a situation like this."

Katie slumped in her chair. She'd been so sure that any lease Seth had written would have anticipated everything. Now what was she going to do?

"But," Seth said, "there also isn't any clause that allows subleasing."

"So . . . ?" Katie asked hopefully.

"You can force—what was her name, Crystal? If Crystal is subleasing from Brittany, and that certainly sounds like what is happening in this case, then you can force Brittany to evict Crystal."

"Thanks, Seth," she said. "I appreciate your help."

She thumbed off the phone. Eviction sounded awful, but Katie didn't see that she had a choice—not any longer.

Fourteen

Katie emerged from her office to find Rose and Erikka sitting together at the table in the vendors' lounge.

"You won't believe this," Rose said, smiling at her, "but Erikka's best friend is the daughter of my new next-door neighbor."

"That's nice," Katie said, trying to care but not doing a very good job.

"Are you all right, dear?" Rose peered at her. "You look troubled."

Katie longed to pour out all her problems, to sit and talk until she couldn't talk any longer, but she had to catch Crystal before she left the building, and besides, her problems weren't Rose's problems. She didn't want to burden her friend unnecessarily. She'd listen, of course, and do what she could, but the job at hand was Katie's and Katie's alone.

"I'm fine," she finally said, glancing at her watch. Could

it really be a quarter to eleven? She was due for lunch with Andy at eleven. Since this time she'd slid her phone into her pocket when leaving the office, she pulled it out and sent Andy a quick text that she might be a few minutes late. Then she sent him another that she had someone who was interested in working at Angelo's. She watched the screen, then saw the replies. "OK," to the being-late text, and "Sweet!!" along with five kissy-face emojis to the potential employee text.

"Looks like you have an excellent shot at a job," she said to Erikka. "I'm meeting Andy, the owner of Angelo's, for an early lunch. If you want to hang around for a little while, when I get back I'll let you know when he wants you to stop by for an interview."

To Katie's surprise, Erikka's face crumpled into tears. "I don't know what to say," she choked out. "You're being so nice to me. I hardly even know you, and you're doing all this for me."

Rose leaned over and put an arm around Erikka's shoulders. "Everyone needs a helping hand once or twice in their lives," she said. "This is your turn, that's all."

Katie realized that, due to all the emotion in the room, her own throat was closing up. She swallowed it away and said, "Everyone gets a turn." *If they're lucky*, she thought to herself as she walked through the lobby. Because what she was about to do would be the absolute opposite of a helping hand.

She entered the salon. Inside, the music was soft and the lighting subdued. Katie instantly found herself relaxing, which she knew was the whole point of the decor, but being relaxed wasn't going to help her. Instead, she summoned up images of Godfrey's red face, of the ambulance, and of the letters she might soon be receiving from Godfrey's attorney.

"Good morning, can I . . . Oh, hi, Katie. What's up?" Crystal asked, smiling.

Katie looked longingly at Crystal's glorious hair, then focused. "Do you know what happened out there a few minutes ago?" She nodded toward the lobby.

"Um, no." Crystal darted a glance toward the glass door, but its smoky color revealed little on the other side except for vague shapes. "I was busy with a new client. She wanted new nails and this complicated design. I think it turned out pretty nice; she seemed really happy with it. I think I'm starting to build up a client base." She bounced a little. "This is going to work. I'm sure of it."

Katie shook her head. "It may work, but it can't work here. I'm sorry."

"But . . ." Crystal fumbled for the end of her braid. Toying with the end, she said, "But I've figured out a venting system. I mean, it's not professional or anything, but I found an old shop vacuum at the thrift store. You can reverse those, you know? And I attached it to some of that flexible tubing and put the other end in that outside window in the back."

"It's better," Katie said, "but it's not enough. One of the vendors had an allergic reaction just now and was taken away in an ambulance."

Crystal's hands flew to her face. "That's awful!" Her eyes started to water. "Is he okay? Please tell me he's not going to die."

"The ambulance didn't turn on its siren," Katie said, which was the only information she had. "So I assume it wasn't life-threatening."

"That's good." Crystal returned to fussing with her braid. "I mean, that's really good. I'm so, so, so sorry, Katie. I thought . . . I wish . . . I mean I'd hoped . . ." Her half-formed sentences trailed off to nothing.

"I'm sorry, too," Katie said. "I'd hoped this would work out for you. But you can't stay." She didn't bother mentioning the sublease issue, though she would if she had to.

Tears trickled down Crystal's face. "Do I have to leave right now?"

For the second time that morning, Katie's heart ached for another person. "I can't have you doing any more acrylic nails. None. But I suppose you can stay for another week if you're just doing manicures and nail decorations."

"Thanks," Crystal said softly, her voice cracking on the single word. "I appreciate—" Suddenly, she whirled and ran down the short hallway. A door thumped shut, and then came the sound of a young woman sobbing as if she would never stop.

Katie took a single step in the direction of the weeping.

No. It wasn't her place to comfort Crystal. She wanted to—oh, how she wanted to—but it wouldn't be right. She blew out a breath and left the salon in a sour mood.

Sometimes being a business owner truly sucked.

~~~~~~~

Saturday morning dawned clear and bright. Katie found it easy to go for an extra-long walk before heading into Artisans Alley, and even then she was regretting the fact that she would be spending the rest of that fine-looking day inside.

Every lap of the Square that she walked, more and more store owners appeared, sweeping around doorsteps that were already clean and washing windows that didn't show a speck of dirt. Everyone, Katie thought, was looking for an excuse to be outside.

Katie shivered as she saw in her mind's eye the snow she would soon be trudging through, then she told herself to stop thinking about the inevitable future and just enjoy the day.

She turned her face to the rising sun and basked in its warmth, smiling and imagining that she could feel the radiant heat seep down into her bones.

Still smiling, she finished her walk and entered Artisans Alley with a light heart and filled with purposeful energy. It was Saturday, and the place would be busy from open to close. First off, she needed to make sure the checkout counters were fully stocked. Then she'd do a quick inspection of the restrooms and take a brisk walk around the floors to make sure all the booths were shipshape.

Cash Desk 2 was low on plastic bags, so she ferried a couple of boxes of them from the storeroom. A quick glance of the restrooms showed that everything was in order, so she was ahead of her self-imposed schedule when she went up the stairs to check the upper sales floor.

Glancing at her watch, she was pleased to see there were almost forty-five minutes until the building opened to the public. If she didn't get caught in a conversation with an early-arriving vendor, she would have time to take care of a few things in her office before the day got busy.

One of her favorite things was to run the register, to see what people purchased and ask questions about who the item was for and why it had been purchased. She'd learned a lot from asking those simple questions.

She smiled, remembering that not all of what she'd discovered was retail-oriented. Some people were willing to share the most bizarre details of their lives. There was the man who'd told her the reason he was buying a pale pink pendant for his wife was because he'd bought something similar for his first girlfriend and hadn't stopped thinking of her for thirty years. And there was the woman who'd purchased one of Sam Amato's metal sculptures because it "spoke to her."

What it might have said, Katie had no idea, other than "I'm a piece of metal," but then her taste in art ran more to the Impressionists, and anyway, wasn't it the aim of Artisans Alley to bring all kinds of artists together under one roof?

Katie mused over that idea as she walked. Did Artisans Alley have an aim? Was there a clear-cut goal, other than to make money? Maybe what she needed to do was write up an official mission statement. Maybe that would help bring everyone together and—

"Oh!" She almost ran smack into Gwen Hardy, who was standing in front of her booth. "I'm sorry, Gwen. I wasn't paying attention to where I was going. I was thinking, and . . ." She stopped talking, because it was obvious that Gwen wasn't paying much attention, either. "Um, are you okay?"

Gwen, who hadn't moved, continued to stare off into space. "It's a beautiful day," she said softly.

"It certainly is." She'd spoken heartily, and Katie winced as she felt her own echoes come back around. "It's a crime to be inside on a day like this."

"A crime," Gwen repeated.

"Yes." Katie studied the pale woman. For the umpteenth time, she wondered how someone who was a big boater managed to keep her skin away from the sun. Then she decided, what the heck, and asked, "You go out boating a lot, don't you? Your skin doesn't show it at all."

Gwen looked at the back of her hands. Then she looked at Katie, and to Katie's horror, tears started streaming down the other woman's face. This was the third person in two days who'd started crying in front of her; if this didn't stop soon she was going to crawl into bed and not get out for a week.

"Let's sit down," Katie suggested. She took Gwen's elbow

and led her into her own booth, where an upholstered chaise was tastefully draped with woven lap blankets. Katie heaped the blankets onto a nearby table, and they sat down. "Do you want to talk about what's bothering you?" she asked.

Gwen, who had by now fished a tissue from one of her apron pockets and was wiping her eyes, shook her head. "Not really, though I suppose I owe you an explanation for breaking down like this. I thought I would be okay, but . . ." She sighed.

"What's the matter?" Katie pressed gently. This had to do with the boat. The boats that had been lurking at the back of Josh's murder. Maybe she'd finally get a solid lead.

"It's our boat." Gwen dabbed at another tear. "Or, actually, it's my husband."

Katie leaned the slightest bit forward. "Yes?" Was she about to hear a confession? Was Ray around? If anyone should hear a murder confession, it should be a former police detective.

"He has arthritis," Gwen said, sighing. "Horrible, debilitating arthritis."

It was a disease Katie had experience with. Her aunt Lizzie had suffered from it, dealing with enlarged knuckles and frozen joints. She shuddered and offered up a hope that arthritis wasn't in her own personal future. "I'm so sorry."

Gwen nodded. "Thanks. It's awful. He's still able to work—he's sales manager at the Chrysler dealership out by the mall—but he can't get out on the boat anymore. He loves to sail. *We* love to sail. It's what brought us together, all those years ago, and now . . . now . . . we're going to have to sell the boat."

Her voice was so low that Katie could hardly make out the words. "I can't sail it alone," Gwen said, "and I won't sail it without him. It would be too hard for both of us. Labor Day was our last time out. It was such a nice day, remember?" She gave a tremulous smile. "A lot like today."

Katie wasn't a die-hard sailor by any means, but she could imagine how hard it must be to be forced to give up something you loved to do. She murmured her sympathies and patted Gwen on the shoulder, saying to let her know if there was anything she could do.

"Thanks, Katie," Gwen said. "You're a good friend."

The good friend felt a little ashamed of herself as she finished her round of the sales floor. Katie had theorized that Gwen might have had something to do with Josh's death because of an odd reaction to the mention of boats, but the reaction had had absolutely nothing to do with Josh.

If Katie had figured wrong about Gwen, what other mistakes was she making?

~~~~~~~

The morning was as busy as Katie had hoped. She thought again how much she was looking forward to having a complete year's worth of sales data so she could begin comparisons. Yes, she was at heart a retail geek and didn't care who knew it.

About two o'clock there was a lull in the action. Katie turned to Edie, who'd been working with her. "Are you okay alone for a half hour or so?"

"Me? Sure thing." Edie nodded. "You've been stuck inside all day. Get out in that sunshine and fresh air and hunt yourself down some lunch. You must be starving."

"I am, actually." It had been easy to ignore her hunger with a line of customers at the register, but now the gnawing pangs were getting downright uncomfortable. "If you need anything, I'll have my phone."

Edie waved her away, and in short order, Katie had grabbed her purse from her office and was on her way across the Square to talk to Andy. Their lunch the day before had been so short, due to yet another frantic phone call from Andy's assistant manager, that she'd hardly had time to tell him about Erikka, let alone ask him why he'd stopped at Artisans Alley that morning.

She'd hung around the pizzeria after dinner, lending a hand whenever it was needed and planning to talk to Andy when things slowed down, but before that could happen, fatigue from events of the long day caught up with her, and she made her way upstairs and crawled into bed before ten o'clock.

But today was a fresh new day, and she was determined to figure out what was going on with her boyfriend. Because something *was* going on; she'd known him long enough and well enough to know that for a fact. Though Andy was by no means a touch-feely kind of guy, he had a knack for sensing her moods and was great at helping her talk through problems.

The reverse was not so true. Guylike, he preferred to ignore his own emotions. Katie hated when he did that and was continually working to get him to open up. Sometimes she was successful, and sometimes she wasn't. Today, though, on this beautiful, sunshiny afternoon, it was going to work. She'd ask the right question in the right way, he would thoughtfully respond, music would start playing, and their relationship would move to a new and deeper level.

At least that's what she hoped.

Mentally crossing her fingers, she opened the door to Angelo's and walked inside. She wasn't even all the way across the threshold when her hopes were dashed to bits.

"Now?" Andy was practically shouting. "You're quitting now? On a Saturday?"

She heard a low mumble, then Andy said, "What happened to a two weeks' notice? What happened to common courtesy? What happened to a little bit of loyalty to the guy who gave you a hand when you needed it?"

The low voice said a few more words, then came Andy's voice again, even louder. "I don't care what that company is willing to give you. I can't afford to pay you twenty percent more. And right now I wouldn't even if I could!"

Katie winced.

"Fine!" Andy shouted. "I'll take that as your resignation."

Fast footsteps approached, and then Katie gasped to see Jim, the assistant manager that Andy had been depending on for months, march out of the back room, around the counter, through the lobby, and out the front door without a single glance in her direction.

"Oh no," she breathed. What was Andy going to do without an assistant manager? Even with that help he was working too hard, making his cinnamon buns in the morning and pizza and everything else from noon to close.

Andy stormed out into the shop, his face still red. When he saw her standing there, he asked fiercely, "Did you hear that? Did you see?"

"I did and I'm so sorry. You had high hopes for Jim, didn't you?"

He ignored the question. "That Erikka you were talking about at lunch yesterday. Is she any good?"

"She had my old job," Katie said. "Which means she has to be computer literate, organized, and able to deal with unhappy clients."

"Sounds perfect. Can you tell her to get over here pronto?"

"Sure, I have her—"

"Great. Thanks. I've got dough to finish making," he said and charged for the back room. Instead of the calzone she'd been thinking about, Katie decided to grab something from Tanner's bakery. The last thing Andy needed right now was another order. She still hadn't heard why he'd stopped by Artisans Alley days before and wondered if she ever would.

Katie sent a text to Erikka, telling her that Andy wanted to interview her right then and there if she could make it to Angelo's as soon as possible.

"On it!" Erikka texted back, with a huge smiley face following.

With that done, Katie pocketed her phone and went across the Square to Tanner's to see what they might have on hand for a quick lunch.

She ended up with a big muffin and an apple and thought that would do the trick, but by late afternoon it became obvious that she hadn't eaten enough. She also wasn't sure what she'd have for dinner. Usually, she and Andy ate something from the pizzeria up in her apartment, while Jim took care of things downstairs, but without Jim, she was pretty sure that scenario wasn't going to happen.

"Um, Ms. Bonner?"

Katie looked up from the blown glass hummingbird feeder she was gift wrapping for a customer and saw Sadie and Sasha Davenport standing in front of her. "Hello, girls. What can I do for you?"

The sisters looked at each other. Sadie nudged Sasha, who said, "Well, we were just wondering . . ." She ran out of words and looked at her sister imploringly.

Sadie rolled her eyes at her sibling and said, "We wondered if you'd like to have dinner at our house tonight. I know it's short notice," she added quickly, "but still, we thought it would be fun if you came over."

"Tonight?" Katie taped down the end of the package and

reached for a ribbon. "Well, to tell you the truth, I don't have any solid plans."

"Come to our house," Sadie said, practically jumping up and down. "It'll be like a real dinner party. Our first ever."

"Please say you'll come," Sasha begged, holding her hands together in an attitude of prayer. "Please, please, please."

Katie laughed, charmed by the girls' enthusiasm. "Since you said please . . ."

The girls clapped with pleasure. "We'll eat at seven," Sasha said, "if that's all right with you. Are you okay with chicken?"

"And allergies," Sadie said suddenly. "Do you have any allergies? Or any of those diet things so many worry about?"

Katie assured them that chicken would be wonderful and that she had no dietary restrictions. "What would you like me to bring?" she asked. "And don't say nothing. A proper dinner guest always brings something."

They settled on a loaf of fresh bread from the bakery, and the girls ran off, full of chatter about all the things they needed to do.

Smiling, Katie sent Andy a text: "Headed to a friend's house for dinner. Hope that's OK with you. Come up after close, OK?"

She returned her phone into her pocket and went on with the wrapping, hoping that Andy found some new employees sooner rather than later. Having Angelo's short-staffed was wreaking havoc on her love life.

～～～～～

Katie parked at the curb in front of the address Sadie had given her. It was a tidy, cream-colored bungalow in a neighborhood of other tidy bungalows. The neighborhood had a settled, comfortable feel, but the lots were tiny and the houses close together. Katie could see why Ray would want to move out of the rental and into a place with room to stretch out.

She'd barely set foot on the porch when the front door was whipped open.

"Katie, you're here!" Sadie ran to greet her and tugged her toward the front door. "Come on in! We're almost ready. The chicken just needs a few more minutes in the oven. Oh, thanks for the bread. I'll get that into the kitchen. Sasha is finishing the salad. Do you want sour cream with your baked potato? I love sour cream. Sophie—you remember our older sister, Sophie? She says serving sour cream at a dinner party is just way uncool, but since she's not here, we're going to do whatever we want."

The nonstop narrative carried them through the entryway and into the small living room. "Dad just came back from Wood U," Sadie said. "He's washing up and should be here any second. Are you okay waiting by yourself?"

"I'm fine." Katie smiled. "Do you need any help in the kitchen? Or the dining room?" She nodded toward the closed door, behind which she assumed was the dining room.

"Oh no, no, no." Sadie put out her hands in full stop mode. "That's the last thing we want. You just stay here, okay?" She backed toward the door. "Dad's upstairs. When he comes down, then you both can come in, okay?"

"Sure," Katie said. "But I hope he doesn't take long. From what I can smell of dinner, it's going to be delicious."

Sadie flashed her a quick smile, opened the door a tiny amount, eeled through it, and was gone.

Still smiling, Katie shook her head. Had she ever been that young? So nervous about having someone over to dinner? She turned and started a casual inspection of the living room but hardly got farther than a quick glance at the pictures on the fireplace mantel when she heard footsteps on the stairway.

"Katie?" Ray looked casually dressed in a polo shirt and jeans, but he also looked genuinely startled and gave her a frown. "What are *you* doing here?"

"What am *I* doing here?" Katie returned his frown, and then some. "Your daughters invited me. Didn't you know?"

He made a low, growling noise, then said, "All I know is they said they had a surprise for dinner."

They gazed at each other for a moment. "I'm getting a funny feeling about this," Katie said slowly.

"You and me both. And it's time to figure out what's going on." He took three strong steps and was at the door to the dining room. Wrenching it open, he shouted, "Sadie! Sash—" and then his voice stuck.

"What's the matter?" Katie hurried to his side. "Are they—" And then her voice got stuck, too. She took in the scene before her and swallowed, then swallowed again and said, "What are we going to do about this little situation?"

A perturbed Ray heaved a huge sigh. "I have no idea."

~~~~~

Katie opened a beer for Andy, poured it into a glass, then poured a glass of wine for herself. She tried to hand Andy's glass to him, but he was staring at her, openmouthed.

"They'd done what?" he asked.

She pushed the glass into his hand and waited until his instinctive reactions kicked in, forcing him to hold on to the beverage, before she said, "Sadie and Sasha cooked up a romantic dinner for Ray and me. They'd used a linen tablecloth, the best china in the house, lit candles, the whole thing. The food was sitting on platters, steaming hot, and there were only two places set."

Andy downed a huge slug of beer, then asked in a flat tone, "What did you do?"

Laughing, Katie said, "I didn't do anything at first. Their dad, however, steamed straight into the kitchen, ready to give them the tongue-lashing of their lives."

"And?"

"They were already gone." Katie laughed again. "They must have put the food on the table and hightailed it out of the house, hoping their efforts would work."

"And did they?" Andy asked, raising an inquisitive eyebrow.

She reached out to touch his glass with hers, creating a slight tinking noise. "If their goal was to make their father so angry that his face turned almost purple, then sure, it worked. And if another goal was to make me remember how manipulative teenaged girls can be, then that worked, too."

"Why would they do something like that?" Andy asked.

"That's what Ray kept muttering," Katie said, amused. "I told him to be grateful he had daughters that were so concerned about his emotional well-being that they'd go to such lengths to get him a girlfriend."

"Didn't his wife die just a year ago?" Andy eyed her. "Seems a little weird those kids would be so interested in finding a stepmother at all, let alone so soon after their mom died."

Katie shrugged. She'd asked the same question of Ray and then heard a little more than she'd wanted to know about his deceased wife. "Sounds as if she may have been a contender for sainthood."

"So what did you do?" Andy rotated his glass and didn't look at her. "With the room set for romance and all. Did you sit down and eat?"

"Oh, we ate." Katie smiled. "But we piled it on plates and

ate it in front of the television, Ray in his big recliner and me on the couch. He's a big fan of Syracuse football, so we watched them play Wake Forest and then I came home."

She looked at Andy, who didn't seem to be finding the foiled matchmaking episode nearly as funny as she did. "Are you okay? You seem a little out of sorts."

"Just busy," he said. "By the way, that Erikka you sent over is working out great. So thanks for that."

"I'm glad." And she was. Erikka would need an additional source of income, but at least she'd be getting some sort of paycheck.

Andy yawned. "Busy and tired," he said and stood. "I think I'll head home."

"Oh." Katie blinked. He hadn't even finished his beer. "Um, okay." She'd planned on staying up late with him, maybe watching an old movie, but he did look worn-out. She walked him to the door. "I'll see you tomorrow."

He gave her a quick hug and a kiss, and she closed the door behind him.

Could Andy really be jealous of Ray Davenport?

Had she given him reason to do so?

Katie pondered that thought a little too long as she puttered around her kitchen, tidying up before she gathered her cats and went to bed. But instead of a restful sleep, she spent the night tormented by dreams of overcooked chicken dinners served on boats captained by faceless men covered in algae who laughed and laughed and laughed.

Fifteen

The next morning, Katie woke with the itchy feeling that she should be working harder on figuring out what happened to Josh. Her original wish, which was to keep Don and Nick's reputation clean, had edged into worry that Don was . . . well, not guilty of murder, of course, but serious worry that the police might *think* he was guilty. And if they were convinced he was guilty, then they'd work hard to build a case against him and not spend much time working on who else might have killed her former boss. And if that happened . . .

"What do you two think?" she asked Mason and Della.

The cats, who were sitting in the middle of the kitchen floor, staring at her with twin "feed me" expressions, didn't respond to her question. This was probably just as well, because in spite of her question, she wasn't quite ready to take advice from her cats. But that didn't mean she couldn't talk to them.

"I'm working on the assumption," she said, "that it wasn't Don or Nick who killed Josh. That's a given."

Mason yawned, which she took as agreement.

"Right. So then we have to figure out who else might have done it." She ticked off the suspects on her fingers. "There's Marcie and her attorney friend, Rob. I still think they're the most likely suspects, no matter what Ray says. I used to think maybe Erikka might be involved, but now I'm sure the main reason she was so upset at Josh's death was that she knew she was going to be out of a job."

Della began to wash her front paws.

"Glad we're thinking the same," Katie said. "So now we're down to the boat people. Yes, I know it's a huge leap to think that boat ownership by someone on Victoria Square could have anything to do with Josh's death, but consider the connection. Josh's body was left in Sassy Sally's, remember? How many people knew that Josh was even staying there?"

The more Katie thought about it, the more she realized what a good question it was. She hadn't known Josh was a guest at the B and B. Who had? Though there was no way of knowing who Josh had told, she was willing to bet it wasn't many. His wife had kicked him out, after all, and he wasn't likely to tell everyone on the street that little fact. No, she'd known Josh well enough to predict that he'd have to lick his wounds for a few days before trumpeting the "fact" that he'd left his wife.

"That's something I need to figure out," she told the cats. "Who besides Don and Nick knew that Josh was staying at the bed-and-breakfast?" She had no idea how she was going to figure that out, so she tucked it into the back of her mind and continued on.

"Back to boats. Duncan, Gwen, and Vance all acted weird when I started asking about their boats. I know now why

Gwen did, but what about Duncan? And . . ." She sighed, not wanting to suspect her assistant manager of having anything to do with Josh's death. She needed to ask Vance some questions, but maybe she could do it gently, in such a way that he wouldn't think she was asking about anything having to do with Josh's murder.

But it was Sunday, and Vance wouldn't be back at Artisans Alley until Tuesday.

Katie looked at the cats. "What should I do?" she asked. "What can I do today? Marcie's gone, and I don't know where her attorney friend lives. I can talk to Vance the day after tomorrow, and I'm not sure what to do about Duncan."

She wondered for a moment about Fred Cunningham, who seemed to be enamored of Marcie. Was that enough to suspect him of murder? Then again, it seemed as if the police might be suspecting Don or Nick of murder for ending up with a body in their bathtub, so—

"Got it," Katie said out loud. "Thanks for your help." She patted the cats on their heads and stood, knowing exactly where she was headed.

~~~~~~~

Katie took her foot off her car's accelerator as she approached the address where she'd followed Don a few nights earlier. She recognized the strange cluster of buildings of varying shapes and sizes and slowed even further.

The other night it had been dark and spattering rain, and now that the world was bright and sunshiny, she was seeing things she hadn't noticed earlier. Primarily the big sign that proclaimed to all and sundry that this was SHATTERED SEAGULL ART GALLERY, but also the number of sculptures that were placed around the grounds.

A seagull, naturally, was front and center; a seagull created from scraps of metal and then welded together in a way that left gaps, giving it the appearance of being a Humpty Dumpty seagull that had been put back together again.

There was also a sculpture of multiple metal rings that rotated in the light breeze, a pair of dancers that looked as if they'd been carved from a single log, a carefully constructed pile of rocks that glittered in the sun, and a three-foot-high three-dimensional trio of maple leaves made of . . . resin?

"Which one is your favorite?"

Katie hadn't noticed the man's approach. She jumped a little as he spoke. Turning, she saw the man she'd seen with Don, or at least it was someone about the same size and wearing the same kind of newsboy hat that she'd caught a glimpse of that rainy evening.

He had his hands in his pockets and was smiling, the very picture of ease and nonconfrontation, so she relaxed and nodded toward a metal framework that held a collection of colorful scarves, all fluttering as the wind caught them. "It's beautiful, but I have to wonder how it's going to look after a Western New York winter."

"You're the practical type," he said, tipping his head to one side. "Form follows fucntion?"

Katie recognized the intentional misuse of the Louis Sullivan quote. "I don't see why it can't be function *and* form. Why do we have to give one a higher priority over the other?"

He laughed. "You know, I'm not sure I ever thought about it that way. I'm Shaw Jennings, by the way; owner and proprietor of this eclectic establishment."

"And I'm Katie Bonner. I own Artisans Alley, over in Victoria Square."

Shaw took off his hat, revealing a bald pate, scratched the top of his head, then replaced the hat. "I've heard about your place. If you're looking for more artists, I'm not interested, but I might know some folks who are."

"That's not why I'm here, but I'd appreciate it if you'd spread the word. I have some openings that benefit artists in time for the holidays."

"Not a problem."

"Thank you." Katie hesitated, then said, "You know Don Parsons."

"Don?" Shaw nodded. "Sure, I know him. He and his partner are opening up . . ." The man's gaze sharpened on her. "Opening up a bed-and-breakfast on Victoria Square. So you know them?"

"They're good guys. I wonder if you'd mind telling me why Don was here the other night?"

Shaw's gaze slid past her. "You seem like a nice enough person, but I'm not sure that's any of your business."

"Normally, it wouldn't be," she conceded. "But if you know Don and Nick at all, you know that a dead body was found in Sassy Sally's not long ago. The police haven't made any arrests, and they're starting to spend a lot of time at Don and Nick's place."

Shifting his weight from one foot to the other, Shaw said, "I heard about that. But I'm not sure what that has to do with me."

"Don and Nick said they were at a party the night of the murder," Katie said. "Unfortunately, there was a point when Don was gone for quite a while."

"He doesn't have an alibi for the murder?"

Katie shook her head. "He's told me that there was a good reason he was gone, and I believe him. I'm not sure that the police will, though. And I'm not sure Don's taking this whole thing seriously enough."

Shaw's smile was ironic. "That sounds like Don."

"Which brings me to the other night. I'm worried about Don and Nick, and when I saw Don sneaking out of Sassy Sally's, I followed him here. Then I saw . . ." She stopped and waited to see what Shaw would say.

"You saw him give me a bear hug. And now you're thinking that Don is cheating on Nick and that's why he won't talk about his alibi." Shaw studied her. "I could tell you you've got the wrong end of the stick, but you don't have any reason to believe me."

She smiled. She was liking this guy. "Nothing personal."

"No offense taken." He gestured toward the largest outbuilding, the one he'd walked out of that rainy night to greet Don. "Let me show you something." He smiled. "A couple of things, actually."

Katie glanced around. Three other cars were parked in the driveway, indicating that other people must be around somewhere, so she followed Shaw across the gravel and through the plain metal door.

Inside, the noise was tremendous. Saws shrieked, hammers banged, and from ceiling-mounted loudspeakers, classic rock from decades earlier poured out. Katie counted at least four people working on various projects of varying sizes. A man wielding a three-foot-long tool stood in front of a whirling wood lathe, a woman was feeding a thick piece of wood into a buzzing table saw, and two young men were banging on a massive hunk of metal.

Shaw didn't give her time to gawk, though; he led her across the room and stopped in front of a large cabinet with holes all over. "It's for drying," he said. "The cabinet is lined with filters, and we can hook it up to a blower system. Speeds the drying process tremendously and keeps the dust off.

He unlatched the cabinet. "I need you to swear that you won't tell Nick, or even give the slightest hint."

"As long as it's not illegal or immoral," Katie said, "I'm good."

"Okay then." Shaw opened the cabinet door and stood back. "Don stopped by the other day to see how I was getting along on this."

The *this* in question was a small table, the size and shape of what Katie had always thought of as a card table. The darkly stained wood reflected back the light so well that Katie put up a hand to shield her eyes. The top of the table was inlaid with an intricate pattern of vines and leaves. It was gorgeous, and Katie felt the stirrings of table envy.

"Marquetry," Shaw said, nodding at the tabletop. "That's my specialty these days. Nick has a big birthday coming up, and Don wanted to surprise him with something special. He left that party to come finalize the details with me."

The saw's noise cut off, and the woman who'd been pushing wood through it looked over. "Showing it off again?"

Shaw smiled, a little sheepishly, Katie thought. The woman approached, and Shaw slung his arm around her shoulders. "My wife," he said, "thinks I'm getting a little too proud of my work."

His wife reached up to give him a peck on the cheek. "Just the tiniest bit. It's kind of cute, actually."

"You should be proud," Katie said, honestly. "It's beautiful."

"That's the best part about making things and giving them away." Shaw eyed the table critically. "You don't have to live with the flaws."

Katie laughed. "I'm sure Nick will never notice anything. And I'm sure he'll love it."

"They're a lucky couple," Shaw's wife said. "They're one of *the* best matches I've ever seen."

"Hey, now," Shaw said, protesting. "What about you and me?"

"I said *one* of the best." She grinned. "We're obviously *the* best match ever."

Katie chatted with the couple for a few minutes, gave them a few of her cards to distribute to any of their friends who might want to rent a booth at Artisans Alley, and headed out. The second she got outside and out of the din, she pulled out her cell phone and called Sassy Sally's. Luckily, Don answered.

"Can you talk?" she asked.

"Well, sort of. I'm trying to figure out how much we should spend on holiday decorations for this place."

"Is Nick around?"

"He's upstairs. I can get him if—"

"No," she said quickly. "I need to talk to you about Shaw Jennings."

There was a long pause, then Don said, "Umm."

"Umm, yourself. If all you're doing is buying something special for Nick's birthday, why on earth didn't you just say so? And why haven't you told the police?"

"How did you find out?" he asked.

"Never mind that. Why wouldn't you tell me?"

A long sigh gusted into the phone. "Because if I told you, then you'd know. And you might tell Rose, who might tell Edie, who might tell someone who might tell Nick."

"I can keep a secret," Katie said, more than a little stiffly.

"And you can keep it even easier if you don't know what the secret is," Don replied. "Now don't go all huffy on me. I'm just accustomed to not saying anything to anyone about things. And if I tell the police, the first thing they'll do is go to Shaw, then they'll talk to Nick, asking about his birthday and what kind of thing I normally get him, and then he'll know something's up and the surprise will be ruined. All I want is to surprise him."

Katie rolled her eyes. "If you're not careful, your need to surprise him could land you in jail."

"Nick's birthday is next week," Don assured her. "What can it hurt to wait until then to explain?"

"Well . . ."

"Please don't tell. Please?" Don begged.

Feeling almost as if she were making a pact with a five-year-old, Katie sighed and hoped that she wouldn't live to regret the promise.

~~~~~~~

Monday was Katie's only day off. Theoretically, at least. She had to spend a good chunk of the day printing lists of the vendors' sales and their checks. Thankfully, she usually had help on Tuesday morning sealing and stuffing envelopes and distributing them in the mail slots in the Alley's tag room.

By Tuesday morning the warmth of the previous few days had waned. Katie hated to turn on the big furnace at Artisans Alley before October, but she also knew that cold vendors and cold customers wouldn't make for a pleasant shopping experience. Cold Katies weren't all that pleasant either, so she was standing in the vendors' lounge with her hands wrapped around her mug, hoping that the heat from the coffee would transmit through her hands and into her bones. She had a small auxiliary heater in her office, but every time she turned that on, she could almost see the electric meter spinning. She hoped the customers would arrive clad in jackets.

Katie liked to hike the aisles of the Alley before it opened and hoped to find one particular vendor on that gloomy morning. She paused. "Vance, can I talk to you for a minute?"

Vance, who'd been wheeling one of the Alley's vacuum cleaners back to the storage area that ran behind the salon, said, "Sure. Hang on just a second." A few rattles and thumps later, he came out, dusting off his hands. "What's up?"

"Do you think it's time to turn on the furnace?"

He squinted, which somehow made him look even more like Santa. A skinny version, the kind that Mrs. Claus would need to fatten up before the holiday. "Now?" he asked. "Is it cold in here?"

"You've worked up a sweat vacuuming. It's sixty-two," Katie said. "Given the extended forecast, I doubt it's going to warm up anytime soon."

Vance pushed up his glasses. "I sure hate to turn it on before October."

Katie shivered. The coffee's warmth wasn't helping as much as she'd expected. "I just hope this isn't an indication of a long winter."

Vance grinned as they advanced toward the vendors' lounge. "That's right, you're not a big fan of snow, are you?"

"If I can ever retire," she said, "I will be moving south. Snow is fine on two days, Christmas Eve and Christmas Day. Other than that, it should stay in the mountains where it belongs."

Vance laughed. "Where's your sense of adventure? Every winter day can be a thrill. Will I make it to work without sliding into someone, or someone sliding into me? Will I be able to walk out to get the mail without falling flat on my face? Will our flight to visit my brother over Thanksgiving be delayed due to a blizzard?"

Katie winced. "You shouldn't joke about things like that."

"Ah, it'll be spring before you know it," Vance said as they entered the lounge. He stopped at the sink and turned on the water to wash his hands. "Time ticks away pretty fast, seems like."

"It sure does." Katie studied her assistant manager, a man she considered a friend. The conversation had opened up a perfect opportunity to question him, but did she really suspect him of murdering Josh? She wouldn't have except for his oddly fierce reaction to her gentle probing about his boat ownership. Which was worse, thinking Vance might have had something to do with Josh's death, or not asking enough questions and maybe having the deputies arrest the wrong person for murder?

Katie thought about what would await Don in prison and shivered again. Then she said, "But you must be a big fan of summer. That's the best boating weather, after all, and what's the point of having a boat if you don't go out on it?"

"I have no idea why anyone would want to own a boat." Vance turned off the faucet, shook the extra water off his hands, and reached for a paper towel.

Since he had his back to her, Katie couldn't see his facial expressions but did detect a stiffening of his shoulders. She thought about what to say and what to ask, and she finally said, "I didn't really like boating at all until Seth started taking me out this summer."

The shoulders remained stiff, but Vance turned to face her. "You took to it like a duck to water, is what I heard."

She smiled. "It took me a couple of times. I was scared stiff at first. I mean, they call Ontario a Great Lake for a reason."

The tension started to ease out of Vance's shoulders. "Exactly," he said. "Ships go down out there. Sometimes they never find any trace of boats that vanish."

Katie nodded. "And they're expensive. The gas alone costs a small fortune."

Vance was nodding along with her. "That's just what I told Janey. We're not boaters, I keep saying to her. Why should we keep this boat, just because my uncle Archibald left it to me? He didn't have any children is the only reason it came to me. There's no reason we shouldn't just sell the beast and be done with it."

"The beast?" Katie asked. "What kind of boat is it?"

"Big." Vance spread his arms out wide. "Way too big for us. The only boat I've ever been on is a canoe, for crying out loud. What do I know about boats? Nothing!"

Katie chose her next words carefully. "Big boats can be intimidating."

"You're darn tooting they are," Vance said firmly. "Intimidating and . . ." He stopped, then looked down at his feet. He sighed. "To tell you the truth, I'm a little scared of it. And that's downright embarrassing for a man to admit. I guess that's why I lashed out at you. Sorry."

"I won't tell a soul," Katie promised, then she asked, "Did you care for your uncle?"

Vance smiled. "Best uncle a guy could ask for. Taught me how to drive. Taught me how to play hockey, too. My dad was great, but he wasn't a sports kind of guy." His voice went distant. "It was my uncle who got me interested in woodworking, come to think of it."

"I bet your uncle would appreciate it if you gave his boat a chance," Katie said. "Don't you think?" She patted Vance on the shoulder and headed to her office.

Now she knew why he reacted as he did when she'd asked about the boat earlier. She was glad it was simple fear of the unknown that had spurred his reaction. Gwen was out as a suspect, and now Vance was, too.

She sat at her desk and glanced at the wall clock. She was trying not to worry for Don, but time was ticking away there, too.

~~~~~~~

The days sped by so fast that on Wednesday afternoon Katie found it so hard to believe that it was mid-week that she checked the Internet to make sure. When she got confirmation, she still wasn't completely convinced. She pushed back her chair and went out front to the Alley's lobby.

"What day is it?" she asked Rose, who was admiring and tweaking the harvest decorations. "Is it really Wednesday?"

Rose rotated a wagon wheel the slightest bit then stepped back, studying her work. "What day do you want it to be?"

The day before Labor Day, Katie thought with a pang. If she could have known then what she knew now, Don wouldn't be under suspicion of murder, because she would have told him not to leave the party. She would also have told Brittany she couldn't sublease her space to Crystal, and she certainly would never have gone to the Davenports' house for a dinner. Andy was still being a little standoffish about that whole thing, which didn't seem fair, but then she probably wouldn't have been completely forgiving if the situation had been reversed.

But instead of all that, she asked Rose, "Why is it that whenever I don't have much to do, time crawls, but when I'm trying to get something done, time zips by too fast?"

"It's a corollary to Murphy's Law," Rose said, smiling.

"You think?" Ray Davenport, who'd just walked in from the back, made a snorting noise. "I'd say it's more someone isn't paying attention to the clock. And speaking of not paying attention, I have some news for you, Ms. Bonner."

Katie's eyebrows went up. "Ms. Bonner? You haven't called me that in months. Have we regressed?"

He shook his head. "More the company I was just keeping. Have you had lunch?"

"Not yet."

"Me neither." He made a come-along gesture. "I'll even buy, since you won't have any appetite in a minute."

Katie and Rose exchanged glances. "Sounds like an offer I better not refuse," she said dryly, and within five minutes they were sitting in a booth at Del's. It was where she often sat with Andy, and she automatically chose the side where she always sat.

Sandy came over with the coffeepot and two mugs. "Haven't seen you in a few days," she said to Katie. "Is Andy too good to eat here anymore?"

"No," Katie said, "he's just . . . busy." At least that's what she hoped was going on. "His assistant manager quit on him last weekend, and he was understaffed even before that." He had hired Erikka straightaway, but even with the hours she was willing to put in, there were still gaps.

"Well, tell him I miss his ugly face." Sandy filled the mugs. "I'll be back in a minute to get your orders."

Ray watched her walk away. "Wish I'd had shoes like hers when I was on the force. Those things don't make a sound."

Shoes were not of interest to Katie, not just then anyway. "So what news do you have that's going to make me lose my appetite? Because you should know that I'm pretty hungry."

"Remember the other day when we were talking about Kimper's murder?"

"Of course I do." Katie pulled the plastic menu from the rack and flipped it open. There wasn't much chance she was going to eat anything other than tomato soup and a grilled cheese sandwich, but it never hurt to look. "You were pooh-poohing my theory that Marcie and Rob killed him."

"For good reason," he said, pushing the small dish of creamer over to her.

She looked up, frowning. "What do you mean?"

"What I mean is both Marcie and her lover boy have alibis. I stopped by the office the other day, and Hamilton checked that out first thing. They're both in the clear."

He grinned, looked straight at her, and Katie, way deep down inside, felt a spark of . . . something. Hurriedly, she glanced down and started working on getting creamer into her coffee. The man was old enough to be her father, for heaven's sake. There was no way she was attracted to him. No possible way. Besides, she had Andy, who was young and extremely good-looking and smart and busy, of course, but wasn't everyone?

"Solid alibis?" she asked, concentrating on stirring the creamer into her coffee without slopping any on the table.

"Solid as they get. The lawyer was at a fund-raiser for clean water, and the future widow and her children were at a friend's house for a sleepover with two other women and their kids. They stopped getting corroborative statements when they hit five each."

Katie removed her spoon from the cup. That was good news for Marcie and Rob, she supposed, and she was glad that Marcie and Josh's girls didn't have to endure the heartbreak of a mother in prison, but the woman and her lover had been the easiest people to suspect.

She looked at Ray. "Do the police have any other leads?"

"Yeah." He looked away. "Why don't we do this part after we eat? If you're still hungry, that is. I know how being wrong can mess with your meal plans."

Katie wasn't having any of that. She laid her hands flat on the table. "Tell me."

"It can wait until—"

"No, it can't. Tell me now."

Ray grimaced but said, "Hamilton told me he's putting together a case against Don Parsons."

Though he kept talking, Katie didn't hear a word. Because Don had left that party and wouldn't tell anyone why, he was going to be arrested for Josh's murder. She clenched her fists. Don was being so stupid about this that he wasn't going to see that the publicity surrounding an arrest, even if it was later proven wrong, was going to damage Sassy Sally's future.

She had to do something to save her friend from his own stupidity, but what could she do that she hadn't already done?

Damn. Why had she promised silence? Should she break that pact?

Nearly choking down a mouthful of coffee, Katie knew Ray had been right. She wasn't going to be able to eat a thing.

Sixteen

Katie had scarcely set foot inside Artisans Alley when she felt presences on both sides of her. Before she had a chance to react, her upper arms were gripped by strong hands, and she was brought to an abrupt halt.

"You're coming with me," growled a low female voice on her right.

"No ifs, ands, or buts," said the voice on her left, which Katie realized belonged to Rose. On the other side was Brittany.

She relaxed, since her two friends were obviously not going to drag her to the Sheriff's Office for interfering with official business or take her to an undisclosed location where she'd be locked up forever because she'd come too close to fingering Josh's killer. "Where are we going?" she asked.

The two women exchanged a loaded glance. "Seriously?" Brittany asked.

"I told you," Rose said. "She's been ignoring the problem for weeks now."

"That part is obvious," Brittany said grimly.

Rose sighed. "I've discussed this with her over and over again, and though she keeps telling me she'll take care of it, nothing gets done."

"Which is why we needed to intervene." Brittany grinned. "Yes, Katie Bonner, this is an intervention. The best part about this one is it'll have a hundred percent chance of success in less than half an hour."

Katie laughed, because she finally clued in to what was happening. "The ponytail thing isn't working out very well, is it?"

"It's fine," Rose said, but her tone didn't convey much sincerity. "But I think you should give Brittany a chance to do something different."

"How different are we talking?" Katie asked, her internal radar sounding off. "The last time I let a stylist try something different on me, I ended up wearing a baseball cap for six weeks."

Brittany opened the door of the salon and ushered her in. "Ah, but you can trust me."

"That's what the last one said," Katie muttered, but she walked to the first chair of her own volition. A smiling Rose waved good-bye, and the door closed behind her.

"Let's get you settled." Brittany whirled a cutting cape around her front and fastened it around her neck. "Now, do you trust me?"

"With what?" Katie asked warily.

"To give you a good cut without knowing what it is beforehand."

That was easy. "Not a chance."

Brittany laughed. "Fair enough. I'm not sure I'd trust

anyone to do that, either. How about this, because I still want to surprise you with what I'm thinking. Are you okay with bangs?"

"I haven't had bangs in years." Katie brushed at the hair draped against her forehead. "But I guess I'm not completely dead set against them."

"Excellent. Are you okay with a style that touches your face?"

"Absolutely not." Katie shook her head. "Can't stand styles like that. I'll end up putting it back with bobby pins or barrettes."

Brittany sighed. "Somehow I figured you'd say that." She asked a few more questions, then tipped the chair back and turned on the water to warm it up before she started shampooing. "And now that I have you where I want you, I'd like to talk about Crystal. No, you sit back and relax." The warm water hit Katie's scalp. "I'm not going to hold you hostage or anything, or give you a horrible haircut because of what you told Crystal." Brittany pumped out some shampoo and started lathering Katie's hair. There was something luxurious about closing her eyes and having her hair washed by someone else that always put her into a dreamlike state.

Almost against her will, Katie felt her muscles loosen. "I'm not sure there's much to say at this point. But I do regret that Crystal has to leave. She's very talented."

"Bright as a shiny penny, as my grandpa used to say." Brittany rinsed out the shampoo, blotted out Katie's hair with a towel, and sat her upright in the chair. "I've known her for a long time, and she has success written all over her. She's bright and energetic and intelligent, and the only thing she lacks is a little self-confidence."

"I know the feeling," Katie murmured.

"I'd guess all women do, right?" Brittany combed out Katie's hair and sectioned it off. "So that's why I'm asking you to let Crystal stay."

Katie wanted to shake her head but didn't dare, not with those sharp scissors starting to snip away. "I can't. We already had a vendor go to the hospital with an allergic reaction." She realized she hadn't seen Godfrey since, either. Strange. "Those fumes are just too strong. Manicures and nail painting are fine, but I can't allow the acrylic nails. I just can't."

"Hmm." Brittany cut and combed and cut some more. "And that won't work for Crystal. The acrylic business is too lucrative."

Katie opened her mouth to apologize, but really, what did she need to apologize for? Instead, she said, "It's too bad this didn't work out. I'd like to give Crystal the chance to succeed, I really would."

For a few minutes, the only sounds in the salon were the soft music and the scissors. Finally, Brittany said, "I know she tried candles and the air fresheners and trying to route the smell out the window, but what if there's another solution?"

"The only thing that will work," Katie said firmly, "is a true ventilation system, and that will cost thousands."

"Hmm." Brittany put away the comb and scissors and started up the roaring blow-dryer. When Katie's hair was dry, Brittany went at it with a flat iron. "What if there's another way to get at the problem?" she asked. "What if there's another way altogether?"

Katie sighed. She didn't want Brittany to get her hopes up. "If there's another way, I'd be glad to hear it."

"Great! When I think of it, I'll let you know." Brittany beamed and turned the chair to the mirror. "So, what do you think?"

Katie blinked. "Wow," she said slowly. "With a capital W."

~~~~~~~

It was hard to believe that a haircut could make so much difference, but two days later, Katie was still feeling the effects of Brittany's skill. Everyone from Andy to Rose to Vance to Del at the diner complimented her new look. Sitting at her desk, Katie ran her hand through the layered locks and felt her hair settle back down into what Brittany had intended: a simple style that framed her face and made the most of the cheekbones she'd always thought were invisible to the naked eye.

Though Katie was reluctant to admit it, the cut had given her a much-needed boost of self-confidence. Not only that, but she was still mulling over what Brittany had said about finding a new solution for Crystal's problem. It had been an impassioned speech, and Katie felt Brittany's persuasive words pushing her to reconsider a lot of things, things far beyond the fumes issue.

Her relationship with Andy, for one, which seemed to have grown more complicated for reasons she wasn't sure she wanted to delve into. Plus there was her vague intention to get more exercise and eat better. And then there was Josh's murder. And Don's stupidity in not giving the police his real alibi.

Katie abruptly stood. She wasn't going to come up with new solutions to old problems spending a fruitless half hour trying to convince him of the error of his ways.

She made her way to the Alley's lobby, which was devoid of life, and took in the completed harvest decorations. It had all turned out wonderful, and it never would have looked so great without a group effort.

"What's going on over there?"

Katie turned to see Sharon Reece, the photographer who'd rented space on the upper level.

Not knowing what she was talking about, Katie turned to see the photographer staring out the front window. From where she stood, Katie couldn't see anything unusual, so she walked toward the plate glass doors and peered out in the direction of Sassy Sally's. A cold, hard ball immediately formed in the bottom of her stomach.

"What . . . the heck?" Sharon asked slowly.

The two of them watched in shock as Don was led down the stairs of the bed-and-breakfast and put into the backseat of a patrol car. A uniformed deputy shut the door behind him got into the driver's side, and the car pulled away.

As the vehicle went past, Don turned to look into Artisans Alley. Katie felt a chill as her horrified gaze met his for the briefest of seconds before the car moved out of view.

Sharon shook her head. "That doesn't look good. Did you see the expression on Parsons's face? I haven't seen anyone look that scared since back in high school when my BFF thought she might be pregnant."

Katie wasn't paying attention to Sharon's comments, because she, too, had recognized Don's panicky fear. She needed a new answer, a new solution, and she needed it fast.

"Do you think they arrested him?" Sharon asked. "He wasn't in handcuffs, but I hear they don't always do that, if they don't think there's a risk of violence or running away."

"I don't know." But what did she know?

Sharon turned to her. "Do you think they think he killed Josh Kimper?"

"No!" Katie said automatically.

"Okay, but what really matters is what the police think, right?"

She was right, but Katie didn't want to go there. She *knew* that Don was innocent. She *knew* that Josh's widow hadn't killed him. She *knew* that her former boss had been promising people he'd get them good deals on pre-owned boats. She knew that he'd drowned in Lake Ontario. And she knew that Vance and Gwen had nothing to do with it. She'd rejected Erikka as a suspect because she so clearly hadn't been in love with Josh, but . . .

What was it Erikka had said? That Josh had told her not to write up any policies that had anything to do with boats. That she was to send boat insurance referrals to three companies. Katie had worked in the insurance business for years and had never heard of any of the three.

The possibility of a new solution hovered in the air, just out of her reach. She wanted with all her might to grab on to it, but it was still too insubstantial, still just a possibility.

"I'll be back," she said vaguely, not even noticing that Sharon had already left her side minutes earlier. She hurried to her office, grabbed her purse and coat, and headed out. She needed time to think. But all too soon, she was heading for downtown Rochester.

She parked her car in a nearby ramp garage and headed for the county office building. She mounted the steps and walked along a lengthy corridor until she came to one particular door. Ten minutes later, a voice called out, "Next!" Katie stepped forward.

"Can I help you?" The middle-aged woman at the Monroe County Clerk's Office looked at Katie expectantly. Her thick, long hair was so bright it was almost orange, and she wore glasses that looked permanently affixed to the end of her nose. Her name tag said BARBARA.

"I'm looking for whatever public information is available on three companies, all of which were formed last October or November." Just after she'd walked out of Kimper Insurance for what she'd assumed would be the last time.

"Are these DBA companies?" Barbara asked. "Doing Business As?"

"I have no idea, but that's probably a good place to start."

Barbara nodded and pulled a computer keyboard toward her. "What are the names?"

Katie recited them from memory. "Fairport Insurance, McKinlay Insurance, and Parma Insurance."

"And how do you spell McKinlay?" At Katie's answer, Barbara's fingers flew across the keyboard. "Like the town, then. Finding out if they're DBAs won't take . . . And here they are." She tipped her head back to read the monitor through her glasses. "Well, kind of. All three were indeed created as DBAs, but the names are slightly different."

"How do you mean?" Katie asked.

"Well, there's a Fairport Assurance, a McKinlay Surety, and a Parma Assured Protection, all formed in early November of last year."

"That's weird," Katie murmured. "Do your records show who created the companies?"

"It's required by state statute." She tapped at the keyboard again. "Here we go . . . That's odd," she said, frowning at the monitor. "All three were formed by the same person on the same exact date."

"What's the name?" Katie asked with a dry mouth.

Barbara pushed at her glasses again and said, "Joshua Kimper."

~~~~~~~

All the way back to McKinlay Mill, Katie's thoughts were more on insurance than on her driving. Luckily, the roads weren't overcrowded at that time of day, before post-work traffic would begin, and she made it back without incident.

She parked her car in front of Artisans Alley, waving at Gilda, who was rearranging her basket store's window display, but not slowing her pace a smidge, and rushed into the building and to the main sales floor.

"Ray?" she called, hurrying to the back corner. "Ray, are you here?"

But he wasn't. She muttered a minor curse word, spun on her heel, and went back outside, heading across the Square to Wood U. The lights were on, but she didn't see anyone inside, not even Warren Noth, who shouldn't have been far, because his contractor's pickup truck was sitting at the curb.

She tried the front door, and it was unlocked. Poking her head inside, she called, "Ray? Are you in here?"

From the back, she heard a rumble of male voices, and then Ray, Noth, and another man whom Katie was pretty sure she'd seen working on the Sassy Sally's renovation walked into what was going to be the main retail space.

"Hey, Katie," Ray said, looking surprised and pleased. "What brings you over here? I'm not late on my rent, am I?"

She rolled her eyes. He knew perfectly well that he'd paid for the full month. "No, I have a police question, if you have a minute."

"Sure." He glanced at the other two men. "We're done here, right?"

Noth, who'd nodded a hello to Katie, said, "As long as Norm here remembers that he needs to put in two-twenty electrical back there and not one-ten, we'll be all set."

"Two-twenty outlets on the back and east walls," Norm said, not even looking at the clipboard in his hand, "one-ten outlets in strips above the wall bench, an outlet reel over the main bench, and three outlets on the west wall, one on the south, and enough florescent lighting that you could do brain surgery."

"Sounds about right," Ray said. "Thanks, guys." The two men headed out, and he turned to Katie. "What's up? You look like you're about to spill a huge secret. Don't tell me you already bought my Christmas present, because you shouldn't have."

Katie shook her head. "I didn't," she said. "Do you know what's happened to Don? He was taken away in a police car this morning."

"Yeah, I figured you saw that." Ray leaned against a structure of two-by-fours that were shaped into what would someday become a display counter. "I'm surprised you're not over at Sassy Sally's, holding his hand."

"He's back home?" Katie was thrilled that Don was home and not in a jail cell, but she was also confused. "I thought—"

"They questioned and released him. And before you ask," he said, holding up a hand, "I have no idea if they're going to arrest him. And I'm not going to waste Hamilton's time by calling, because he won't tell me. We'll just have to wait and see."

"That's what I'm trying to tell you," Katie burst out. "I think I figured something out, maybe something really important."

"Oh?" The expression on Ray's face clicked from interested bystander to active police officer. "If you have any information, you need to—"

"I know, I know," she said impatiently. "I'm not sure if it's important or not. That's why I wanted to talk to you."

"All right." He put one arm across his future counter and suddenly started looking like the detective he'd been for so many years. "I'm listening. Talk away."

So Katie did. She told him what Erikka had said about the insurance companies. Told him about the boat that Del had never been able to purchase. Told him about the three com-

panies that sounded like the names of insurance companies
but probably weren't. Told him that Josh had created all three
on the very same day, a little less than a year ago.

But when she finished, Ray was frowning. "I'm not sure
where this gets us."

"Don't you see?" Katie asked. "Josh was running some
sort of boat insurance scam. I don't know what, exactly, it was
or how it worked, but why else would he set up three shell
companies? And he did it after I left, because I'd been there
long enough to know if something weird was going on. Erikka is smart, but she didn't have any experience with insurance. He probably intentionally hired someone who'd never
worked in the industry before. When he told her there wasn't
any money in maritime insurance, she had no reason not to
believe him."

"And that's not true?" Ray rubbed his chin.

"Of course it's not." After she'd returned from Rochester,
Katie had made a few phone calls to colleagues she'd once
worked with in other agencies and confirmed. "Those policies are low risk, for the most part, but people with big boats
tend to want to over-insure their property."

"So how does this tie into Kimper's death?"

Katie sighed. "I don't know. But there must have been
something illegal going on. Why would he lie to Erikka otherwise? And creating three new shell companies on the same
day seems suspicious to me."

"There could be perfectly innocent reasons for all of that."

"Like what?" she challenged him. "I've tried to think of
one and I can't."

Ray stared at the ceiling, whistled tunelessly, then must
have come to some sort of conclusion, because he nodded and
looked at her. "I think this is worth taking to Hamilton about.
Hang on, hang on," he said, seeing her excitement. "It's late

in the afternoon. There's no point going over there now. Even if he's still at his desk by the time we get there, he won't give us his full attention."

"But this is about murder!"

"And there isn't any imminent murder going on right now, is there? Trust me, we'll get more attention and focus out of him in the morning."

Though Katie reluctantly agreed, she also knew something else.

Maybe Detective Hamilton could live without making progress on the case until the next day, but she wasn't sure she could wait that long.

Seventeen

Katie looked around Sassy Sally's beautiful new kitchen, placed her hands on her hips, and scowled. "Why are you such an idiot?"

"I must have been born that way," Don answered. He looked over his shoulder, then, turning back to her, he said in a low voice, "I don't know where Nick is, but I don't want him to overhear any of this."

Her eyes went wide with surprise. "He doesn't know the police were questioning your—"

"Shhh!" Don made frantic shushing motions with his hands. "This is all going to blow over. There's no need for him to know anything about it until the whole situation is cleared up."

"And how are you going to do that, exactly?"

He offered her a sheepish grin. "By doing what you said I should do to begin with. Go to the police and tell them that

I left the party to commission a piece of art. Shaw Jennings will corroborate what I said, and there were a couple of people out at his studio working that night. That should be easy enough to give me a solid alibi."

"You're such an idiot," she repeated. "What are you going to say when the police ask you why you didn't explain that at the beginning? They're going to find that really strange, and I have to say I agree with them."

"Piece of cake," Don said confidently. "All I have to do is tell them how much I love my husband and how much I want to do something wonderful for the birthday of such a handsome, loving, attractive man, and then I do this." He lowered his head and looked up at Katie through his eyelashes, then batted his eyes.

"That's your argument? You're going to play the gay card?" Katie flung her arms out wide in exasperation. "Are you kidding me? This is the twenty-first century."

Don shrugged. "Some people accept the LGBT community, sure. Maybe even most, depending on the accuracy of whatever poll is asking the questions. But do not doubt that there are people out there who hate the fact that gay and lesbian couples exist."

"A few people, maybe."

Don's face had lost all trace of humor. "More than a few. It's something we have to live with and accept."

Katie sighed. "I'm sure you're right. It's not as if discrimination against women is over, either."

"Right." Don's grin returned. "So we might as well use our disadvantage to our advantage whenever we can, right?" He batted his eyes again. "Love your haircut, by the way."

Ignoring the comment about her coiffure, she wasn't sure he was right about using the disadvantage. It seemed more than a little manipulative and at least the slightest bit dishonest, but since she'd never had to walk in shoes the shape of his or Nick's or Seth's, who was she to judge?

"Go home and stop worrying," Don said. "Nick's birthday is on Wednesday. This can all wait until after that."

Though Katie wasn't so sure, she didn't disagree with him, not out loud anyway. Partly because it wouldn't have done any good, and partly because she'd just had a brilliant idea about how to learn what Josh had been up to.

Once she'd learned that, then, and only then, would she stop worrying.

~~~~~~~~

All afternoon Katie had been thinking about what she planned to do. Now she had to find the courage to actually do it when what she'd prefer to do was curl up on the couch with Andy, the cats, a couple of thick slices of pizza, and a movie or two.

Instead, fifteen minutes after she walked up the stairs to her apartment, she walked back down again, only now she had some food in her stomach and had changed clothes from the business casual she wore to work into dark jeans, a black turtleneck, and a hooded black fleece jacket.

She felt a little silly dressing as if she was going to a burglary, but told herself it was all in her head, that no casual observer would think twice about her choice of clothing. Lots of people wore black. She'd even overheard a customer, who was looking at some of Gwen's woven shawls, say that black was the new black. Whatever that meant.

Outside, the sky was turning its own shade of non-trendy black. Katie drove north, peering up at the thick cloud cover that had rolled in and trying to remember what time the sun set. Was it really getting dark this fast, or was a storm coming in? In the gloomy half-light, it was hard to tell.

A fat raindrop spattered the windshield. "Swell," she said, then wondered if maybe this wasn't a good thing for what she was intending to do. Not that it mattered. She was committed to this journey, for better or worse, and a little thing like rain wasn't going to stop her.

It didn't take long for Thompson's Landing to show up in her car's headlights. Katie stared through the murk and found the driveway she wanted, the driveway she'd entered so many times during the summer to go sailing with Seth, and the same driveway she'd left after seeing Josh Kimper for the last time.

Well, the last time she'd seen him alive, anyway. In her dreams she was still catching glimpses of a body floating in a bathtub. Sometimes it was Josh, sometimes it was a stranger, and one awful night, it had been her own body.

"Get a grip," she said out loud. If she was going to poke around the marina, trying to figure out the scam Josh had been working with boat insurance, she needed a clear head. This was no time to creep herself out.

But as she parked in the far corner of the parking lot, she started to think that hanging around the mostly deserted marina was enough to put her in a creeped-out frame of mind all by itself.

Most of the boat slips were empty. A few boats of various shapes and sizes were scattered about, gently bobbing up and down in the water. At least half of them, Katie saw, were sailboats. She shivered, finding it hard to believe that people would go out on any pleasure boat in temperatures less than sixty-five degrees, let alone a sailboat, when most of the time you had to be on deck.

"It takes all kinds," she murmured, quoting her aunt Lizzie, and headed in the direction of the boats.

She'd only vaguely remembered the boat Josh had pointed out as his, but she had remembered it being a Carver, sleekly white and gorgeous. That afternoon, she'd refreshed her memory of the boat via the Internet and knew she'd recognize it if she saw it again.

Since Josh had been a brand-new boat owner, she was willing to bet that he hadn't had it pulled out of the water the day she'd run into him. New owners had a tendency to think the weather would stay warm in September for an extended boating season. They also tended to forget how early the sun went down, which made getting out on a weeknight difficult for people with day jobs, and the odds of decent weekend weather went down significantly with every passing week.

Katie walked down the wooden docks, her soft-soled shoes almost silent, studying each of the boats still in the water and rejecting every one. She'd hoped that Marcie had asked the marina to take care of the boat's winterizing, which meant that it would be one of the last ones out of the water. If the boat was still there, she should be able to sneak aboard. The police had undoubtedly gone over the whole thing, but they'd only been looking for evidence of murder, not evidence of insurance fraud.

But when Katie reached the far end of the marina, she still hadn't seen a single boat that looked anything like the Carver. While she'd hoped she'd find the boat in the water, she hadn't really expected it. Which meant it was time for plan B.

She turned and studied the half dozen large buildings that were scattered at the back of the marina's property. Around each of the buildings were trailered boats, many covered in bright blue shrink-wrap, but many still without the protective winter plastic.

Though Katie didn't know if they were waiting to get

wrapped or if they went without, she walked toward the boat storage yard, crossing her fingers that Josh's boat wasn't being stored inside, and that it didn't have the shrink-wrap on. It would be hard to recognize the boat if it was covered in that thick blue plastic, and she wasn't sure if she could bring herself to cut her way in, even if she did.

The asphalt of the parking lot turned to gravel as she got closer to the boats, then to grass when she reached the multiple rows of shuttered craft. Behind the warehouses lay more boats than she'd ever seen in her life, all lined up nice and tidy and empty.

"Swell," she said to herself. This was going to take forever. She looked up at the sky. Now that her eyes had adjusted, it didn't seem quite as dark as it had when she'd been driving. Plus, the storage yard had automatic lights that were starting to turn themselves on, creating shadows that stretched long across the grass. She should have enough light to at least identify Josh's boat even if it took until midnight.

Heading to the farthest corner, she walked up and down the rows of boats, methodically checking each one for size and shape. It didn't take as long as she'd thought it might, but even still, all the light was gone from the sky when she reached the last line of boats.

The temperature had dropped, too, and Katie shivered inside her fleece jacket, wishing she'd brought a hat, or at least gloves. She put her hands in her coat pockets and trudged along the boats, more than a little disappointed that she'd wasted the night on a fool's errand.

She'd truly expected to find Josh's boat and had half expected to find something on the boat that would explain the insurance scam. Well, maybe not half expected, but she'd certainly convinced herself it was a realistic possibility.

A wind gust blew down the back of her neck, and once again she shivered. Halloween was more than a month away, but the deserted grounds were starting to give her the willies. She reached the last of the boats, a craft half again as long as Josh's, and came to a stop.

There were possibilities at this point: Had Marcie already sold Josh's boat, or was it being stored inside one of the warehouses? Okay, there was a third possibility, that Marcie was storing the boat somewhere else, but Katie didn't see that as likely.

She eyed the warehouses with their multiple sets of doors, both large and small. Well, it didn't hurt to try, she supposed. Starting at the building closest to her, she tried the doorknob of the human-sized door. Locked. Which was what she'd assumed, but you never knew.

The wind picked up, and she zipped her jacket all the way to the top. Five more buildings to check, five more doors to test, and then she was out of there. It was all kind of silly, anyway. The Sheriff's Office hadn't arrested Don, after all. And even if she found the boat, what had made her think she'd find anything that would help her learn how the scam had operated?

The second, third, fourth, and fifth buildings were also locked, and Katie headed to the sixth and final building, as due diligence, really, already thinking about the hot chocolate she'd make when she got home and wondering if she'd stay awake or fall asleep if she started watching *Casablanca*. She put her hand on the sixth doorknob, tried the door, and it opened.

She gave a start and was so surprised that she almost shut it again.

Light poured through the small gap, which seemed strange.

She hadn't seen a soul or a single vehicle since she'd arrived. She had begun to assume that someone had left the lights on and the door unlocked by mistake, when she heard a radio broadcasting a football game.

Hmm.

She poked her head inside but saw only boats, boats, and more boats. Inching inside, she debated calling out, and almost did. Something kept her quiet, though, and she moved silently among the mothballed boats, both looking for Josh's Carver and trying to see who might be in the building.

The warehouse seemed even bigger on the inside than it did on the outside, and the voice of what she assumed was a local high school football radio announcer bounced around, echoing off all the hard surfaces.

She crept closer, keeping to the back wall, in the shadows and out of sight. There was a good chance it was just an employee working on winterizing a boat. If so, she'd sneak back out, no harm, no foul. But the whole thing seemed odd. Why would a single employee winterize boats so late at night? And why wasn't a car parked outside?

For the first time, Katie was glad for the black clothing she'd chosen. Unless someone looked directly at her and saw her pale skin, she should be essentially invisible.

She edged deeper into the building. All kinds of boats lined the outside walls, and there was an open aisle in the center for hauling the craft in and out. The floor was concrete, and she carefully kept her shoes from making any sound as she moved.

A metal *clang* startled her. At the same time a man cursed, and she realized he must have dropped a tool.

So, a guy working on a boat.

Still, she wanted to get a closer look. She made her way

carefully forward, step by cautious step, half of her trying to
think of what she'd say to this guy if he happened to look up
and see her, the other half sure that she was close to finding
out why Josh had been murdered.

Peering around the end of a bright red vessel, she caught a
glimpse of a blue-jeaned pant leg. She poked her head around
a little further and saw that he was facing the stern end of a
big, beautiful boat, using some sort of small power tool on the
top of the hull.

Katie watched, trying to figure out what was going on.
This was no part of winterizing; even she knew that. Winterizing was almost entirely about taking care of the motor. The
only thing anyone would do to a hull was wax it, and that was
clearly not what was happening.

Curious, she slid forward to get a better look, trying to
remember everything Seth had ever told her about boats. Everything she'd ever learned about everything, really, because
judging from the furtive way the man kept looking around,
he was obviously doing something he shouldn't.

What could he be up to? What was on a hull? What was . . .
And then Katie suddenly knew what the man was doing. She
remembered sitting on the back of Seth's boat, putting her
hands on the edge—the gunwale—to steady herself, and feeling something under her fingertips. She leaned over and had
seen a serial number.

"Done," the man said and stepped back. He turned, and
Katie pulled in a quick breath.

It was Warren Noth.

She slid backward, back into the depths of the shadows.
This was enough for Detective Hamilton. It had to be. All
she had to do now was get back to her car, leave quickly, and
call 911. She could report what was going on here, and they'd
arrest Noth, and—

There was a noise behind her, which made no sense because she knew Noth was still in front of her. But there was no time to wonder, no time to think, because she heard a fast whir of air, felt a monstrous *bang!* on the back of her head, and then crumbled to the ground.

Eighteen

~~~~~~~~~~

Pain. Pounding pain. That was the first thing that registered in Katie's foggy brain. A pounding headache beyond belief. With her eyes still closed, Katie tried to move—only her wrists were attached to each other. Then she realized her ankles were in the same situation.

She tried to sit up and immediately banged her head on something immovable. "Ow!" Her cry of pain sounded weakly pathetic even to her own ears.

Flopping back down, she waited for the sharp throbbing in her head to subside. It took about a year and a day, but the pain eventually subsided to a level that didn't make her want to whimper like a whiny child.

Then, when she thought she could think about something else other than her head, she slowly opened her eyes and saw . . . nothing.

Well, not exactly nothing, she amended silently. There

was a small amount of light, but only enough to let her make out the outlines of large shapes. She was lying on a narrow bed that had a ceiling two feet above her. To her left she could make out cabinets and a table with banquet seating.

She studied the arrangement, her fuzzy brain trying to make sense of it all. Though the place looked vaguely familiar, she felt no sense of ever having been there in her life. Yet . . . where was she, exactly?

That's when she noticed she was moving. Up and down with a little side to side thrown in for good measure. Suddenly, she clued in to the noise that had been rumbling in the background all along.

"Oh no," she whispered.

Because she was on a boat.

Tied up.

And no one knew where she was.

How could she have been so stupid? She started cursing herself but stopped almost as soon as she started. Berating herself was going to have to come later, after she figured a way out of this mess. Right now she had better things to do.

She looked over to what she now recognized as the boat's galley. If it was a functioning kitchen, surely there'd be a knife she could use to cut her bonds. Feeling around with her fingers, she deduced they'd wrapped duct tape around her wrists and ankles as a restraint. For a moment she was grateful they hadn't slapped her mouth shut, then she felt stupid for a second time. Why should they bother? There wasn't a soul around to hear any cries for help.

That fact might give her an edge. They would expect her to start screaming the second she regained consciousness; if she stayed silent and stealthlike, maybe, just maybe, she could use that to her advantage. How, exactly, she didn't know, but there had to be a way.

After trying unsuccessfully to unstick the tape from her ankles—her fingers were also half covered with tape, and she couldn't grip for beans—she wriggled to the edge of the bunk, lowered her feet to the floor, and listened. No voices, no footsteps, no thumping of any kind, just the boat's motor humming along as it carried her farther and farther away from safety.

Panic stirred somewhere in her middle and started to flow outward.

Take a deep breath, she told herself and pulled in a couple. She had to stay calm if she was going to survive. And at this point, survival was the only thing that mattered. Everything else could wait. Had to wait, really, and since the second—and the only other—thing on her mental task list was to slap Warren Noth and whoever else was working with him in jail, she had to get control of her emotions.

First, she had to get her hands and feet free. Then she needed to figure out a plan for getting to shore. Then she could work on the jailing issue. Whoever it was would eventually pay for what they'd done to Josh and were doing to her.

But, as she stood and hopped her way across the floor toward the galley, she couldn't help wondering: Who was the "they" in question? Warren Noth, yes, but there was at least one other person involved, the one who had clonked her on the head. So, two, at least. And maybe more, for all she knew.

The footsteps, the ones she'd heard behind her for the fraction of a second before she'd been whacked on the head, had sounded heavy and male, but she wouldn't want to assume that. Women could be plenty mean and murderous; she knew that for a fact.

She hopped forward, trying to make no noise as she did so. The whisper of her soft-soled shoes against the carpet was slight, but it seemed as loud as cymbal crashes to her. Though there was no possible way her movements could be heard up above, over the sound of the grumbling engine, she was still wary, stopping between every hop and cocking her head, listening.

Forty-million hops later, she stood in front of the galley sink. Awkwardly, she pulled open the first drawer she could grab.

Empty.

"Dammit," she whispered and tried the next drawer.

That one was empty, too, as were the cabinets above and the cabinets below. Not a single utensil, not a single pot or pan. Not even a Tupperware lid.

Her nascent plans to cut herself free and then use the knife to threaten whoever it was driving the boat instantly vaporized. No wonder they'd felt free to leave her down there; they'd emptied the boat of anything useful.

"Jerks," Katie muttered. But they were murderous jerks, and she couldn't let herself forget that.

Because now what was she going to do?

Turning in a slow circle by virtue of a series of coordinated hops, she surveyed the contents of her prison by the dim light that filtered down through the skylights from what she assumed was the cockpit.

Seth's boat, the one with which she was most familiar, was a sailboat, but except for the width—sailboats were skinnier— the two interiors had a lot in common. Low ceiling, narrow walkway, wraparound seats for a banquet table that could be lowered to become another berth, compact galley, built-in couch/berth. Up toward the boat's forward end, Katie could see hints of a master cabin and a tiny bathroom.

All probably as empty as the kitchen had been. Still, she had to try.

She gave the kitchen one last going-over, just to be sure,

and for a second time, found absolutely nothing, not even a take-out packet of pepper.

Getting down on her hands and knees, she checked the cabinets under the seats and found nothing except a book of matches and a small packet of tissues, which she shoved in her pocket. How they could possibly be useful as part of an escape plan, she didn't know, but she wasn't about to reject anything.

She started to stand but came to the sudden and very abrupt realization that getting up from a hands-and-knees position when your wrists and ankles were tied together was a lot harder to do than it sounded.

"Never mind," she muttered to herself and inched her way to the front of the boat on her knees and elbows, feeling like a large and awkward human caterpillar. She made a slightly hysterical mental note to bring knee pads to her next kidnapping, then firmly battened down the hysteria and concentrated on the task at hand, ignoring the sharp sting of carpet burns.

Reaching the master cabin took longer than she would have liked, but at least she hadn't been detected.. She wanted to sigh with relief because she now had the ability to close a door between herself and her kidnappers, but she knew she wasn't safe, and no closer to escape. Speaking of escape . . .

No light filtered farther than the cabin's door, so she searched the cabinets, shelves, and bunks strictly by feel. Just like the kitchen, they were completely empty. Not even a book of matches this time.

Deep in her stomach she felt the stirrings of despair. She was never going to get out of this. Somewhere out in the middle of Lake Ontario, Warren Noth was going to toss her overboard, and she would drown, just like Josh. She had no idea how far from shore they were, but she'd lived near the big lake most of her life and was more than familiar with what the temperature of the water was likely to be at this time of year and the effects of hypothermia.

She wasn't cold; in fact, she was sweating from all her caterpillaring efforts, but she shivered.

Bathroom, she told herself. Check out the head. It would be an excellent place to leave a small pair of scissors. A nail file. Anything.

As she shuffled/hopped out of the main cabin, she thought somewhat desperately about detaching a plumbing fixture to use as a cutting instrument. Maybe the faucet was a little loose. Maybe she could get it off and there'd be a sharp edge and she could saw through all those layers of thick tape. Maybe . . .

But there was nothing.

A tiny bit of light helped Katie quickly establish that no fixture was even remotely loose. Not the faucet, not the shower head, and nothing in the under-sink cabinet.

"Dammit," she said under her breath as she grabbed onto the edge of the cabinet and pulled herself to her feet. She flinched as she saw movement in front of her, then felt stupid as she realized she'd caught sight of her own reflection in the mirror.

The mirror.

Hope surged through her. The mirror! She could break the mirror and use a shard to cut the tape. She'd get out the packet of tissues—so useful!—to protect her hand during the cutting job. This would work, this would really work. She was as good as free, and when she was free, surely she would figure out a way to get back to shore. A boat this size was bound to have a lifeboat.

Excited, she reached out . . . and her hopes died in an instant.

The mirror was made of plastic.

She blew out a disgusted breath. It probably made sense, safety-wise, to have plastic mirror on something like a boat, but it sure would have been nice to catch a break for once.

And now what was she going to do?

Her legs were starting to cramp, so she hopped over to the small commode and sat down, putting her elbows on her knees. The next obvious step was to come up with options. Unfortunately, she couldn't think of a single one. She'd been so intent on getting her hands and feet free that she hadn't considered anything else.

"Dammit," she muttered and sagged a little. Her right elbow slid off her knee and banged against the toilet paper roll.

The toilet paper . . .

She scrabbled at the roll, telling herself not to get too excited, maybe it wasn't the right kind, maybe it wouldn't work, maybe she was nuts, maybe . . .

Her taped-together fingers reached around the toilet paper, trying to figure out how it was attached, feeling the holder, thinking hard, begging *please don't let it be plastic, please, please, please* . . .

It wasn't. It was metal.

She smiled into the dark and grasped the metal cylinder with her fingers. Pushing it to one side, she loosened it from the holder. Letting the toilet paper drop to the floor, she pulled the two halves of the cylinder apart. Inside was a metal spring. She put her index finger on the end and nearly laughed. It was so sharp it almost pierced her skin.

Perfect.

Leaning down, she ran the sharp end of the spring across the tape. It made a skittering noise that was like music to her ears. Pressing down a little harder, she drew the spring across the layers of duct tape over and over and over again.

Every so often, she'd use her fingers to check her progress.

When the top layer parted, she almost cheered out loud but instead kept bearing down. Second layer cut through . . . third . . . fourth . . . fifth . . . and then she was free!

Well, her ankles, anyway.

Katie stood and walked—no, *strode*—out of the bathroom, feeling a huge psychological boost. If she could get her feet free, she could get her hands free, and then she'd be able to get going on the serious business of getting back to shore.

She went into the master cabin and sat on the bunk. With her fingers half taped up, it was going to be harder to use the spring, but she had a lot of motivation, and there was no way she was going to just sit there and give Warren Noth and his buddies an easy time of it.

Turning the spindle around, she tried to aim the sharp end at the tape around her wrists, but the metal made it slick, and it rolled out of her fingers and hit the floor.

Swell, she thought, and slid to the carpet. It took a little searching to find her tool, and when she did, she just stayed on the floor. If the thing had slipped out of her hands once, it might do it again.

She levered the spindle every which way she could think of, aiming it this way and that, getting cramps in her hands and ignoring them, but the noise she'd loved so much just wasn't possible.

Now what? There had to be a way. She was not going to give up. Just. Was. Not.

She started to stand, thinking that in her earlier exploration of the kitchen maybe she'd missed something. Probably not, most likely not, but maybe, and what else did she have to do?

In her effort to stand in the dark, her foot caught the corner of the bunk, and she fell back to the floor.

Silly foot, she thought and gathered herself up to make another attempt to stand.

Then . . . she didn't.

It wasn't a silly foot at all. Because it had given her an idea.

She drew her feet together, inserted the spring between her shoes, and held it tight. Holding her breath, she leaned forward and ran her wrists over the sharp end. The sawing noise wasn't as loud, but it was there.

This was going to work. It might take a lot longer to get her wrists free than it had her ankles, but this was going to work.

Katie almost hummed with satisfaction as she worked, dragging her hands forward and backward, forward and backward, forward and backward. Though she couldn't reach her fingers around to check on her progress, she could feel her bonds loosening. Slowly, horribly slowly, but loosening they were.

Forward and backward.

Over and over and over.

The task was mind-numbingly boring. Katie had drifted into a sort of daze so deep that when she cut through the last layer of tape, she didn't realize what she'd done until the sharpest part of the spindle scraped across her exposed skin.

She yelped a little, then blinked in the dark. Her hands were loose. She was free!

Saying a fast prayer to the heavens, she jumped to her feet. It was time to get on with the next part of her escape plan. Not that she'd come up with one yet, but it had been hard to plan that far ahead when her hands and feet had been taped together.

Katie's head swam with dizziness, and she grabbed at the doorway to steady herself.

Careful, she told herself. *You had a good crack on the skull.*

She raised a hand and felt her head, wincing when she found the tender spot. She had no idea whether or not she had a concussion, but since she didn't have an emergency room handy, there wasn't much point in wondering about it. That could wait until later.

What she needed was a way off the boat. She had to get back to shore. She had to—

The noise of the engine, which had been her sole companion ever since she'd woken up, suddenly subsided.

Katie froze. If the boat had stopped, that had to mean something was going to happen, and it was a certainty that that something wasn't going to be in her best interests.

She soft-footed it to the bottom of the short flight of stairs and listened. No footsteps approached, which was good. Her only weapon was the toilet paper spindle, and while that sharp end could do some serious damage, to use it she would have to get closer to Noth than she wanted. And there was still the stomach-clenching question of his associates. Who were they? How many were there? Was it just one, or . . .

Katie shook her head at herself and focused on listening.

But there was nothing to hear, nothing but the slap of waves against the boat's hull. Nothing but the sound of a low wind. Nothing but—

"You ready?"

Katie's gaze flicked overhead. That had been Noth's voice. He must have been the one at the wheel.

"Give me a minute."

The second voice was farther away and hard to make out over the waves. Katie strained to hear.

". . . do you figure?"

"An hour should do it," Noth said.

Katie, looking up, tracked his footsteps across the ceiling. She tensed. Was he going to come down into the cabin? If he did, she had to scramble up and out. Get outside and over-board; it was her only chance.

She felt a shuddering bump against the boat. What the . . . ?

When the second voice called, "Tie up the stern, will you?" she realized the bump had been a second boat coming up alongside.

"Got it," Noth said. Through the skylight, Katie saw a flashlight's beam playing over the boat. "Let's move, Luke. I don't want to be out here any longer than I have to."

Katie's brain tickled at the name. Luke? She'd met a Luke recently, but where?

"Hang on. Got to get my dive light."

Dive light? Katie frowned. Why on earth would anyone be diving in the middle of the night?

A loud splash at the boat's stern shifted Katie's attention, followed by more bumps. These bumps, however, were quieter and came from underneath her feet, underneath the boat.

The smaller bumps traveled forward and then back again.

"Got them," Luke called.

Noth grunted. "Good. Let's get going."

The boat rocked a little, and Katie heard the unmistakable sound of a body climbing out of the water. Seconds later, the engine of the other boat turned over, gurgling a little as the pro-pellers started churning the water.

"Untie us," Noth said.

"Did you take the key?"

"Don't be stupid. Of course I took the key."

"How long before we get the money for this one?" Luke asked.

Noth laughed. "Greedy little jackass, aren't you?"

"All I want is my fair share—"

Then Noth must have slammed on the throttle, because

the other boat's engine roared to life and hurtled across the water, away from Katie and the boat she was on.

As she stood there, two facts popped into her head at the same time. First was that the Luke in question was Luke Stafford, Erikka's ex-boyfriend. But that fact was completely eclipsed by the knowledge that the boat in which she'd been imprisoned was about to sink.

With her in it.

Nineteen
~~~~~~~~~~~~~~~

Katie's panic, which she'd been successfully keeping at a low level, burst into full flower. "Come back!" she yelled. "You can't leave me here!"

But they had, in fact, left her alone on a sinking boat. And they knew they had. They were trying to kill her, and with her body contained inside the cabin, no one would ever know what had happened to her.

"My car," she said out loud. Her car would be found at the marina, and . . . But no. The keys were in her purse, which she'd undoubtedly left on the floor of that warehouse. Either Noth or Luke would drive the car to some secluded location and leave it.

Maybe a hunter would find it during deer season, or maybe no one would find it until spring, or even later. She would vanish without a trace. People would be shocked, and Andy would run himself ragged trying to find her, but time would move on. The memory of Katie Bonner would fade, and Andy's pain would eventually ease. He'd fall in love with someone else, someone thin and blond, and they'd marry, they'd have three lovely children, and none of the three pregnancies would ruin the blonde's trim figure.

"It isn't fair," Katie said to herself. Then, since no one was around to hear, she shouted at the top of her lungs. "It's not fair!"

The echo of her own words bounced back at her, and she felt a little childish, complaining about fairness at her age. Of course it wasn't fair. Most things weren't. But whining about it wasn't going to help a thing, and if she let herself be distracted by the unfairness of life, her life would end up as short as Noth and Luke hoped.

"Not if I can help it," she said out loud, and this time her words made her feel better. Not a lot, but even a little was a step forward.

What she needed was a plan. A realistic one that didn't include kindly aliens noting her predicament and rescuing her with a beam that would transport her to dry land. Although that would have been nice, she had to assume she was on her own.

And what she needed to do first was get off that boat. Because, if Noth's estimate of one hour had been correct, that was how much time she had before enough water seeped in to send it to the bottom of the lake. She was one hundred percent certain that, on Luke's short dive underneath the boat, he'd been unscrewing the plastic plugs that filled the boat's drain holes, letting water pour inside the hull.

She needed to get outside, she needed to start the bilge pump, she needed to use the radio to call for help, she needed to see if there was a life jacket aboard, she needed to—

"First things first," she said, as firmly as she could. Before she could do anything else, she had to get out of the cabin. She climbed the few stairs and tried the door. It wasn't locked, because what you wanted on a boat was to keep thieves from getting in, not to keep people from getting out, but they must have wedged the door or barricaded it, because she couldn't move it more than an inch or two.

She banged on the door with her fists, used her shoulder to whack at it, and thumped at it with her hips, but none of her efforts made it budge. The boat was quality construction, which made sense, because it had to be worth a hefty sum if Noth and Luke were killing people over the scam they'd set up, but it would have made things a lot easier for her if the door had been made of thinner wood.

Rubbing her shoulder, she retreated down the stairs to think. She glanced up at the skylights. In a movie, the hero would jump up, grab the edges of the light, and pull himself up and through to escape. That wasn't going to work in this case, because the opening was far smaller than she was, and even if it had been big enough, she lacked the upper-body strength to pull herself up like that.

What she needed was a battering ram of sorts. For the thousandth time, she glanced around the small space. Everything was built-in. The kitchen cabinets were built-in, as were the bunks and their upper and lower cabinets. She'd already used the only thing in the bathroom that had been removable without tools, and the spindle wouldn't make a very good battering ram.

"There has to be something," she murmured, crossing her arms and leaning against the table, thinking about the hours she'd spent on Seth's boat. He'd had a fire extinguisher, which would have been ideal, but she hadn't found one under the sink, and if there was another one, it would most likely be up in the cockpit.

The boat gave a wallowing roll, and Katie put her hands behind her on the table to steady herself . . . Table.

Katie flung herself to the floor. On Seth's boat, he'd once shown her how the table could be lowered to be level with the seats. Add the cushions from the under-seat storage and you had extra sleeping accommodations.

But she didn't care about the accommodations; what she wanted to know was if the table, which went down, would also go up. And out.

It was too dark under the table for her to see what she was doing, but it didn't take long for Katie to figure out how to release the table. She gasped with surprise as the surface dropped down onto her shoulders, then pushed up against it, using her legs, using her back and shoulders and arms to push it up . . . up . . . up . . .

The table slid out of its metal pedestals and crashed to the floor.

Bam!

Breathing deep from her efforts, Katie found the table was much heavier than she'd anticipated. "Stupid well-built boat," she muttered, wondering if she had the strength to pick it up and use it to batter anything, let alone a door at the top of the stairs.

She stood and picked up the tabletop. It slid out of her hands and hit the floor with a thud. No way was she going to be able to carry that up the stairs and whack the door with it. If she'd had someone with her, maybe, but not by herself.

As she stood there, staring at the dim outline of the table, a growing despair settled in her chest, and her throat seemed to constrict.

"No," she whispered. "I will not give up." Too many people were counting on her. And what would happen to her cats? Plus, she'd been so looking forward to working with a year's worth of data for Artisans Alley.

There had to be a way. All she had to do was find it. All she had to do was—

"Got it!" she exclaimed, then told herself not to get so excited. Her new idea might work, but it might not.

She picked up one end of the table and jockeyed it around to sit on the bottom stair. So far so good. With a grunting effort, she flipped it up vertically, wavering on her feet a little as she balanced the table on its thin edge.

"This will work," she said as confidently as she could.

She pushed and pulled and slid the table up the stairs. At the top, she wedged the bottom corner of the table into the small gap she'd created. She pushed harder, wedging it in some more, then pushed a little bit more, putting as much of her weight into the shove as she could.

Keeping the tabletop steady with both hands, she maneuvered down the stairs and to the table's opposite end. Singing a pirate heave-ho, she threw her body against the tabletop, which was now a lever, hoping, praying, and begging anyone who was listening to let this work.

Crack!

The noise of wood screeching was sharp and loud, but the door didn't fling itself open. Katie ran up the stairs. The door had opened another inch. Not much, but it was progress. And at that point, any progress was good.

An elated Katie worked on wedging the tabletop deeper into the gap, then she returned to the opposite end and hurled her body against the table a second time.

Crack!

Katie and the tabletop tumbled to the floor in an untidy heap. She pushed it away, scrambled to her feet, and hurried

up the stairs to see what had happened. But even before she'd
reached the top, she felt so much fresh lake air on her face
that she let out a cheer.

Then she ran smack into the door.

"What the . . . ?"

Her plan, which had been to use the tabletop as a lever to
push away whatever barricade blocked the door, hadn't
worked at all. What she and her lever had done instead was
to break the door itself.

"Close enough," she said and jabbed at the broken bits
with her fleece-covered elbow and her sneakered feet. The
more she jabbed and kicked, the more light began to stream
through, and soon she'd broken away enough pieces of door
to squeeze her way through.

"I'm out!" In the moonlight, she could see why she hadn't
been able to push away the barricade; it was the boat's anchor, and he'd lashed it into place.

She stuck out her tongue at the thing and moved on to the
next task on her survival list. Finding a life jacket. A lifeboat.
Anything, really, that might float long enough to get her to
shore. Speaking of shore . . .

Katie looked across the water and saw nothing but a dark,
star-speckled sky merging into black waves. No shore in sight.
She swallowed, knowing that if the shore couldn't be seen, she
was miles from land, much farther than she could swim, and
far enough that, if she was in the water, she'd perish from
hypothermia long before she reached safety.

She turned, starting her search for a lifeboat, and saw a
string of lights off in the distance. "I am so stupid," she said
and almost laughed. She'd been looking in the wrong direction for land, that was all. And though it was still a long way
off, it was within sight, at least.

Squinting, she tried to judge the distance, and also tried to calculate where she was.

A mile off, probably. But she had no idea what part of Lake Ontario she was floating around upon. East of Rochester? West? She couldn't tell. Heck, for all she knew, they could have been boating for some time before she woke and it was the Canadian shoreline she saw.

She studied the sky. The wind was stiff, creating large gaps in the cloud cover, letting glimpses of the moon and the stars show clear. She didn't know much about the constellations, but she did know enough to find the Big Dipper, and up the far edge of the dipper to the North Star.

A cloud bank parted, and she saw what she needed. "Ahh," she murmured. North was in the direction of the dark horizon. That line of lights was to the south.

Now that she was directionally oriented and had some light to work with, she made a quick search of the boat—no key in the ignition, just as Noth had said—and found it as empty as the cabin area had been. No life jackets and no boat. Which, she supposed, made sense, because if they were doing what she thought, scuttling boats, claiming the insurance, then raising the boats and selling them, they would want the boat to vanish without a single trace.

A grim Katie headed for the cockpit. "Wonderful," she said, as she viewed the dashboard. But it wasn't really a surprise to her that the emergency radio had been stripped from the console. Why let it be ruined from immersion in lake water? When Noth and Stafford recovered the boat, they'd just put it back in and sell it as part of the whole package.

So . . . now what?

Katie had no clear idea how much time had passed since the other boat had left, but it had to have been at least thirty

minutes, half the time that Noth had predicted it would take
for the boat to sink. "T-minus thirty," she said.

Assuming Noth was right, she had half an hour to rescue
herself. The boat would be sinking lower and lower into the water
that entire time, wallowing deeper and deeper into the waves
until it would finally drop all the way under.

She smiled to think of the surprise Noth and his sidekick
would feel when they went to salvage the boat and found no
trace of her body. At least she had that satisfaction, knowing
they'd always be wondering what happened to her, wondering how she'd escaped—

Escaped the boat only to—

"No," she said loudly, startling herself. She was not going
to drown out here. She. Was. Not. She'd come this far; she
wouldn't let herself give up now. There had to be something
she could do. There had to be.

Katie walked around the boat a second time, looking for
something, anything, that would help. Since she didn't find
anything that time, she did a third round.

Still nothing.

Okay, she wasn't going to get off the boat, not with any
real chance of making it to shore alive, anyway. So if she
couldn't get off, the only alternative was to get someone to
come rescue her.

It was a brand-new idea, and one she didn't particularly
care for—she was used to doing for herself and had grown to
prefer it that way—but there was a time and a place to ask for
help, and this was it.

Only . . . how? The radio was gone. There was no air
horn. No way of amplifying her voice whatsoever, and
there was no point in shouting; the shore was too far for
anyone to hear. Besides, it had to be either very late at night

or early in the morning, and who would be out at that time of night?

As dispassionately as she could manage, she eyed the distance to shore and tried to estimate how long it would take someone to reach the sinking boat. In a fast boat, probably only a few minutes, but so many boats were already out of the water.

She shook away the question. She couldn't do anything about the boat that might be coming to fetch her, so she wouldn't worry about it. What she had to do was signal that boat, but again . . . how?

Blowing out a breath, she shoved her hands in her coat pockets and was surprised to find something in them. Oh yes. The tissues and the matches. Fat lot of good they were doing her. If she hadn't been dead set against littering, she would have tossed them overboard.

She went back to the cockpit area and got down on her hands and knees. Maybe there was storage for flares. Maybe Noth hadn't seen it. Maybe she'd be able to set one off. Maybe . . .

Only there were no flares.

She sat back on her heels and blinked away the tears that threatened. Signal. She had to have a signal. Without a flare, what else could create a signal in the dark? What would create a light? She didn't have a flashlight, and she had no way to flick on the boat's lights. She had nothing.

Hang on. Matches. She *did* have matches.

She looked around but saw nothing that would burn worth a toot. The wood trim might catch on fire, but there wasn't enough to make the kind of huge blaze that she needed. Sure, the boat's fiberglass would burn, but it would take an accelerant of some kind, and she didn't have anything handy . . . or did she?

Not stopping to think, she scrambled to the boat's stern, slapping her palm against the hull, searching for what she knew had to be there.

"Got you," she breathed, then she unscrewed the gas cap and grinned as the stink of gasoline flowed up into the night air.

She hurried down to the bathroom and hunted around for the toilet paper she'd tossed on the floor way back when getting untied had been the most important thing in her life. With the almost full roll in hand, she rushed back up the stairs and unrolled a long length of toilet paper.

After feeding it into the gas tank, she pulled it back out. She did the same thing with the rest of the toilet paper and ended up with more than half a dozen gas-soaked lengths of paper.

She gathered them up and placed them at strategic locations on the boat, all facing the shore, all in spots that had wood trim or at least vinyl upholstery that would fire up faster than a fiberglass hull.

"Now or never," she said and lit the first match. Once it was burning steadily, she tossed it onto the biggest, wettest pile of paper. It went up with a satisfying *whoosh!* and she moved onto the next pile.

In less than a minute flames shot high, and Katie's nose wrinkled at the stink of burning fiberglass and plastic. She ignored the stench and scanned the shoreline, looking for boat lights that might be headed her way.

The fires burned hot and high, and still, she saw nothing.

The boat settled deeper into the water.

Still nothing.

The fires grew, and she edged to the boat's bow and started to wonder if her attempts at arson had been a little too successful.

But there was still no sign of rescue.

Katie watched the boat sink lower and lower, watched the fires come closer and closer. She would swim, if it came to that. She was a strong swimmer, and maybe shore wasn't as far away as she feared. Maybe she'd make it.

A few minutes later, when the fires had been extinguished by the water that was starting to lap at her toes, she tried not to think about the water's temperature and made her next plan. She'd stay with the boat as long as possible, because it was always better to stay with the boat, even if it was falling away under your feet, and then she'd swim for it.

Even as she made that last plan, the boat took a sudden lurch and dropped away. Katie sucked in a deep breath of air as the cold water surrounded her. She toed off her shoes, put her head down, and started swimming.

Swimming in the dark, cold water.

Swimming for her life.

She didn't think about what she'd miss if she died; she didn't think about who would miss her. Every stroke and every breath was focused on survival, on making it to shore.

Swim, she told herself. *Swim!*

So she did.

And she never knew, later, which came first, the searching spotlight or the young voice that sounded out of the dark. "It had to be about here, Dad. I'm sure of it. I positioned it with that new app I downloaded."

Katie saw the boat about twenty yards away. "I'm here!" she shouted. "Over here!" But her throat was raw from so much time in the water, and only a croak came out.

"Johnny," his dad said reasonably, "I know what you thought you saw, but we've been out here for almost an hour. If you'd seen a burning boat, we'd be seeing flotsam. There's nothing."

"But, Dad—"

"Sorry, son. We've been out here long enough."

Katie saw his hand close down on the throttle. "Help me!" she yelled at the top of her lungs. "Help me!"

"Dad! Dad!" Johnny shouted. "Did you hear?"

His dad must have heard, because he swung the boat around, and soon they'd hauled a wet and shivering Katie onto their boat, where they wrapped her in blankets and rushed her back to shore.

Twenty

"Would you like more coffee?"

Katie, who'd stopped talking and was staring at the contents of her mug, looked up at Detective Hamilton and tried to smile. "Thanks, that would be nice." She actually didn't want any more coffee, but she was beyond tired of talking and would appreciate the time it would take for Hamilton to do the refill.

"No problem." The big man, who'd been sitting across from Katie at the table in the Artisans Alley vendors' lounge, pushed himself to his feet and went for the pot. "I could use more myself."

He probably needed it a lot more than Katie did. After her rescuers had brought her safely back to shore, 911 had been called and the detective had been yanked out of bed. As far as Katie could tell, he hadn't had any sleep since that midnight call, and it was now almost noon.

Hamilton's cell phone rang, and he walked into Katie's office, shutting the door. Privacy for his phone calls was why she'd ended up in the vendors' lounge that morning to begin with, and she was starting to get itchy about all the time a stranger was spending in her creaky office chair.

She got up. Maybe she did want more coffee. What would a little trembling in her fingers hurt?

When the mug was half empty, her office door opened again. Hamilton came out, full of energy and smiling broadly.

"They're starting to talk," he said.

Katie nodded. Both Warren Noth and Luke Stafford had been captured hours before—but neither one had said anything beyond requesting legal representation. "What are they saying?" she asked.

"They're both claiming everything was Kimper's idea," the detective said.

"How convenient." Katie rolled her eyes.

"Oh, sure. But it doesn't matter, really. You can get tossed in jail for being an accomplice, too. And Kimper sure wasn't out there last night."

"No." Katie wrapped her hands around the mug. The few hours of sleep she'd grabbed had been filled with dark dreams, and she'd woken up in a panic so thick that it had taken the combined purrs of Mason and Della to calm her down.

Detective Hamilton looked at his notes. "Noth said he met Luke Stafford about a year ago when Noth happened to stop by the Kimper Insurance office to pay his insurance bill. Stafford was there, doing some maintenance work, and the three of them, Noth, Stafford, and Kimper, started talking about boats."

He glanced at Katie, who was listening raptly, and went on. "Noth and Stafford both claim that all they did was talk about how an insurance scam could be pulled, that if you had the know-how and some equipment, you could sink a boat, claim it was stolen or lost in a storm, claim the insurance, then salvage and sell it. You'd have the insurance money and the money from the sale of the boat."

"In the warehouse," Katie said slowly, "I saw Noth doing something at the stern of the boat, near the top and off to the side."

"Exactly," Hamilton said, smiling. "Do you know what's often on that part of a boat?"

Suddenly, she did. "The serial number. He was making it illegible."

Hamilton gave her an approving nod. "Kimper set up all those insurance companies so the underwriters wouldn't get suspicious about so many claims coming from one agency."

It all made a convoluted sort of sense. But there was still one big mystery that Katie hadn't even come close to solving. "Did Noth or Luke say anything about how Josh ended up in the bathtub at Sassy Sally's?"

"Now there's a story." Hamilton poured coffee into his mug, offered some to Katie, then sat down again. "And I do mean a story."

Katie frowned. "Do you think they were lying?"

The detective shrugged. "It doesn't matter what I think, really. What matters is what we can prove." He eyed her. "You worked for Kimper for years. Do you know if he could swim?"

"If he could . . . ?" Katie gaped at him. "I have no idea."

"Noth and Stafford said they were out boating with him that Labor Day, and that Kimper accidentally fell overboard. They claim they had no idea he couldn't swim, that they thought his flailing around in the water was him just messing around."

Katie shook her head. "I find that hard to believe, but who knows? Maybe he couldn't swim. I'd ask Marcie, his widow."

"We're working on it," he said. "Noth and Stafford said they fished him out of the water still alive. Said they took him back to Sassy Sally's, because they knew that's where he was staying. He was fine when they left him, they said, and that he must have had some water in his lungs and that must have triggered a heart attack or something. Oh, I know, I know," he said, smiling. "It's unlikely to the extreme. But that's their story, and so far they're sticking to it. The prosecutor is going to have the field day of his life ripping them apart in court."

"But assuming he drowned right there in front of them, why on earth did they take him to Sassy Sally's and not just leave him in the lake?"

Detective Hamilton slid his notebook into his jacket pocket. "I doubt we'll ever know why—not for certain—but I have a theory. I think those two are both severely homophobic and saw implicating two innocent men as a big bonus."

Katie sputtered. "But that's . . . that's . . ."

"Awful." The detective stood, nodding. "Horrible and appalling. Makes you want to root for Don Parsons tomorrow all the more, doesn't it?"

"What's tomorrow? Is he playing in some late-season golf tournament?"

Hamilton's eyebrows went up. "Playing, yes. Golf? Not even close. Didn't you know? Parsons and Farrell are big stakes poker players. I hear that's how they met, at a poker tournament in Miami. They're both good enough to play in those Vegas tournaments they show on television. The pot tomorrow will probably go over a million dollars."

"I had no idea," Katie said faintly. A million dollars? That explained the money to renovate the bed-and-breakfast, and it explained why neither one of them seemed to have a job. It also made sense of a few other things that Katie had been puzzled about. She grinned, glad for the explanation.

Hamilton thanked her for her time and said he'd be in touch. As he headed out, Andy came in, exactly at the time they'd arranged earlier.

"Ready for lunch?" he asked, helping her to her feet and giving her a huge hug. "I love you, by the way," he whispered into her ear. "Please don't ever scare me like that again."

"Is that your, um, brother?"

Katie pulled away from Andy, although she didn't really want to, and looked at Ray Davenport's daughters. "No, this is Andy Rust, my boyfriend and the owner of Angelo's Pizzeria."

"B-boyfriend?" Sadie stuttered. She looked Andy up and down, taking in his age, his size, and his unquestionable good looks.

"Um, we didn't know you had a boyfriend," Sasha said, her cheeks turning a bright shade of red.

"And you didn't ask, did you?" Katie's smile took the sting out of the words. "I appreciate that you don't want your dad to be lonely, but I'm sure he can take care of that himself." She thought of Ray, remembering that odd connective spark of . . . something that she'd felt once or twice when with him, then pushed the memory away as ridiculous. She couldn't possibly be attracted to Ray Davenport.

"Boy, do I feel stupid," Sasha said. "Wait until Sophie hears this." She backed out of the vendors' lounge and continued.

"The poor kid," Andy said, then turned back to Katie. "Are you okay?"

She smiled up at him. "I am now."

"Katie?" Rose called from the main sales floor. "Katie!" She charged into the room, flush faced, and her hair, which normally didn't have a single strand out of place, was mussed. "I have to talk to you right this minute." By the tone of her strained voice, it had to be a real emergency.

"What's the matter?" Katie asked, concerned. She'd always thought Rose was unflappable.

"It's that Godfrey Foster," Rose burst out.

Brittany appeared in the doorway. "Is that the big guy with the allergies?"

Katie tensed. She hadn't seen Godfrey since he'd been taken away in the ambulance after that allergic reaction to Crystal's nail fumes. "Is Godfrey all right?" *Please let him be okay*, she thought. The last thing Artisans Alley needed was a lawsuit.

"Yes," Rose said. "And *that's* the problem. He's perfectly all right."

"But that's good." Katie frowned.

"No, no, you don't understand," Rose said, almost frantically. "He's perfectly fine. He was *always* fine. I overheard him on his cell phone, talking to his wife, saying that his fake reaction had worked, that the nail girl would be gone from Artisans Alley by Monday."

"Fake?" Katie's voice was low and surprisingly calm. "Godfrey *faked* an allergy to get rid of Crystal?"

Rose nodded.

Turning to Brittany, Katie said, "Tell Crystal she can stay." She would deal with Godfrey later—as in telling him to leave and refunding him any unused rent—but she first had to make things right with Crystal. "Tell her we'll work out a way to vent the fumes if I have to pay for it myself."

"I'll help."

Katie looked up to see Duncan McAllister standing in the doorway. "You don't have to do that," she said stiffly.

"No, but I will." He nodded. "It's my apology for being so difficult. My only explanation is that when I was coaching kids' hockey, I was falsely accused of abuse. It was hard to deal with, and when you started asking all those questions about boats and whatnot, well, I overreacted. I'm sorry, and I'll show it by helping out with Crystal's project. She's a good kid. She doesn't deserve crap from someone like Godfrey Foster."

"Me, too," Ray said, coming into the room and slinging his arms around his daughters. It was obvious he'd already ditched his cane. "A little bit of money, a lot of labor, and we'll have that venting system finished in no time."

"I'll help." Vance edged into the by now crowded room. "And I'll help double if I can get some boating instruction from Duncan, here, next summer."

"Sounds like a plan," Duncan said agreeably.

As the two men fell into a boating-oriented conversation, Katie got a wonderful idea. Seth didn't like to sail alone, and she couldn't go out as often as he would like, so what she needed to do was introduce him to Gwen, giving him a deckhand and her a way to go sailing.

"What are you grinning about?" Andy asked, squeezing her hand.

She gestured to the room, to the multiple conversations going on, to the plans being made, to the relationships forming and growing. With contentment in her heart, she said, "I'm happy."

Because Artisans Alley was a huge success in all the ways that really counted.

Katie's Recipes

Chocolate-Dipped Madeleines

   10 tablespoons unsalted butter
   ⅔ cup sugar
   3 large eggs, at room temperature
   ½ teaspoon salt
   1 tablespoon vanilla extract
   1 cup all-purpose flour, sifted

Chocolate Glaze

   ¼ cup corn syrup
   ¼ cup water
   ¾ cup sugar
   1 cup chopped bittersweet or semisweet chocolate

Melt the butter, then set it aside to cool to room temperature. In a medium-sized mixing bowl, beat the sugar, eggs, and salt until they're light yellow and very thick. Stir in the vanilla. Add the flour and melted butter alternately, using a gentle folding motion so the batter loses as little volume as possible. Refrigerate the batter, covered, for 45 minutes or so, until it's thick.

Preheat the oven to 375°F. Scoop the batter into the lightly greased wells of a standard-sized madeleine pan, using 1 slightly rounded tablespoon of batter for each cookie. (If you have only one pan, bake in sequence, keeping the remaining batter refrigerated.) Bake the madeleines for 12–14 minutes, until they're light brown at the edges. Cool in the pan for several minutes, then remove and cool completely on a rack.

To prepare the chocolate: In a small pan, combine the corn syrup, water, and sugar. Bring to a full rolling boil, stirring until the sugar melts. Remove from the heat, add the chocolate, and let stand for several minutes; then stir until smooth. Reheat as necessary to keep it soft enough for dipping, adding a bit of extra water if needed. To glaze the madeleines: Gently grasp at one end and dip the other end in the chocolate. Set on a rack until the chocolate hardens.

Store the cookies in an airtight container.

YIELD: VARIES

Almond Cookies

½ cup shortening
¾ cup white sugar
2 eggs
½ teaspoon almond extract
1½ teaspoons baking soda
1½ teaspoons warm water
2 tablespoons milk
1¾ cups all-purpose flour
1 teaspoon cream of tartar
⅛ teaspoon salt
¼ cup ground almonds
Sliced almonds

Preheat the oven to 375°F. In a large bowl, cream the shortening and sugar. Separate the eggs and refrigerate the whites. Add the egg yolks and the almond extract to the creamed mixture. Dissolve the baking soda in the water and stir into the mixture, along with the milk. Combine the flour, cream of tartar, and salt; gradually stir into the sugar mixture. Fold in the almonds. Roll the dough into a log about 2 inches in diameter. Wrap in waxed paper and refrigerate for at least 4 hours. Cut the dough into ⅛-inch-thick slices and place 2 inches apart on ungreased cookie sheets. Brush with the egg whites and sprinkle with sugar. Bake for 10–12 minutes, or until lightly colored. Let cool on wire racks.

YIELD: 36 COOKIES

Apple Raisin Muffins

½ cup vegetable oil (or unsweetened apple sauce)
¼ cup butter
1 cup sugar
2 eggs
1 teaspoon vanilla extract
2 cups all-purpose flour
¾ teaspoon baking soda
¾ teaspoon ground cinnamon
½ teaspoon salt
1½ cup diced apples
½ cup raisins
½ cup walnuts

Preheat the oven to 400°F. Place 12 paper muffin wrappers in a muffin pan. In a large bowl beat the oil, butter, and sugar with an electric mixer for 2 minutes. Add the eggs and vanilla extract; beat for 1 minute. In another bowl, stir the flour, baking soda, cinnamon, and salt. Add the rest of the ingredients to the wet mixture; stir just to combine. Spoon the batter into the prepared muffin cups. Bake 20–25 minutes or until a toothpick inserted in the center of the muffin comes out clean.

Remove the muffin tin to a wire rack. Cool 5 minutes before removing the muffins from the cups; finish cooling on the rack. Serve warm or store in an airtight container at room temperature. These muffins freeze well, and this recipe can be doubled.

YIELD: 12 MUFFINS